"Mr. Decker." Fiona's loud voice yanked Pearl from her reverie. The woman had managed to garner the entire table's attention. "Have you made your choice yet?" She pointedly looked at Amanda and then Pearl.

Amanda gasped and covered her mouth. Pearl attempted to kick Fiona beneath the table but missed. The gentlemen stared with obvious confusion.

"My choice?" Mr. Decker's lips stretched into a charming smile. "Coffee would be most appropriate after dessert, I believe."

The gentlemen all chimed their agreement. Mr. Decker lifted his glass of water in a toast to the fine meal.

Fiona O'Keefe, however, could not be so easily diverted from her purpose. "That's not what I meant, and you know it. Which one of us are you going to marry?"

A small-town girl, **Christine Johnson** has lived in every corner of Michigan's Lower Peninsula. She enjoys creating stories that bring history to life while exploring the characters' spiritual journeys. Though Michigan is still her home base, she and her seafaring husband also spend time exploring the Florida Keys and other fascinating locations. You can contact her through her website at christineelizabethjohnson.com.

Books by Christine Johnson

Love Inspired Historical

Boom Town Brides

Mail Order Mix-Up

The Dressmaker's Daughters

Groom by Design
Suitor by Design
Love by Design

Visit the Author Profile page
at Harlequin.com for more titles.

CHRISTINE JOHNSON

Mail Order Mix-Up

HARLEQUIN® LOVE INSPIRED® HISTORICAL

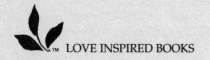

LOVE INSPIRED BOOKS

ISBN-13: 978-0-373-28357-6

Mail Order Mix-Up

Copyright © 2016 by Christine Elizabeth Johnson

www.Harlequin.com

Printed in U.S.A.

Have not I commanded thee? Be strong and of a good courage; be not afraid, neither be thou dismayed: for the Lord thy God is with thee whithersoever thou goest.

—*Joshua* 1:9

For every teacher who inspires and encourages.
Thank you for giving so generously
of the gifts God gave you.

Chapter One

August 1870

"I do hope Garrett Decker is as handsome as that gentleman over there that you find so fascinating."

Pearl Lawson started at her friend's comment and absently adjusted her sleeve while keeping a good grip on the steamship railing. "I can't imagine who you mean."

She hadn't been staring, had she? The striking gentleman standing not twenty feet away on the promenade deck certainly warranted more than a casual glance. He wore an impeccable dark brown suit that matched the color of his hair. The breezes off Lake Michigan ruffled the thick locks that ought to be topped by a hat, but that minor impropriety was not what had drawn Pearl's attention. No, it was the vigor of his gestures during conversation with an older gentleman. Clearly they were discussing something more interesting than the calm seas and clear blue skies. Pearl longed for spirited discussion. Any topic of current concern would do, as long as it didn't dwell on the weather or one's health.

An impish twinkle sparked in Amanda's eye. "He would make a fine beau."

"That's not why we're here. I have a teaching position, and you are getting married."

Amanda fiddled with the clasp of her nearly empty bag. "I'm not so certain about that any longer."

Pearl understood her friend's jitters. Getting married to a man she'd never met must be terrifying. "I'm sure Garrett Decker will be even more charming and handsome than that man."

"How can you know? We only have the advertisement." Amanda slipped the newspaper clipping from her bag. After two weeks of agonized second-guessing, it was frayed and creased to the point of falling apart. "'Widower with handsome inheritance seeks wife in booming town soon to rival Chicago. Well-furnished, comfortable house. Inquire at mercantile for Mr. Garrett Decker. Singapore, Michigan,'" she said. "It says nothing of his appearance." Her hand trembled. "Or his temperament."

Pearl squeezed her friend's arm. "If he doesn't suit, then we shall get along together. My wages ought to support two frugal women." She gave Amanda an encouraging smile. "No one knows better how to stretch a penny."

Amanda answered with a shake of her ebony curls. "You have always done much better than I." She fingered the satin ribbons on her hat. "Is it wrong to be fond of pretty things?"

"Not for someone as lovely as you."

Amanda lifted her violet eyes, which abruptly widened. "Don't look now, but your gentleman has noticed you."

"More likely you. After all, you are the pretty one."

Amanda blushed. "But I am practically spoken for. At least as soon as we arrive in Singapore. This gentleman should be for you."

"You know that I cannot marry. The terms of my teaching contract were quite specific on that point."

"But it's not fair."

Pearl had thought that at first, but upon reflection she could understand their point. "They do not wish to hire a teacher only to lose her shortly afterward. It is no hardship for me to postpone any thoughts of marriage for a year. I have no prospects at present, and a true gentleman would wait as long as necessary. Even if someone should profess undying love, I will be too busy with the school to consider courting, least of all marriage."

"I don't know how you can dismiss romance so easily. If that fine-looking gentleman asked to get acquainted, you couldn't possibly deny him."

"I can, and I will." Yet even as Pearl spoke, she could see her friend's attention drawn down the railing.

"He's looking the other way now. We must do something to attract his interest. Perhaps a stroll in his direction. You could inquire about the weather."

Pearl groaned. "Absolutely not. He is already deep in conversation. It would not be polite to interrupt."

"It's always acceptable for a lady...oh, dear!" Her exclamation was accompanied by a tight grip on Pearl's arm. "He's walking away. You must do something, or you'll lose him."

"I am not chasing after a man."

"If you won't act, then I will." She waved her fan briskly and exclaimed loudly, "The sun is too hot. I feel faint."

"Stop this," Pearl hissed.

Amanda clutched Pearl's arm again. "It worked. He looked our way." She raised her voice again. "I can't seem to draw a breath." She started to slump.

"If you faint, I'll...I'll..." Pearl couldn't think of a thing she would do to the friend who'd grown up with her in the orphanage. They'd stayed close even after Amanda had been placed with a family, while Pearl stayed unclaimed. When Amanda's fiancé jilted her, she turned to Pearl, who convinced her to answer the advertisement that would place Amanda in the very same town as Pearl's schoolhouse. Now Amanda's well-being fell on Pearl's shoulders. But it did not give her friend license to play matchmaker.

"Mr. Decker might not like women who swoon," Pearl pointed out.

"Mr. Decker? Mr. Garrett Decker?" A redhead in an emerald-green silk gown halted beside them. "I could not help but overhear, but I must warn you that that particular gentleman is already spoken for."

"What?" Pearl and Amanda said at the same time.

After days on a cramped, hot train and spending all but a few of their coins on this last passage, Pearl's plan for Amanda could not come to naught.

"It can't be," Amanda whispered, her complexion so pale that Pearl feared she was about to genuinely faint. "The advertisement is only two weeks old."

Two weeks was plenty of time for a man to wed. However, this woman sailed on the same ship as them. If she was already married to him, why wasn't she with her husband?

Pearl thrust back her shoulders, prepared to battle for her friend. "Then you are his wife?"

"Not yet." The woman tossed her head, which was topped by a hat bursting with ribbon and feathers. "But I soon will be."

Pearl could have kicked herself for never considering that other women might respond to the advertisement. "Have you corresponded with him?"

"There wasn't an address to write him," the redhead admitted, "but I intend to win his heart the moment we land in Singapore." She assessed Pearl and finished with a tight smile.

Apparently she felt Pearl was no competition, which she wasn't. Amanda, on the other hand, could surpass any woman in the virtues that counted most. Kind and gentle of spirit, Amanda was also skilled with the needle and an above average housekeeper. Her cooking might suffer from lack of instruction, but then what would a man living in such an outpost expect? Certainly not the finely dressed redhead standing before him, nor the mousy woman who poked her head into the small group.

"Are you talking about Mr. Decker?" the mouse squeaked. Her hands clutched a book so tightly that her knuckles turned white.

Oh, dear. Not another. How many women aboard the *Milwaukee* were traveling to Singapore in answer to the same advertisement? At least three. Amanda had competition. Worse, the handsome gentleman had drawn closer and caught her gaze. Pearl swallowed the flutter in her stomach and tried to concentrate on the trouble at hand.

"How many could there be?" Amanda whispered, her voice shaking.

"It doesn't matter if there are a hundred. Mr. Decker will choose the one who would make the best wife, and that is clearly—"

"A hundred!" Amanda paled. "There couldn't possibly be a hundred."

Why had Amanda seized on that small exaggeration?

"But I've placed all my hopes in him." The mousy bookworm looked close to tears. "I hope he's good and kind."

Pearl felt Amanda tremble. Hugh Bellchamp had not been a kind man. Not only had he betrayed his engagement to Amanda, but he had also done so to elope with the daughter of the family that had taken in Amanda. His note, delivered the morning of the wedding, had spared no cruelty, citing her unknown parentage as the deciding factor. Amanda was not good enough to become a

Bellchamp, not when the Chatsworth money was taken into account.

The redhead snorted. "I want a strong man, not some weakling who spends his time writing love poems."

Pearl cringed, for Hugh had written Amanda dozens of poems during their courtship. She felt her friend sway. Amanda's fan dropped from her hand and plopped into the water far below. "This is useless speculation, ladies. We won't know the man's character until we meet him."

The ship turned just enough to cut off the breeze. The thick August air could make any woman perspire, but drops poured off Amanda's forehead. Her ringlets looked damp beneath the small straw hat that afforded no shade whatsoever, and her color had paled even further. Since Pearl didn't carry a fan, she tugged off her gloves and waved them in front of Amanda's face.

"Perhaps we should find somewhere to sit." She felt Amanda's grip loosening.

"Oh, dear." The bookworm's eyes widened as she recognized the imminent danger. She looked left and right. "The only chairs are in the ladies' lounge or upstairs."

Too late. Amanda gasped ever so softly before slumping. Pearl reacted to her friend's collapse, cradling her on the way down and taking the brunt of the impact. Her knees smacked against the wood deck, but Amanda landed without injury.

"Is she all right?" the mouse whispered.

The redhead pulled smelling salts from her bag and offered them to Pearl.

One whiff of the astringent contents sent Amanda into a coughing fit.

Pearl stroked the damp curls from Amanda's face. "We need air, ladies, and some water would be nice."

"I'll fetch some." The mousy woman hurried off.

That left the redhead. Pearl tried to hand back the

smelling salts, but the woman's attention was focused on something behind Pearl.

"Ladies." A rich masculine voice rolled over Pearl's head with the calming effect of a lapping wave. "Do you have need of a doctor?"

Without looking, she knew it was him. The hatless man. The man whose animated gestures had intrigued her. Her pulse raced. She didn't dare look at him lest she lose her head. That would not help Amanda. So she kept her gaze focused on her friend and tried to ignore the girlish pounding of her heart.

The redhead seized the opportunity to extend a gloved hand. "We are most grateful for your assistance. This woman swooned."

The man ignored her and peered at Amanda. "I can fetch a physician."

"That's not necessary," Pearl said quickly. They could not afford the services of a doctor. "See, the color is already coming back to her cheeks."

"She doesn't have a fever?"

Pearl detected genuine concern in his question. "I think it was just the heat." She left out the real cause. No gentleman wanted to hear that three women had cast themselves into the marriage market for the same man. "A glass of water is on its way."

"You're certain you don't need a physician?"

Amanda managed to flutter her eyelids at him. "No, thank you, kind sir."

That little flirtation stirred a most unwelcome feeling in Pearl's heart. Amanda was her dearest friend. Pearl should be pleased that any man had pushed the memories of Hugh from Amanda's mind, but why did it have to be this gentleman?

"I think it might be best to send for the doctor." He lifted a hand to catch a porter's attention.

"No!" Amanda shot to a sitting position.

"Opposed to physicians?" the man asked with a hint of amusement.

"Not at all," Pearl replied. Neither of them had much money left after paying the costs of rail and ship travel from New York, even though the indirect route via Chicago proved least expensive. They would need every cent for room and board until Pearl began her new position. "Thank you for your consideration, but we will manage."

Pearl began to stand, and he extended a hand to assist her. She hesitated, but at the redhead's grunt of displeasure accepted his help. At his touch, a sensation like lightning shot from her hand to her shoulder. Her gaze locked on his. He lifted her like a fallen leaf. She didn't feel her feet, couldn't break the gaze, couldn't think a single lucid thought.

He released her hand with a smile that took her breath away. Though dozens of passengers had boarded in Chicago, she had noticed him. Tall, dark-haired and elegant, he looked the picture of a gentleman. Now his manners proved him to be exactly that. No other man had come to their aid. Few even glanced in their direction. She became aware that she was staring again. It didn't hurt that his blue eyes twinkled like the sapphires she'd once seen on display in a New York jeweler's shop window.

After a final smile that dimpled his cheek, he turned to Amanda. "May I help you to your feet?"

"Of course," she said breathlessly.

Pearl stared at her friend, whose gaze was riveted on this handsome gentleman.

He extended his hand. She put one gloved hand in his, and without the slightest effort he pulled her to her feet.

"Thank you," Amanda gushed, gaze still fixed on him.

Pearl fought unconscionable waves of jealousy. Why should she care about Amanda's interest in the gentleman? Amanda was the one who desperately wanted to marry. Pearl couldn't, according to the contract she had signed. But his eyes... She struggled to draw a breath. Something about the man drew her like no other. Curiosity and intelligence and laughter danced in his eyes. He made her feel as if she had always known him, even though they'd just met.

He turned back to Pearl. "Are you well, miss?"

Pearl swallowed and found her throat dry and her voice missing. She settled for nodding.

"Can I have my salts back?" The redhead stuck out her hand.

Pearl dropped the vial into it.

The woman then turned a dazzling smile on the gentleman. "We're fortunate that you were here, sir. I'm Miss O'Keefe, but you may call me Fiona."

He bowed with the perfection of a diplomat. "Pleased to meet you, Miss O'Keefe. I am Mr. Decker."

The three women stared at Roland with mouths agape. What on earth was wrong with them? The brunette had recovered sufficiently that he did not expect a repeat of the fainting spell, but they all looked as if he had just said the most shocking thing possible. Yet all he had done was introduce himself.

Behind Fiona O'Keefe a fourth woman squeaked and dropped a glass of water. The liquid splashed on Fiona's skirts while the glass rolled over the edge and into the lake far below.

The redhead turned on a tiny mouse of a woman. "How could you be so clumsy? Do you know how much this dress cost?"

The startled young woman looked ready to burst into tears. "I'm sorry."

Fiona O'Keefe relented, though she looked none too

pleased. "I planned to wear it to dinner at the captain's table. Now what will I wear?" She turned back to Roland. "I had hoped to make a fine impression."

Roland stifled a groan. Clearly she intended to impress more than the captain. "I can assure you, that you cannot help but impress anyone you meet."

That turned Fiona O'Keefe's distress into triumph. "I hope to see you later, *Mr.* Decker."

Her emphasis on his title perplexed him, as did the peculiar looks the other three women shot in his direction. The mousy woman hid behind the others as if afraid he would strike her. The brunette kept glancing between him and her friend with an almost wistful look. That friend, on the other hand, had rapidly moved from shock to confusion to disappointment. A moment later, she straightened her elegant neck, tossed back her loose chestnut locks and steeled her shoulders in much the same way Eva once had.

He choked back the bitter memory and turned his attention back to Fiona. "Perhaps we shall meet again."

He would do his best to avoid her. Fiona O'Keefe had all the makings of a woman intent on capturing a husband, and marriage was the last thing Roland sought. Even if he was the marrying type, he certainly wouldn't choose the fiery redhead. The no-nonsense lady who had stuck by her stricken friend was much more intriguing. From her unusual height to her lively green eyes, she was a woman worth knowing. Alas, he had no time for pleasantries, not with a potential investor at his elbow.

"Perhaps I might convince the captain to add you to our company," Fiona O'Keefe suggested with a coy smile.

Roland wished he wasn't already included at the captain's table. With Miss O'Keefe present, he would not be able to conduct a moment's business with Mr. Edward Holmes, the investor from Chicago that he was trying to interest in his plans for a glass factory. He chose his words with care. "I have been invited already."

After warbling her delight, Fiona O'Keefe swept down the promenade deck and into the nearest door.

"I know it's not the Christian thing to say, but that woman is insufferable," the take-charge woman muttered.

Roland had to stifle a grin. He liked a woman who spoke her mind.

"Now, Pearl," the brunette scolded with a touch to her friend's arm. "She did help me."

Pearl. Roland rolled the name around on his tongue. A pearl was a bit of sand that irritated an oyster long enough to become a gem. He had a feeling the name fit.

The brunette had settled her attention on him. "Thank you, Mr. Decker. Your assistance was most gallant."

Her wide eyes and stunning dark curls would captivate most men. Perhaps they might interest his brother, who desperately needed a wife. Maybe he could convince Garrett to come aboard long enough to meet her when the ship stopped in Singapore. If the purser refused to let him board, Roland would bring the lady to Garrett. A simple dockside meeting might set ablaze the dried-out tinder of his brother's heart.

He answered the brunette but couldn't stop watching the lady named Pearl. "Thank you, miss, but any gentleman would do the same."

None of the women pointed out that no one else had come to assist them.

Instead, the victim graciously accepted his response. "I am pleased to make your acquaintance, Mr. Decker. I am Miss Amanda Porter, and this is my friend, Miss Pearl Lawson." She paused, apparently hoping he would give his Christian name, thus putting them on a level of intimacy that he did not care to initiate.

"Pleased to meet you, ladies."

Amanda frowned. "Pearl is the new schoolteacher in Singapore, Michigan."

"Is that so?" He had not imagined any of them would be getting off at Singapore. He looked at Pearl anew. Her take-charge, plainspoken demeanor might fare well in the rough-edged society of Singapore. "I wasn't aware we needed a new teacher."

"You clearly don't have children, then," Pearl stated.

"Uh, no." His brother might have mentioned the need for a schoolteacher, but as a bachelor Roland had little interest in such matters.

"Pearl," Amanda cautioned her friend before turning back to him. "I'm afraid the long journey from New York has wearied us. Pearl isn't usually this forward."

Roland suspected Miss Pearl Lawson was behaving exactly as she always did. Those thrust-back shoulders and strong chin indicated she took no nonsense from anyone. Rather refreshing. Usually women simpered around him. He'd endured cloying attention, batted eyelashes and every manner of feminine wile down to the feigned swoon. He didn't know if Amanda Porter's fainting spell had been genuine, but he doubted Pearl would ever stoop to that deceit. She seemed honest and straightforward, without one bit of artifice.

"I'm Louise Smythe," a voice squeaked from behind the two women, drawing his attention from Pearl.

Roland had forgotten about the fourth woman. "Miss Smythe."

Her cheeks flushed. "Mrs. Smythe, actually. But my husband was killed in the war."

"My sympathies, ma'am. Most families lost someone. Two of my cousins never returned."

She bowed her head, as if overcome.

Roland glanced back to see Holmes had joined them at some point. He made further introductions and then began to angle the investor toward the gentlemen's lounge. "If you will excuse me, Mr. Holmes and I have business to attend to. I hope to see you ladies later."

"You will hardly be able to avoid Fiona," Pearl noted, "since she will join you at dinner."

"Ah, yes…dinner." Why did she have to remind him of that now-onerous task?

He opened his mouth to say more, but Holmes interrupted with an even more unwelcome proposition. "Why don't all of you join us?"

Roland couldn't stifle this groan. Four women would hinder any attempt at striking a deal before they reached Singapore. "I doubt there would be enough room at the captain's table."

"I—I have other plans," Louise Smythe spluttered, slipping into the background again.

Mr. Holmes accepted her regrets but not the protests of Pearl and Amanda. "I happen to know that there is ample room."

Pearl's expression had tightened, as if she dreaded the thought of dining with them, but Amanda clapped her hands with delight.

"The captain's table! It will be wonderful, won't it, Pearl?"

The no-nonsense woman looked like she was about to make an excuse, but after a pleading look from Amanda, she gave in. "We would be delighted."

"It will be an excellent opportunity to get better acquainted," Amanda said, again glancing between Pearl and him. "Won't it?"

"We will have plenty of time to get acquainted once we all disembark in Singapore," Pearl stated.

"All?" Roland didn't miss that little word. "You're all going to Singapore? Why? There's nothing for women to do there. Except the school, of course."

Now Pearl looked perplexed. "But you are expecting us."

"What?" He backed up a step. "I'm not expecting anyone, least of all four women."

Amanda looked like she would burst into tears. Louise Smythe bit her lip.

Only Pearl stood strong. "Then there has been a very grave mistake, Mr. Decker."

Prickles ran up Roland's spine. Whatever mistaken impression these ladies had come to believe, he wanted no part of it.

"Indeed there has." He bowed stiffly. "Good afternoon, ladies. Mr. Holmes and I have business to attend to."

Then, like a coward, he escaped to the safety of the gentlemen's lounge to decipher what had just happened and figure out how he was going to get out of the mess.

The thought of dining with Mr. Decker knotted Pearl's stomach. Gazing at him from afar had been pleasant. More than pleasant. Those brilliant blue eyes drew her in like no other man, but she'd let her fancy roam where it had no business going. Pearl Lawson was a schoolteacher, under contract to teach, not marry. Despite his peculiar behavior, Mr. Decker must want to marry at once. His advertisement had drawn three eligible women. Thus far. There could be many more already in Singapore. To give Amanda equal footing with Fiona, she'd agreed to her friend's pleas to join him for dinner, but it would be difficult not to let her suddenly unruly emotions run wild.

She shouldn't be concerned. Handsome men had never flocked to her side. Amanda was the pretty one, the one who drew men's attention. Amanda desperately wanted to marry and have a family. She was the one who was responding to Mr. Decker's advertisement. Pearl had no business thinking of Mr. Decker in any manner except as the object of Amanda's affection. Still, it would be difficult to sit with the man at dinner and not let her thoughts roam into forbidden territory.

Provided they were even admitted into the dining saloon. Third-class tickets did not entitle them to meals, and they could not afford to purchase them. This invitation promised to turn into an embarrassing fiasco.

She worried her gloves while Amanda tidied up before dinner. Since they were already wearing their best gowns, they could not change, but a little brushing off of the dust and adjusting of the hair might make them more presentable.

"I wish I had a silk gown like Fiona's." Amanda sighed.

"Yours is infinitely prettier."

Amanda blushed. "But it's not silk, and it's handmade."

"By an expert seamstress."

"You don't think he knows I made it, do you?"

"I doubt his business is tailoring or dressmaking." Pearl brushed at the wrinkles creasing her rust-colored skirt. "Besides, why would he look at your gown when your features are so much more pleasing?"

"Do you think so?" Even more color dotted Amanda's cheeks. She turned back to the tiny mirror loaned to them by another third-class passenger. "I think he was more interested in you."

A shock bolted through Pearl. Could a handsome, well-off man like Mr. Decker be attracted to a tall, ungainly woman like her? "Impossible. Moreover, I am not the one responding to his advertisement."

Amanda bit her lower lip as a frown creased her brow. "Did you notice how he reacted when you pointed out that he must be expecting us?"

Pearl had to admit that she'd noticed. "Perhaps he didn't understand." Surely a man who advertised for a wife would expect someone to answer that advertisement. What if Mr. Decker turned out little better than Hugh Bellchamp, first luring women to Singapore and then dashing their hopes? "He must have misunderstood."

"Perhaps." But Amanda looked as skeptical as Pearl felt.

"We could send our regrets and dine on our cheese and biscuits as planned."

"Oh, no. We must attend," Amanda urged. "I couldn't send regrets. Not now."

Thus they found themselves approaching the doors of the dining saloon at precisely seven o'clock. Many passengers milled about waiting to be seated. Pearl hung back to look for Mr. Decker, but he found them first.

"Miss Lawson. Miss Porter."

She couldn't help noticing that he addressed her first and lingered longer over her hand. If Amanda noticed, she did not remark upon it. They then proceeded to discuss the day's weather, the prognosis for that night and the usual inquiries into health and well-being.

At last the steward indicated he was ready to seat Mr. Decker's party. Soon Pearl would find out if she and Amanda would be refused entry.

When Amanda moved toward the steward, Mr. Decker pulled Pearl aside. "I hate to ask this of you upon such short acquaintance, but I beg you to remind Mr. Holmes that you are the town's schoolteacher."

Pearl frowned. "Why?"

Instead of answering, he retrieved Amanda and nestled her on his left arm while holding out his right for Pearl.

She shook her head. This moment must belong to Amanda.

Without a single comment, the steward led them to the table situated at the front of the room. The captain, resplendent in his uniform, stood to greet them. Pearl breathed out in relief. They would not be refused. Naturally Fiona O'Keefe was already there. Judging by her expression she was not pleased to see that Mr. Decker had brought guests. When he seated Pearl next to Fiona, the woman's irritation visibly rose.

The entire seating arrangement was peculiar. Considering Mr. Decker's request, Pearl had expected to be seated next to Mr. Holmes. Instead, Amanda took that place, with Mr. Decker on her other side. From this distance, Pearl would have to shout for Mr. Holmes to hear her.

The meal began with a light beef broth, elegantly served in china bowls emblazoned with the ship's insignia. On a less calm sea, those bowls would spill their contents all over the linen tablecloths, but tonight the bowls remained perfectly in place.

The gentlemen maintained the bulk of conversation, first complimenting each of the ladies and then discussing the voyage before drifting into talk of business. To each man's delight, Amanda gave them her full attention, irritating Fiona even more.

At the first lull in the conversation, Fiona proclaimed, "This is the finest ship I have ever sailed on, Captain. Is it new?"

Her comment drew the desired attention from all the gentlemen at the table.

"I'm afraid not, Miss O'Keefe," the captain said, "but it has been recently serviced. Do you sail often?"

"Recently, I sailed from New York City." Fiona looked each man in the eye. "I was a rising star on the stage."

That startled Pearl but intrigued the men, who asked where she had appeared.

"Smaller theaters," Fiona replied, her color high. "As a soprano."

Pearl wasn't certain she believed the story, but it did make an impression on Mr. Holmes.

"What manner of songs did you sing?" the man asked.

Mr. Decker cleared his throat. "Wholesome songs, I imagine."

His pointed look must have gotten through to Fiona, for she smiled coyly and replied, "But of course, gentlemen. I would never sing anything else."

Though the men quickly returned to their business discussion, Pearl wondered at Fiona's story. Why admit any alliance that could sully her reputation before the man she wanted to marry? A man seeking a wife certainly wouldn't look in music halls. Yet there was a desperation in Fiona's eyes that a man might miss. Regardless of the reason, this woman needed the marriage. That made her a dangerous opponent for Amanda.

Pearl glanced back at her friend, whose attention had flagged somewhat.

"Where do you hail from, Miss Lawson?" the captain asked.

Pearl reluctantly turned from her friend. "Amanda and I are also from New York."

"New York?" Holmes bellowed above the din of conversation and flatware clinking against china. "Decker, you didn't tell me you had to send to New York for a teacher."

Mr. Decker took the comment in stride. "We want the most highly educated instructor for our children."

Now that was peculiar. Hadn't he said earlier that he didn't even know they'd hired a new teacher? Now he claimed she possessed higher qualifications than she did. Though she'd studied hard, she didn't have a university degree. That's why she'd applied to a small, remote posting. They did not quibble over her credentials, yet here was Mr. Decker touting her education. Couple that with his request that she remind Holmes of her position, and she could not make heads nor tails of Mr. Decker.

He was gracious, charming and could talk a fish onto a

hook. She would give him that. His stunning good looks couldn't be denied, either. From perfectly chiseled cheek-bones and jaw to impeccable attire, he was a sight to behold. Judging by the smooth cheeks and manicured haircut, he had visited the ship's barber after seeing them this afternoon.

Yet he spoke with confidence of things he knew nothing about. Pearl couldn't condone that. It was one shade short of stretching the truth, and she began to wonder if he was the right man for Amanda.

Or her. She pushed away that thought. Three women sought to marry Mr. Decker. She was not one of them.

Their steward removed her empty soup bowl and replaced it with a steaming plate that carried the most delicious smell. She closed her eyes and savored the delicate poached fish in a buttery sauce and steamed new potatoes dusted with parsley. Sautéed early carrots completed the plate.

Pearl had never eaten so well. It took every bit of restraint not to gobble down the fare. After each bite, she counted to thirty, smiled at Amanda, who was also reveling in the delicious food, and attempted to interject a comment into the conversation.

The captain had managed to engage Fiona, though she watched Mr. Decker like a hawk. When Amanda smiled at him, Fiona frowned. When Mr. Decker glanced in her direction, the redhead fluttered her eyelids.

Amanda, on the other hand, smiled at everything the men said but contributed nothing. That would not do. Pearl caught Amanda's attention and motioned for her to speak. Amanda averted her gaze and took another bite of food. Now was no time for Amanda to succumb to her tendency toward shyness. If she didn't say something soon, Mr. Decker would never notice her fine qualities.

Pearl seized a lull in the conversation to guide the gentleman's attention in the proper direction. "Amanda is an accomplished pianist."

"Is that so?" Mr. Holmes said.

Alas, the wrong man had seized the bait.

Amanda blushed. "Not so very accomplished."

"Nonsense. You play Mozart beautifully, and that is not easy," Pearl pointed out.

"Indeed," Holmes said. "Do you also play hymns?"

Amanda brightened. "Yes. My favorite is 'Amazing Grace.'"

That initiated a lively discussion in which Mr. Decker and Fiona O'Keefe did not participate. Pearl watched him closely. Either he had no favorite hymn or was not the churchgoing sort. For Amanda's sake, she hoped it was the former.

Next came the dessert course, a delicious spiced cake with candied peaches. Pearl closed her eyes and let the flavors melt on her tongue. It might be years before she tasted such fare again, but one day she would wend her way west, where fortunes could still be made.

"Mr. Decker." Fiona's loud voice yanked Pearl from her reverie. The woman had managed to garner the entire table's attention. "Have you made your choice yet?" She pointedly looked at Amanda and then Pearl.

Amanda gasped and covered her mouth. Pearl attempted to kick Fiona beneath the table but missed. The gentlemen stared with obvious confusion.

"My choice?" Mr. Decker's lips stretched into a charming smile. "Coffee would be most appropriate after dessert, I believe."

The gentlemen all chimed their agreement. Mr. Decker lifted his glass of water in a toast to the fine meal.

Fiona O'Keefe, however, could not be so easily diverted from her purpose. "That's not what I meant, and you know it. Which one of us are you going to marry?"

Chapter Two

Roland gagged on a mouthful of water.

"What?" He coughed. Repeatedly. "Marry?"

"Yes, marry." Fiona O'Keefe's gaze bored into him. "You've met us. Now which one do you choose?"

What on earth had gotten into that woman? He had not once stated he was in the market for a wife, yet she seemed to think he was supposed to pick one this very instant. Moreover, this choice was supposed to come from some undefined group of women that he had supposedly met, and which clearly included her.

He took a gulp of water to give himself time to rein in his shock and replace it with the calm of a placid lake. "I believe there has been some mistake."

"Don't think you can wiggle out of this," Fiona replied. "Pearl and Amanda and that Louise Smythe also want to know your answer."

He instinctively looked to Pearl, whose lips were pressed into a grim line. Amanda, on the other hand, had paled to the point that he wondered if she would faint again. He searched his memory for the last woman mentioned. Smythe. Smythe. Ah, yes, the small mousy woman who lost her husband in the war. She was not at the table. Given

Fiona's obvious designs on him, he was surprised she mentioned the other women. By his count, that put the eager prospects at four.

Whatever those ladies were up to, he was not going to marry. Not now. Not in the foreseeable future. He couldn't imagine where they'd gotten that idea. For a moment he recalled the fake advertisement he'd written as a joke to jolt his brother out of mourning, but he'd thrown that into the fire. None of them could possibly have seen it.

Judging by each woman's rapt attention, they expected an answer.

Well, if there was one thing Roland Decker excelled at, it was his ability to escape from tight situations. No woman was going to snare him in her net.

So he guffawed and turned to Holmes. "Isn't that like a woman, always looking for a husband?"

He could feel Fiona's indignation boring into the side of his head.

Holmes, after an initial chuckle, turned serious. "Domestication never hurt a man."

"Except when it cuts into his attention and time starting up and running a new operation," Roland pointed out.

He took great care not to look any of the women in the eye, though he could not miss Amanda's distress, for she was seated between him and Holmes. Moreover, Pearl shuffled in her seat. He could imagine the glare she'd fixed on him.

Instead of agreeing with him, Holmes continued to press his point. "A diligent wife understands the demands placed on her husband and assists him in every possible way."

That wasn't Roland's experience. His brother's late wife had placed demands on him. Eva had hated Singapore, hated his work, pleaded with him to move back to the city. Garrett had nearly caved in to her demands before the accident.

"Mr. Holmes is right," Pearl chimed in, the high color dotting her cheeks mirroring the strands of red in her chestnut hair. "Marriage is a true partnership of like interests. Husband and wife working in unison can accomplish much more together than apart. Did not King Solomon note that a two-strand cord is stronger than one?"

Roland savored her persuasive determination. She might be a worthy partner—if he was in the market for a wife. But experience had taught him that words meant nothing. Promises made in the heat of first attraction vanished once the wedding bells stopped pealing.

"Clearly you have not been married, Miss Lawson," Roland said.

That would have silenced most women. Not Pearl.

"Have you, Mr. Decker?"

He laughed. "Touché. I have witnessed many marriages, though."

"And those have jaded you on the institution?"

"Let's say I've seen its shortcomings."

The captain cleared his throat. "Fascinating as this debate is, I am needed in the wheelhouse." He rose. "Please excuse me, Miss O'Keefe. Miss Lawson. Miss Porter. Gentlemen."

"Of course," Pearl murmured.

Though the captain had admirably engaged Fiona O'Keefe most of the evening, his departure now set her attention squarely on Roland. "You did not answer my question, Mr. Decker."

He folded his napkin and set it on the table. "I thought I did, but if you must hear it plainly, I am not in the market for a wife." He rose. "The day has been long, and tomorrow I must rise early to attend to business. I bid you good night, ladies."

* * *

"What are we going to do?" Amanda whispered to Pearl when they'd reached the promenade deck.

Pearl scrambled to come up with an answer. Mr. Decker's denial might have disheartened Amanda, but it infuriated her. After the first flush of selfish excitement that he was not interested in Fiona, the full import of his words struck home. He did not want to marry *anyone*. Yet he had placed an advertisement in a New York newspaper.

What sort of man did such a thing? She had thought him solicitous and compassionate, not the type who would tempt women to leave their lives behind only to disavow he'd ever suggested they do so. If not for the many diners surrounding them and for Amanda's fragile state, she would have given Mr. Decker a piece of her mind.

He must have sensed the imminent danger. That's why he'd left so quickly. Good riddance, in her estimation. However, that did not ease Amanda's distress. Pearl had to set aside her anger and find a way to soothe her friend. So, she paused at the railing and took a deep breath.

Overhead, stars sprinkled the moonless sky. The seas were still calm, and the *Milwaukee* plied the water with ease. The night temperatures were pleasant. Under other circumstances, they might while away the hours pointing out the constellations. Instead she must find some way to turn wormy crab apples into apple pie.

Pearl made her decision in an instant. "We continue on to Singapore." She hoped her certainty would bolster her friend's rapidly sinking hopes. "Something good will come of this. I'm certain of it."

"How can you be so sure? Not only did Mr. Decker not expect us, but he doesn't want to marry. What happened? Was the advertisement a cruel joke?"

Pearl could not tell her that she'd begun to think it was. Possible explanations tumbled through her head. The most far-fetched she discarded at once, but one lodged and refused to let go. Mr. Decker had claimed that marriage would take away from running a new business. What if the promise of marriage was simply a ploy to bring inexpensive labor to Singapore? What if he was the worst sort of scoundrel, someone who would take advantage of a woman when she was at her most vulnerable?

No, she couldn't let herself think that. She certainly couldn't allow Amanda's thoughts to drift in that direction.

"We will get by," she said firmly. "My new position includes room and board. We will share the room and make do on my earnings."

"But you wanted to save enough to go to California."

Pearl shoved aside that dream. Friends were more important. She had been abandoned by her parents. She would not abandon her friend.

She squeezed Amanda's hand. "That can wait until we sort this all out."

"I will find a job," Amanda declared. "I can be a ladies' maid."

Pearl doubted there were many frontier ladies needing that sort of maid, but she didn't point it out. "You do keep a tidy house and sew beautifully."

"I love to sew, but do you think anyone will need a seamstress?"

"We won't speculate on what people do or don't need. We'll trust that things will turn out for the best."

"All things will work together for good for those who love the Lord," Amanda said, paraphrasing scripture. "We must rely on that."

"Yes, we must." Pearl drew in a deep breath. Perhaps her friend was stronger than she appeared. "I'm tired and tomorrow will be busy. Shall we go below to find a spot to sleep?" Third class granted them passage but not sleeping quarters or a meal.

"Let's not. It's so noisy with everyone squeezed in there. I'd rather stand here and look at the stars."

Pearl had to agree. "We will search for some chairs, then, or a spot on the upper deck, and lift our gaze to the skies. You'll see. In the morning, everything will seem better."

Especially after she cornered Mr. Decker.

Morning dawned with scarcely a breeze. The cloudless sky stretched overhead like a blank canvas. This day would usher in a new life for Pearl as a schoolteacher. The prospect excited her even while she kept watch for the man who had crushed her dear friend's hopes.

Pearl stood at the railing with Amanda, their carpetbags at their feet, as the ship glided toward the mouth of a river guarded by a small lighthouse. Shimmering dunes rose on either side, dotted by clumps of green. Grass or shrubs, she guessed. Any trees were hidden from view behind the sand hills. In both directions the shoreline stretched unbroken except for a small, smoke-belching enterprise a distance to the north. If not for the lighthouse, she would think they were headed into the wilderness.

"How pretty." Amanda sighed. "I wonder where the town is."

Pearl wondered that, too. The marriage advertisement had promised a booming town. The employment posting had proclaimed a "bright future in the next Chicago." She saw no sign of habitation, least of all a thriving city.

"It must be upriver." At least Pearl hoped it was. She could manage the wilderness, but Amanda deserved a more genteel life. Despite Amanda's labors in the Chatsworth household, she was ill-equipped for backbreaking drudgery. The Chatsworths kept several servants, including a housekeeper and cook. Rather than being taken in as a daughter, Amanda had worked, but she had never taken on the care of an entire family. Pearl gripped the rail, for the first time doubting her decision to convince Amanda to join her.

Her friend's fragile hope had been dashed last night by yet another unfeeling man. First she'd suffered Hugh's unconscionable jilting. Now Garrett Decker had dismissed her. Just thinking of the man made Pearl's blood boil.

Her first objective of the day had been thwarted when Mr. Decker, despite claiming last night that he must rise early, did not appear on deck. Apparently that early morning business was conducted in the sanctuary of the gentlemen's lounge, where none of the women he'd injured could reach him.

Not interested in marrying? He had some nerve sending out an advertisement and then withdrawing it once he'd met the prospective brides. Fiona might be a little too forward and Louise Smythe a little too reticent, but Amanda shone like the rising sun. He had seemed to enjoy her companionship last night. Then why snuff out her hopes so cruelly?

She tapped her fingers on the railing. If he could not explain himself, she had a mind to give him a thorough tongue-lashing. Providing she could find him. The wily fox had ducked into his den. He might be able to hide aboard ship, but eventually he must leave. She would nab him ashore.

The ship entered the river, and Pearl spotted the first sign of life. A thin trail of smoke rose from a building on the left-hand shore. Farther upriver, another dark column lifted against the rising sun. The ship rounded a corner, and she heard the growl of engines and a piercing whine that made Amanda clap her hands over her ears.

"What is that?" Amanda asked.

Pearl shook her head. The tooth-shaking howl wasn't familiar. As they rounded the next bend, the source became obvious. Rafts of logs floated near shore. Sawdust coated the ground. Big, open wood-frame buildings roared with the hum of engines and the scream of huge saws.

Amanda's eyes rounded, and her hands stayed pressed to her ears.

The ship's whistle blew, and the vessel glided toward the dock that lined the shore. Beyond the dock stood a scattering of weathered wood buildings tucked between sand dunes. Most were single-story cabins or houses. A few had two stories. One building was particularly large. None bore the markings of a schoolhouse. Boardwalks and streets crisscrossed between buildings, but she saw no carriages or buggies. A couple of wagons waited near the waterfront. Though workers crowded the sawmills and docks, not a single soul walked through town.

Pearl's heart sank.

"Is this Singapore?" Amanda asked.

"Yes, ma'am," replied a sweat-stained laborer standing nearby. "Stockton's town."

"Stockton?" Pearl asked, her thoughts immediately drifting toward another man. "I thought perhaps Mr. Decker was in charge."

The man guffawed and slapped his thigh. "That's a funny one, miss. No sirree, Stockton owns the mills and the store and pert near everythin' else in town. Decker works for him. Runs the store."

Oh, dear. In spite of Mr. Decker's fine clothes and silver tongue, he was not important at all. Moreover, Singapore was no bustling metropolis. "Then it's a company town."

The man grinned, revealing a few missing teeth. "Wildest town on the coast."

Amanda paled. Pearl gripped her arm, afraid her friend would faint. Surely the man was mistaken.

"Do you live here, sir?"

"Board in one of the cabins." The man gestured in the general direction of town. "Been workin' here 'most two years now. This was the first chance ta head back home ta see the folks. Heard the mill's running full steam again." He rubbed his hands together. "Hopin' ta make enough ta git me a bride."

Oh, dear. She hoped the man didn't see them as prospects. Though a hard-working man was a blessing, both she and Amanda had hoped for someone a bit more sophisticated. Nevertheless, she offered a faint smile, all the while considering what they would face.

"Where is the boardinghouse?"

He waved at one of the two-story buildings set back from the waterfront. "And that there big building is the Astor House."

"Astor House?" Amanda exclaimed. "Like the hotel in New York?"

"The very same."

Except it looked nothing like the famed hotel. Clearly the citizens of Singapore thought a great deal more of their town than a stranger could see at first glance. Pearl wondered about the boardinghouse. She had envisioned a pleasant atmosphere with tea served at four o'clock in a formal parlor, not a place filled with rougher sorts in a town with a bad reputation.

"There must be families," Pearl said, "since there's a school."

He shrugged. "A few between here'n the tannery 'n Saugatuck."

"Saugatuck?" That place hadn't been mentioned in the employment posting.

"Upriver a bit."

Pearl struggled to keep her composure. None of this was turning out as expected.

A snort of disgust from behind echoed her thoughts. "This isn't a boomtown," said Fiona O'Keefe.

Beside the redhead stood the diminutive Louise Smythe, who looked as pale and frightened as Amanda.

"Maybe looks are deceiving," Pearl said with more hope than certainty. She had wanted a frontier experience, but this wasn't at all like the stories she'd read. She had imagined tidy cabins with whitewashed fences. Any Indians would be friendly and helpful. After all, the advertisement had boasted of a civilized and prosperous town.

The crew threw out thick lines and men on the docks wrapped them around large pilings. A gangway was extended and the passengers began moving toward it. Pearl picked up her bag and shuffled forward with Amanda and the other ladies. Below, the first passengers streamed out of the ship. All were men, mostly laborers. One older couple disembarked, but not one other woman. From what she could see, the four of them were the only single women leaving the ship at Singapore. The rest must be going on. That meant they were the only ladies whose hopes of marriage had been dashed by Mr. Decker.

There that fox was! She leaned over the rail to be certain. Sure enough, there he stood on the gangway as tall and proud as the day they'd met, gesturing this way and that while conversing with Mr. Holmes.

The two men stepped ashore, and then Mr. Holmes stopped to talk to a porter. Mr. Decker, on the other hand, roamed down the dock. Pearl followed his movements, determined to find the man once she'd disembarked. He strode the dock, chatting with the men who'd helped tie the ship to the moorings. Judging by the laughter and smiles he received, he was well liked by every one of them.

Slowly she inched forward. Amanda gripped her arm. She'd seen Mr. Decker.

He waved at someone far down the dock, just this side

of the large sawmill. That person must not have noticed him, because Mr. Decker cupped his hands around his mouth and yelled, "Garrett! Over here."

"Garrett?" all four women exclaimed at once.

That was the name on the advertisement. Could there be two Garretts in Singapore? Or was there more than one Mr. Decker?

Chapter Three

It was good to be home, which is what Singapore had become to Roland since he'd moved here eight years ago. At the time he'd been a clerk in Mr. Stockton's Chicago emporium. His boss offered him the management of the Singapore general store, and he had leaped at the opportunity. It got him away from the scene of his greatest disappointment.

He had not expected his older brother to follow four years later. Garrett was as different from him as night from day. Garrett preferred to work with his hands. He boasted a massive frame and their father's auburn hair. He never opened a book other than the Bible and enjoyed playing a harmonica at night. He was as rustic as the society in this lumber town.

What had Eva seen in him?

That's the question that had haunted Roland for over eight years. He and Eva were the same age, while Garrett was four years older. Roland had taken her to the finest shows in Chicago. He'd spent every spare dollar on gifts for her. He'd shared his excitement over the latest scientific discoveries with her. He sought progress whereas Garrett preferred the stability of tradition. Roland thought

Eva loved him, yet she had chosen his brother. She had married Garrett and in rapid succession bore him a son and a daughter.

Then they moved to Singapore.

Seeing her again had been difficult. He had kept his distance, but they could not avoid each other in such a small town. Disputes arose until brother separated from brother. Few words passed between them until Eva died. Even now, the memory of that day scored him to the bone. Every time he looked at Garrett's son and daughter, he saw her. Garrett must have felt the same way, for he holed up with his grief and ignored the children. Roland made the first move. For the sake of the children. He could still hear Garrett's hollow refusal. Yet in the end his brother relented and moved in with Roland.

The brothers reached a truce. The children were their bond. The two men did their best, but the children hadn't rebounded. Little Isaac carried the weight of the world on his seven-year-old shoulders, and Sadie wouldn't say a word.

"Give it time," Mrs. Calloway, over at the boardinghouse, had told him. "It'll take a while for those young'uns to get over losing their ma."

Months and months had gone by, and it hadn't seemed to help. Maybe this glassworks factory would be just the thing to pull those children from their self-imposed isolation. With success, he could provide the finest of everything. New toys for Isaac. Fancy dresses for Sadie. The prettiest dolls. Whatever their hearts desired.

To get the factory off the ground, Roland needed investors. Stockton had held back, calling the venture shaky at best, but if Roland could get Holmes on board, Stockton might follow. Two days in Chicago and another aboard ship showed him that Holmes valued honest labor and deep morality—the latter in short supply here, with the exception of his brother.

He called out again to Garrett, who apparently couldn't hear him above the whine of the saws.

His brother looked this way and that.

Roland waved and pushed past the passengers and curious onlookers. Again he cupped his hands around his mouth. "Garrett!"

"Garrett?" The sharp question came from that new schoolteacher, Pearl Lawson, who stood an arm's length away with her hands perched on her hips.

If she hadn't been so obviously miffed, he might have found her flushed cheeks and flashing eyes irresistible. Instead he looked for his brother, who had disappeared again.

"Miss Lawson. I am busy."

Holmes was walking toward him. He didn't have time to deal with ladies who mistakenly thought he was in the market for a wife.

She stepped in front of him. "You are not too busy to answer a simple question."

"Excuse me." He skirted around her, using his long strides to reach Holmes before she could catch up. "Did Charlie agree to take your bags to the hotel?"

"Yes, he did," Holmes said with a shake of his head. "Wouldn't take a penny for his efforts."

That's what Roland had hoped would be the outcome when he told Holmes to inform the lad that Roland Decker had suggested him. Later, he would add a little extra to the lad's wages, but now he had to catch Garrett. "There's someone I'd like you to meet."

"Mr. Decker!" That schoolteacher was pestering him again. "I must have a word with you. In private."

Roland bit back frustration. The candor that he'd once

found refreshing was now beginning to irritate him. "As I said, I have business to attend to."

"It will only take a minute." Her jaw was set and her gaze did not waver. "It is most urgent."

Holmes nudged Roland forward. "I can wait. Please take care of the lady."

Roland did not care to address what he was certain she would ask, but to deny her would throw doubt on Holmes's opinion of him and his project. He glanced up to see his brother had halted on the docks, staring up at the steamship, doubtless looking for him. Roland had a moment to calm the brewing storm.

"What is it, Miss Lawson?"

Holmes had thoughtfully stepped out of hearing range.

She rummaged through her bag and pulled out a tattered newspaper clipping, which she held out to him. "Did you or did you not place this advertisement?"

Roland had placed an advertisement in the Chicago papers looking for investors, but he couldn't imagine why Pearl Lawson would get upset over that. He accepted the clipping from her gloved hand. It took only seconds to recognize the wording, but how on earth had it leaped out of the fire and onto the pages of a newspaper?

Garrett. It had to be. He must have taken Roland's prodding seriously and rewrote the advertisement from memory. Roland pulled off his stifling hat. His brother's memory was better than he'd figured. This advertisement was word for word what Roland had written as a joke.

"Where did you get this?" he asked Pearl.

"From the New York newspaper."

"New York?" He faintly recalled that all the ladies attempting to claim his affections hailed from that city. He swallowed the lump building in his throat. How it had gotten to New York was only the tip of the problem. The fact that it offered no means to whittle down prospective brides meant these four women might be the first in a deluge.

"When?" he choked out.

"When what?"

"When did this advertisement appear?"

"Two weeks ago."

"Two weeks." He attempted to calculate precisely how many women might arrive in Singapore, for this advertisement stated that all applicants must apply in person. Why, it could be hundreds. "How many of you are there?"

One perfectly arched eyebrow lifted. "I assume you are referring to candidates for your hand, not a twin, which I do not have. In answer to your question, there are three. On *this* ship."

"Including you?" Something about the idea of his brother marrying Pearl Lawson set Roland's teeth on edge.

"As I told you, I am here to teach school." For the briefest moment, disappointment flashed across her face before she reined it in. "Then you did place the advertisement."

He swallowed again. "In truth, I'm not sure how it got in the newspaper."

She snorted in disbelief. "It didn't happen by itself. Are you or are you not Mr. Garrett Decker?"

At least on that he could speak with certainty. "I am not."

Both her eyebrows shot up this time.

"Let me explain," he said before she could get spitting mad again. "I am *Roland* Decker. My brother—my older brother—is Garrett."

She breathed out with what looked suspiciously like relief, and a little chuckle escaped her lips. "Then you are not the one seeking a wife."

"I am not." But he wasn't entirely certain his brother was, either. Surely he would have said something if that was the case.

Since Garrett had finally spotted him and was striding in their direction, they would soon have the answer. Then Roland could send the hopeful ladies off with his brother and get back to the business of courting Mr. Holmes's patronage.

Pearl struggled to hide her relief. Mr. Decker—Roland—had proven not to be a scoundrel. She mentally reviewed all his responses on the voyage. He had answered truthfully in every instance. No treachery or deceit had been involved, though she could not imagine why he didn't know his brother was seeking a wife, especially since the advertisement stated that all interested parties needed to inquire at the mercantile. That laborer had told her that Roland ran the store. Surely there could not be more than one general store in such a small town.

Regardless, she owed him an apology. "Please forgive me. When we heard your name and that you hailed from Singapore, we naturally assumed you were the one who sought a wife."

"An understandable mistake. I hope it did not cause you too much trouble."

His smile sent her insides fluttering again. She pressed a hand to her stomach. It must be a result of overindulgence at last night's meal. She was not accustomed to such rich food. He grinned, and she realized she had not replied to whatever he had asked. She searched her mind. Oh, yes, something about troubling them.

"Not at all. Amanda will be relieved that it wasn't you." *But not as much as I am.*

"Is that so? Your friend finds me lacking as a potential husband?"

Oh, dear. Heat rose to her cheeks as she realized what she'd said. "I didn't mean to infer that she thought you inferior in any way. Because you aren't." She fanned her face with her hand. "My, it's hot in the sun."

He ignored her discomfort. "And you know her mind on such matters?"

Now he was having fun at her expense. "Mr. Decker!"

He chuckled. "Roland, please."

She warmed to the change of direction. "Like the valiant knight."

A grin spread across his face. "Precisely. I aim to bring progress and prosperity to Singapore." He swept his arms wide, encompassing the less-than-impressive array of buildings. "That is why I cannot consider marriage at this time."

For some irrational reason, her buoying spirits plummeted. She averted her gaze and took a deep breath. After all, she could not consider marriage, either. "I understand, Mr. Decker."

"Roland."

"Roland." His name rolled off her tongue with such pleasantness that she could easily imagine saying it every day of her life. She sighed. "Too bad business and marriage are mutually exclusive propositions."

His smile never wavered. "They might not be for some men, but I would never subject the woman I loved to such loneliness. I work long hours, Miss Lawson."

"Pearl."

That smile of his softened, and the blue eyes twinkled. "Pearl. It would not be fair to her."

"Shouldn't that be her decision?"

Once again he cocked his head in that charming manner. "You are rather an independent sort, Pearl."

She had heard that sentiment before. She was too outspoken, too insistent, too independent. That's why men walked away after their first meeting. Roland would, too, though for different reasons. "I consider independence a virtue."

He let loose a great burst of laughter. "Do you turn everything on its head?"

"Only things that need turning about. An independent woman can take care of herself while providing all that her family needs."

"Is there no room for a man to assist her?"

Her stomach fluttered alarmingly. He could not seriously want a relationship with her, not after stating he would not marry anyone.

She touched a hand to her hot cheek. "Of course. If he is committed to her."

His gaze narrowed. "I see."

She dropped her hand as her silly hopes deflated. What had she thought would happen? He was a confirmed bachelor. She could not marry without losing her new position.

"First and foremost, Mr. Decker, I am a schoolteacher."

Roland stiffened and bowed ever so slightly. "And I am a businessman with duties waiting."

Her gaze sought Amanda, who waited on the dock with their carpetbags and the other two bride hopefuls. It had taken a stern warning to keep Fiona at bay, but Louise had gratefully accepted her help sorting this out. All three women watched intently. Fiona clutched the handle of her fine parasol. Louise pressed a book to her chest. Amanda nibbled on her lower lip. In Pearl's estimation, Amanda was the loveliest by far, but none of them could predict what a man might think.

"Good day, Miss Lawson." Her companion bowed to take his leave.

"Roland?"

He halted and gave her an inquiring look.

She took a deep breath. "Might you introduce us to your brother?"

* * *

Something about Pearl captivated Roland. Maybe it was the determined set of her chin or the flash of fire in her eyes. Maybe it was the way she protected her friend or took charge in difficult situations. She wasn't afraid. Except perhaps of him. He'd noticed the pleasant flush of her cheeks and didn't think for a minute that it had anything to do with the sun. Rather, he'd been relieved to learn that she not only wasn't answering the advertisement for a wife, but also accepted his statement that he would not marry.

She had a good head on her shoulders and would make a fine teacher.

Once he'd introduced her to Garrett, he asked her to tell her friends to wait a moment. He must warn his brother before unleashing the women on him. Pearl gave him a peculiar look before returning to them. She didn't trust him. He probably deserved that. If he'd been the object of the women's attention, he would have run back on the ship and headed for the next port. Garrett, on the other hand, needed a wife. And Roland needed to determine if his brother had placed the advertisement.

Garrett gazed at Pearl's retreating back. "Seems like a decent schoolteacher."

"The children will like her." Roland had to settle that point before he got to the next. "I had ample time to talk with her aboard ship. She will do well. But there's another matter we need to discuss, and we haven't much time."

In fact, the three bride hopefuls were staring at him as Pearl talked. It wouldn't take long before they realized Garrett was the object of their hopes. He doubted even Pearl could hold them back then.

"No investors?" Garrett asked.

Roland shook his head. "That's not it. I've brought Edward Holmes to look over the project site and layout of the land." A second urgent thought occurred to him. "In fact, I'm hoping you can join us. He will be impressed by your work. I could convince him that you should be the factory manager."

"Manager?" Garrett's brow creased as if the job was the worst he could imagine.

"Added responsibility comes with additional wages."

Garrett scowled. "If I told you once, I told you a thousand times. I'm not interested in managing anything. I like to work with my hands."

"Mr. Decker!" The fiery Fiona O'Keefe interjected herself into their discussion without waiting for introductions.

Roland shouldn't have expected less. After all, she had done the same with him. This time, her attention centered on Garrett, whose ordinarily ruddy complexion grew even more so at the sight of the elegantly dressed redhead. As usual, Roland's brother was at a loss for words.

"Garrett, may I introduce Miss Fiona O'Keefe." Roland gestured to the redhead and then proceeded to introduce the other women. His gaze drifted to Pearl, who hung outside the ring of anxious women, but she was scanning the town.

Garrett cleared his throat, obviously uncomfortable. "Pleased to meet you, ladies." He managed to look each one in the eye but showed no sign of particular interest in any of them. "What brings you to town?"

Roland groaned. That meant his brother either did not place the advertisement or had forgotten about it. Unfortunately, Roland had not had time to tell Garrett what to expect. Judging by the expression on Fiona's face, he would soon feel the wrath of four upset women if Roland didn't step in.

"Now, ladies, shouldn't you settle in at the hotel or boardinghouse before we get down to business?"

"Business?" Garrett questioned, so obviously perplexed that Roland pitied him.

"We most certainly will not," Fiona stated. "We have come all the way from New York in answer to this." She waved the advertisement in front of Garrett's nose. "And we expect an answer."

Roland's brother blanched. "An answer to what?"

This was going in a terrible direction, and to make matters worse, Holmes had drawn close enough to overhear the entire discussion. If this went the way Roland expected, his brother would lose the goodwill of four women, and Roland would lose an investor.

"Now, now," he said calmly. "You can't expect my brother to make a decision without getting to know each of you."

"A decision on what?" Garrett asked.

But Roland had managed to quiet the fire in Fiona O'Keefe's eyes.

Her anger subsided. "I suppose you're right. When do you want to begin getting to know us? At dinner this afternoon?"

"Uh, uh," Garrett stammered, backing away.

Roland noticed Pearl's expressive lips begin to tilt upward. He might be able to save both his project and his brother. "Supper would be better. If you ladies agree, we would be delighted to invite you all to supper tonight."

"We would?" Garrett said.

"Yes, we would." If nothing else, it would give the women their first glimpse of the children—a detail not mentioned in the advertisement. "The invitation extends to you, too, Miss Lawson. Shall we say six o'clock? I shall personally escort all of you from your lodgings."

Pearl nodded slightly. "We will be at the boarding-house."

Amanda and Louise Smythe drank in his words without question.

Fiona O'Keefe relented. "Very well, then, we shall see you tonight at the boardinghouse." She turned her gaze back to Garrett. "But I expect a decision soon, Mr. Decker."

"Decision on what?" Garrett choked out.

Roland motioned for his brother to stop, but he must not have noticed, for he plowed right on.

"I can't see what decision I could make that would affect you ladies."

Fiona O'Keefe twirled her parasol and cast Garrett a provocative smile. "Why, which one of us will become your wife, of course."

Chapter Four

"What will we do?" Amanda blurted once they'd reached the sanctity of their room in the boardinghouse.

Pearl scanned the sparse furnishings. "We will have to share the bed, just like in the orphanage." She pulled open each of the four drawers in the bureau. Though battered, it was clean and free of insects. "There's more than enough room for our belongings, and our Sunday dresses can hang on the pegs. I will have to do all my planning for classes at the school, but that's neither here nor there. Yes. We will make do."

"I didn't mean that. I meant for tonight. With all of us together, how will I ever make a good impression?"

Pearl settled beside her friend on the rather lumpy mattress, which at least felt like a feather tick rather than straw or horsehair. "You can't help but make a good impression. My concern is if Garrett Decker made a favorable impression on you."

Amanda blushed and picked at a thread on her skirt. "He is rather different from his brother, isn't he?"

"In looks, yes, but we mustn't judge a man on looks alone."

"Of course not." Still, Amanda scrunched her face. "He didn't seem at all pleased to see us."

Pearl had noticed that. Rather than answer Fiona's direct question, he had hurried off on the pretense of needing to return to work at the mill. The glare he'd shot at Roland hadn't escaped her notice, either. He did not think much of inviting the four ladies to sup with them. She was a little leery, too. Bringing all of them together at once meant just one thing.

"I fear we will be put to the test tonight."

Amanda blanched. "Will he ask us questions? What should I say about the Chatsworths...and Hugh?"

"Nothing. It's none of their business."

"But it would be if we married."

"Even if you and Garrett are a perfect match, you won't be getting married tonight. If you ask me, since he is the one who placed the advertisement, he's the one who needs to do the talking. Once you're convinced he would make a good husband, then you can reveal more details about yourself."

"But no man likes to hear that his intended was rejected by another. And then there's the orphanage."

Pearl hugged her friend. "If he's a godly man, those things won't make one bit of difference. If they do, then he's not the man for you."

"That's easy for you to say. You're not the one who wants to marry."

An image of Roland flashed through Pearl's mind, but that was pure foolishness. He'd made it clear that he would not marry, and she was prohibited from doing so. Restless, she walked to the window, which overlooked the smattering of houses on the sandy streets.

"Do you believe all things will work for the best for those who love the Lord?" Nothing was turning out as planned. Pearl hoped that didn't extend to her teaching position.

"O-of course."

"It will work out. You must believe that."

"I hope so." Yet Amanda's shoulders drooped.

Pearl must bolster her friend's confidence. "You will wear your Sunday dress, and I will ask Mrs. Calloway if she has any curling tongs."

Amanda sucked in her breath. "If I only had a pretty necklace. Not just this old half of a locket." She touched the tiny silver pendant hanging around her neck on a silver chain.

"The locket is perfect, for it invites conversation. Garrett will want to know where the other half is, and then you can tell him about your brother."

Amanda's eyes shone. "Maybe he will help me search for him."

"Perhaps he will."

Pearl smiled for her friend's benefit, but Garrett hadn't been the brother to travel to Chicago. Roland seemed more likely to take on such an adventure—provided it fit into his plans. That man was impossible to pin down.

"You don't think he will." Amanda's crestfallen expression told Pearl she'd let her thoughts run wild again.

She mustered another smile. "Everything will work out for the best. Now, let's get you ready for supper. We don't want Roland showing up before you're picture-perfect."

"What did you do?" Garrett growled once they reached the mercantile's stockroom. "Off to Chicago on another one of your larks and you bring back four women who seem to think I'm going to marry one of them."

Roland struggled to stifle a grin. If this whole situation didn't threaten to start a war between the men and women, it would be hilarious. Unfortunately, he and his brother were outnumbered and, in spite of Garrett's current irritation, out-enraged.

"Well," Garrett demanded. "Spit it out. What do you mean by bringing those ladies to Singapore?"

Roland shrugged, as if it meant nothing. "First of all, Pearl Lawson was hired to teach school. You must have known that."

Garrett simmered down a bit. "I forgot her name." He shuffled his feet against the rough plank flooring. "Or maybe I never heard it. It's not like I'm on the committee that makes the decisions."

"You sit in on the meetings. We've had to bring Isaac and Sadie to Mrs. Calloway so you could attend."

"That doesn't explain the other three women."

Roland slapped his hat onto the hat rack, slipped from his good suit jacket and donned an apron. Three days away meant he'd have a lot of work to accomplish in the store and not much time left in this work day.

"I can't explain the other three." Roland couldn't hide the chuckle. His brother would have his hands full with those ladies. Garrett should have thought of that before placing the advertisement. He looked his brother in the eye. "They seem to have some misguided idea that you are looking for a wife."

"I'm not, and you know it!" Garrett stormed, his face beet red.

As a child, Roland had enjoyed teasing his older brother until Garrett's temper blew like a steam whistle. Ma and Pa had frowned on Roland's shenanigans, but he never got the strap. Now that Garrett was older and beefier, he looked like he could tear off a man's head. Roland knew better. Garrett subscribed to that turn-the-other-cheek nonsense from the Bible. Roland did not let people trample on him. He wouldn't mind seeing his brother squirm, though. Garrett needed a wife, whether he realized it or not.

He pulled Pearl's crumpled newspaper advertisement from his watch pocket and spread it on the counter before his brother. "Maybe you can tell me why you placed this, then."

Garrett stared at him a moment before reading the advertisement. He hung over it so long that he must have read it ten times. "Where did you get this?"

"Pearl had it. Apparently it appeared in the New York newspaper, but then you know that."

"I do not." Garrett backed away from the advertisement as if it had been dipped in poison. "I sure didn't put it in the newspaper." He waved toward the clipping with his index finger. "You're the one who wrote it. Don't go trying to put the blame on me. This is your problem. You fix it."

"That's why I invited the ladies to supper tonight."

"That isn't fixing anything—it's stoking the fire!"

A chuckle escaped, and Garrett nearly connected on a blow to Roland's shoulder.

"Whoa!" Roland stepped back, hands up in surrender. "I figured we could clear everything up once and for all. Then the ladies can head back to New York on the next boat out of here."

That quieted his brother for a few seconds before worry returned. "What if they won't leave?"

Roland rather hoped that would be the case for at least one of the women, though which one suited his brother best was still in question. Thus the supper.

"I'm sure they're reasonable. Once you tell them that you did not place the advertisement—"

"You did it!"

"I didn't. But someone clearly did, someone who knew about my little joke. Did you tell anyone about it?"

Garrett flushed. "I might have mentioned something at the mill."

That might have explained it except that the advertisement followed his joke word for word. No sawmill worker would be able to recount each word, even if Garrett had. "If neither one of us placed the advertisement, how it got there is a mystery. One I intend to get to the bottom of tonight."

Garrett sighed, resigned. "Should I ask Mrs. Calloway to watch the children?"

"Sure—no." The brilliant idea he'd had earlier popped back into his head. "The advertisement doesn't say anything about children. None of them realizes you have a son and daughter. I'll introduce Isaac and Sadie. You watch each woman's reaction. You'll want a woman who loves children."

The sudden ache in his heart couldn't be that he feared who that woman would be. Pearl. As schoolteacher, she would have a natural affinity for children.

"You're forgetting something." Garrett was scowling again. "I don't want to get married."

As promised, Roland met them at them at the boardinghouse at precisely six o'clock. Pearl commanded the top porch step beside Amanda, whose raven curls far outshone Fiona's satin gown. The rival had donned a more tasteful sapphire-blue this evening. In comparison, Louise and Pearl faded into the background. Yet Pearl couldn't help but notice that Roland's gaze landed first and longest on her.

"Good evening, ladies."

He headed for Pearl, but Fiona glided down the wide steps to meet him first, all smiles and chatter. Pearl, Amanda and Louise had to trail behind Roland and the talkative redhead, taking care not to snag a hem on the rough wooden boardwalk.

Pearl lifted her brown gingham skirts a couple inches and placed each sturdy boot in the middle of the board. Unlike the wharves, the boards had been laid lengthwise on occasional crosswise planks. Though sand crested onto the boards in some places, in other areas the long boards drooped above the sand, creating an unsteady platform.

Amanda stepped off the edge and teetered precariously before Pearl reeled her back in.

"This is as unstable as the ship," Louise commented in that soft voice of hers.

That had to be the most Louise Smythe had said since Pearl met her. The woman did have the sense not to drag a book with her tonight, but she, like Pearl, had not worn her Sunday best. That gave Amanda the advantage, especially if Fiona continued to claim Roland's attention.

At present, Amanda's face blazed, either from the late-afternoon heat rising off the sand or from embarrassment. Either way, she needed to regain control before they met Garrett Decker. Louise's comment had been meant kindly, but lately Amanda took everything in the worst way.

Pearl sighed and wrapped her arm around Amanda's. "It's better than walking in the sand. Think how that would get in your shoes."

"I suppose you're right."

Pearl eyed the redhead, who now clung to Roland's arm and leaned closer by the minute. Her laughter and vivaciousness rubbed Pearl the wrong way. The fact that he looked her way repeatedly poured vinegar into the wound.

"They're not right for each other," Amanda whispered as she picked her way along the boardwalk.

"I don't know who you mean."

"Fiona and Roland."

Though seeing Roland and Fiona in close conversation

hurt more than it should, Pearl focused on what was more important. "All that matters is what you think of Garrett."

Amanda trembled. "I'm afraid."

"That's natural, but remember that this is only a first meeting. It's your opportunity to determine if he is the sort of man you might consider marrying." She squeezed Amanda's hand to reassure her. "You can always decide not to marry."

Amanda's lip quivered. "What will I do then?"

That was the question. This town did not appear to have more than a couple of saloons, the hotel, the store and the boardinghouse in the way of businesses. The first would gladly hire a woman of Amanda's beauty, but Pearl would starve before she let her friend work in a drinking establishment. The hotel and boardinghouse were better prospects, but Pearl hated to think of lovely Amanda as a maid. That left the store, which would give Amanda ample time with the Decker brothers.

Perhaps too much time. What if Amanda fell for Roland? She had been drawn to him aboard the *Milwaukee*. No. There must be another solution. Amanda was good with the needle.

Pearl latched onto that. "I'll ask Mrs. Calloway if she knows of anyone who might need sewing or fancywork."

Amanda brightened. "I'm sure there would be, unless there's already a seamstress in town."

Pearl recalled that only one elderly couple had disembarked here. She'd seen no other women aside from Mrs. Calloway. "I doubt there is."

Roland led them to a two-story building on the wharves leading to the large sawmill. Pearl expected him to walk in the front door, but he led Fiona up a rickety outside staircase leading to the second story. He waited on the landing at the top for the other three to climb.

"Here we are, ladies. Our humble home." He flung open the door and motioned all of them inside ahead of him.

Fiona entered first, followed by Louise. Pearl waited for Amanda to enter. She felt a hand to her elbow.

"Don't let my brother's gruffness fool you," he said in a low voice. "He has a good heart."

Her heart sank. Amanda would not bear up under a gruff man. One scowl and she'd start edging for the door.

"Thanks for the warning," she murmured before stepping through the door.

The interior was dimly lit, and one could hear a pin drop. The three ladies all stared to Pearl's right. She followed their gaze, and her jaw dropped. The advertisement had omitted one key detail. Garrett Decker had children.

Chapter Five

That was not the only discrepancy in the advertisement. It took Pearl mere seconds to ascertain that Garrett Decker was not wealthy. The rooms were furnished with the barest necessities. Two rather faded stuffed chairs faced the woodstove. A rude bench sat just inside the door, and pegs held jackets and coats and hats. The only fine piece of furniture was a walnut sideboard, but it needed a good polishing. Across the room an unvarnished table was surrounded by six mismatched chairs. That left them two short by her calculations. No curtains or paintings or the slightest hint of a woman's touch.

Yet before them stood a boy and a girl, both quite young, six or seven she would guess. When had they lost their mother? Her heart tugged her nearer.

"What sweet children."

They eyed her solemnly and silently. Their father pulled them close.

Gruff was not the word she would use to describe Garrett Decker. Stony. Unyielding. Clearly not pleased to find four women invading his home. He seemed even less pleased that she had approached his children, almost as if he feared she would take them away.

Roland swooped between Pearl and the children. "Miss Lawson is going to be your new teacher this year." He then shot his brother a glare.

Pearl wondered what that was about, but she was more curious about the children. Their expressions did not change, though they assessed her from head to toe. Not one word or even a sound. They must be shy.

Roland motioned to the boy. "This is Isaac." He pushed the boy forward a step. "And this is Sadie."

Pearl dropped to one knee so she would be at eye level. "Isaac, I'm pleased to meet you. What grade will you be in?"

The boy didn't answer.

"He finished one year," Garrett said with a defensive snarl.

She turned to the girl, who looked younger. "Have you begun school yet, Sadie?"

She stuck her thumb in her mouth.

Pearl smiled. "I like your doll."

The rag doll had seen better days. A button eye was missing, half the yarn hair was gone and it hadn't seen the wash in a long time.

"I had one like that when I—" Pearl halted. They did not need to know she grew up in an orphanage or that she, too, had refused to let anyone touch her Dollie. That rag doll had been her last connection to her parents. She'd clung to it as if that would bring her mama and papa back. Sadie must have suffered similar loss. "I loved my Dollie. Does yours have a name?"

Sadie just looked back with solemn eyes.

Pearl rose, having made no progress. School would be difficult for Isaac and Sadie if they refused to talk.

"She calls it Baby," Garrett mumbled, his color high.

"Pearl—Miss Lawson—is not here in response to the advertisement," Roland needlessly pointed out.

Garrett's gaze drifted to the other three women, and Roland once again swooped into action.

"Where are my manners?" Roland introduced each of the ladies in turn.

Fiona no longer bubbled over with witty comments. Her gaze circled the room repeatedly, and she looked ready to accuse the men of what Pearl had already noticed. The advertisement had misled them. Louise didn't even look up at Garrett. She hung back and said little more than the children. Pearl walked her trembling friend closer to the prospective groom once Roland introduced her.

"Amanda and I have been friends since we were Sadie's age."

Amanda instinctively looked at the little girl and smiled softly. "Would you like me to make you a pretty new dress?"

Sadie's eyes widened, and she nodded her head while holding out her rag doll.

"Oh, a matching one for your doll, too?"

Amanda had always had a gift with children. Where Pearl loved to see a child learn and grow, Amanda took them into her confidence. As a consequence, children adored her. Already she had made progress with little Sadie.

Her father's expression had soured, however. "I'm not wasting money on frivolous things."

That startled Amanda, who stared at Garrett as if he'd just confessed to murder. "A new dress for school is hardly frivolous."

Pearl could have cheered. While adults might make her friend nervous, Amanda would rise to defend any child. Clearly, Sadie needed some encouragement, which she wasn't getting from her father. Unless, of course, he couldn't afford a new dress.

Pearl looked Garrett Decker in the eye. "We will work

something out. Amanda can create beautiful things with the needle."

His set jaw told her she'd meddled where she didn't belong. Oh, dear, this wasn't going well for Amanda. Not at all.

"Come to think of it," Roland interjected, "we've got some odds and ends of fabric at the store that I was going to throw away. If you and Miss Porter would like to look through them, I'd give you any that you think you can use."

Amanda gushed her thanks, but Roland wasn't looking at her. He sought Pearl's approval. She had to swallow the lump in her throat. Even though the scraps were probably too small to make a dress, the gesture meant a lot, for it smoothed over the differences that had sprung up between his brother and Amanda.

Pearl couldn't help but smile. "We are most grateful."

His trace of sheepish concern vanished in a brilliant smile. "Then we accept, don't we, Garrett?"

Roland's brother had not unlocked his jaw, even though his little girl looked up at him with the most hopeful, tremulous expression that Pearl had ever seen. Her heart just about broke. She would do anything to bring a smile to that little girl's lips. Anything.

Garrett puffed out his breath. "I don't want to owe anyone."

"I'll pay any costs," Amanda offered.

Pearl stared at her friend. Between them, they had only enough for room and board until school began. Where was she going to get money to pay for thread and ribbon and whatever else she needed?

Roland laughed and clapped his brother on the shoulder. "Isn't that like you, always counting your pennies?"

A snort from behind Pearl reminded her that Fiona and Louise were also in the room. She turned to see Fiona standing with her arms crossed and a fire brewing in her eyes.

"Pennies?" Fiona said now that everyone's attention had shifted to her. "Your advertisement said you were wealthy. Now you're talking about counting pennies? What kind of man are you to lure us here under false pretenses?"

Though Louise didn't verbally second the sentiment, her dismay spoke volumes. Amanda, naturally, said nothing, but Pearl had never shied from speaking her mind.

"The advertisement did hint that you were a man of means. I believe it said you had a handsome inheritance." She dug in her bag to find the crumpled bit of paper and came up empty. What had she done with it?

"Now, ladies, I'm sure this little misunderstanding can all be cleared up over supper." Roland waved them toward the table. "Have a seat, and I'll be right back with the stew." He scooted through the door beyond the table faster than a rat abandoning a sinking ship.

"Little misunderstanding?" Fiona shook her head. "This is not a misunderstanding. This is deception, pure and simple. I know better than to throw good after bad. I'm here to make a good match, not marry a pauper. I could have had that in New York."

Pearl wondered why Fiona hadn't stayed in New York. A thriving musical career should have brought her to the attention of men of wealth. For her to throw herself into such an uncertain situation, something must have happened.

She didn't have time to contemplate it, for with a final toss of her head, sending the feathers on her hat dancing, Fiona stomped toward the door. "Come, Louise, Amanda. We can't let these men get away with this. Stew!" She said the word as if it was the final insult.

Louise meekly followed, but Amanda hesitated, torn

between obeying Fiona and staying behind with the children. She looked to Pearl for answers, but Pearl would not tell her friend what to do. Amanda must learn to trust her instincts and the Lord instead of relying on the advice of others.

Amanda looked back at little Sadie, who clung to her father's hand. "I like stew. Do you?"

For the first time, Garrett Decker's expression cracked. "She doesn't talk. Not since…" He stroked his daughter's head.

Pearl squeezed back a tear. He didn't have to finish for both her and Amanda to understand. Little Sadie hadn't spoken since her mama died or left. The vivid memory of watching her father walk away returned with an ache. *Be a good girl, Pearl.* Her papa's admonition had carried with it the hope that if she was good enough, maybe then her mama would get well and her parents would come back for her.

They never did.

Roland walked back into the room carrying a pot of stew. "Can you fetch the bowls, Isaac? The spoons, Sadie?"

The children hurried off.

He looked around the room and then at his brother. "You sure do know how to clear out a room."

Pearl again noted the six chairs. Maybe that had been the plan the whole time.

Roland's brother had barely finished saying grace when Pearl began to point out her friend's virtues.

"Amanda is an excellent housekeeper, and she's wonderful with children."

What Pearl said mattered far less to Roland than the charming tilt of her head and spark in her eyes. The two individuals at the center of her persuasion paid the potato and cabbage stew an uncommon amount of interest. Pearl barely touched hers, while the children watched the two ladies with a mix of curiosity and fear.

Most men would find Amanda the prettier of the two ladies, but he preferred Pearl's chestnut hair and lively green eyes. The fact that her spoon spent more time pointing at Garrett than in the bowl struck him as hilarious. His brother wouldn't know what to do with a spitfire like Pearl. He, on the other hand... That was foolish thinking. She'd flat-out told him that her teaching contract prohibited marriage, and he wasn't ready to settle down, Mr. Holmes's cajoling aside. He had a factory to build.

"What are you going to do?" Pearl's demand settled on him.

He had no idea what she was talking about, but a little charm usually settled down whatever chafed a woman. "Proceed with my plans."

Her stormy expression told him he'd failed to hit the mark.

"And *your* plans do not include cleaning up after the mess *you* caused."

The sparking eyes weren't quite so wonderful when her fury was directed at him.

He tried to placate her. "As I told you, I did not place that advertisement."

"Neither did I," Garrett stated in no uncertain terms.

The children looked down at their bowls of stew the moment Roland glanced in their direction. Odd. They were never this interested in eating. Garrett must not have given them a good midday meal. He began to address Pearl when out of the corner of his eye he saw Isaac whisper something to Sadie. No doubt about it. Something was going on between those two.

"I don't care which of you placed that advertisement." Pearl pointed her spoon first at Garrett and then at Roland. "Three women have spent their savings and traveled a great distance in response to it. I expect you to honor your words."

Garrett's jaw dropped.

Roland stifled a snicker. Seeing his older brother squirm was worth the trouble.

"I'm not marrying," Garrett stated. "I don't care what you threaten."

Sadie made an odd squeaking sound, and Isaac wiggled like his chair was on fire.

Finally the boy stood. "May we be excused? Sadie don't feel good."

"Doesn't," Pearl said, correcting Isaac.

Garrett ignored her. "You may go. Take your bowls and spoons to the kitchen."

The children clattered out of the room with their dishes. No doubt they would head outdoors after dropping the bowls and spoons in the washtub. That left just four at the table. Amanda picked at her stew, head bowed. Pearl had a strange expression on her face, and Garrett scowled.

"Why did you have to bring up that advertisement in front of the children?" Garrett was not happy. "Isaac keeps begging me for a new ma. Says Sadie needs a woman about the house, but we're doing just fine. She can get all the womanly time she needs with Mrs. Calloway or Mrs. Elder."

Color highlighted Pearl's cheeks. "I'm sorry. I shouldn't have spoken with the children present."

Garrett accepted the apology with a stiff nod.

"They'll get over it." Roland tried to make light of things in order to bring back the sparkle in Pearl's eye. "They're young."

Pearl turned back to him. "When did they lose their mother?"

Garrett frowned, but the question hit Roland like a

bullet. He shivered. The chill of that day still hadn't left his bones. The water. The ice. Eva. He shook his head.

"Almost a year and a half ago," Garrett stated, his gaze piercing through Roland.

Both women drew in a breath.

"So tragic." Amanda sighed.

Pearl started to ask something but stopped. Unusual. She seldom bridled what she said. "I'm sorry for your loss."

Roland decided to put into words what she'd refused to say. "That's why my brother needs a wife."

Garrett looked like he would spit nails at him. "I am not marrying. Sorry to disappoint you, ladies, but you've come here for no reason. Now that you know, you can catch a boat back home."

Amanda paled, but Pearl looked livid.

Roland aimed to cut her off. "I will help with the fare to Chicago."

Pearl's pressed lips indicated she wasn't buying his generous offer. "Mr. Decker—"

"Which one of us?" Roland asked.

"Both." She spat out the word. "I am not leaving and neither is Amanda. Fiona and Louise deserve better than a token effort to appease us. You brought them here. You will ensure all three ladies have enough money to get home."

Roland's jaw dropped. "I can't do that. It would cost..." He quickly calculated in his head. "A month's wages. At least."

His brother was now grinning.

Pearl was not done. "I do not want your money, and I doubt the other ladies would take it, either. We are perfectly capable of earning it. What they need is employment. Since you are responsible for this situation, I suggest you find jobs for them."

Roland could feel his temper rise. "There aren't many jobs in Singapore, unless they plan to saw timber or work in one of the saloons."

Garrett coughed. Amanda gasped.

Pearl glared. "I expect you to find them *respectable* jobs."

"Like I said, there aren't many jobs here."

"Your general store must need another clerk."

Roland sputtered, "Impossible."

Garrett snickered.

Pearl persisted. "If not the store, then at another respectable establishment."

"I might be able to find something for your friend." The brunette was pretty enough to attract the interest of someone. Maybe the hotel needed housekeepers.

"For all three ladies." Pearl apparently considered that closed the conversation, for she rose. "Thank you for supper, gentlemen. I look forward to hearing from you, Roland. Garrett, I expect to see your children at the schoolhouse on the first day of class."

Roland stood, but he couldn't think of a thing to say. Three jobs? Impossible.

Pearl tugged on her gloves. "Come, Amanda. I believe our business here is done."

Garrett pushed back his chair. "Thank you for visiting, ladies."

Amanda shot him a shy smile, but Pearl merely nodded, apparently still peeved. After another curt nod, she swirled out of the house with Amanda in her wake.

Roland sat down, exhausted.

"That didn't go well," he murmured.

Garrett laughed. "It's good to see you take the brunt of feminine ire for a change."

"Don't think you're safe yet. Those women aren't leaving Singapore anytime soon." Therein lay the problem.

Roland pulled the crumpled clipping from his watch pocket and smoothed it out on the table. "'Widower with handsome inheritance seeks wife in booming town soon to rival Chicago. Well-furnished, comfortable house.'"

"Your words."

"My words exactly, none of them true."

"I am a widower," Garrett pointed out.

"All right. One true statement. It's easy to see why the women expected more. The advertisement specifies a house, not the top floor of a general store with sparse furnishings and cracks so wide that the snow drifts across the floor in the winter."

Garrett shrugged.

"Then there's the mention of a handsome inheritance."

"Ma's sideboard."

"It is handsome, and you did inherit it."

"Eva loved it."

"I'm surprised you didn't lock it away in the stockroom with everything else." Garrett had stripped the place of anything personal. Curtains, pictures and treasured furnishings all went into storage. "You can't hide from the past."

Garrett glared at him. "Is that what you're doing? Trying to push me into marriage when I'm not ready?" He pointed at the scrap of newspaper. "You placed that advertisement."

Roland shook his head. "I didn't. That's what's so perplexing. No one had any reason to do that, even as a joke. If it had turned up in one of the local newspapers, I could see someone playing a joke on you, but not New York. What man at the mill would even think to send it to New York? Chicago's closer."

Garrett still didn't look convinced. "If you didn't do it and no one in town did it, then who?"

"It would have to be someone who stood to gain from it. Who would want to see you married?"

"You."

"Besides me."

Garrett leaped up and paced to the window.

Roland joined him. "Did you notice Sadie's expression when Pearl mentioned the advertisement?"

His brother said nothing.

"And how Isaac reacted when you said you weren't going to remarry? Not just disappointed. He almost looked guilty. Then he asked to be excused."

Garrett scrubbed his jaw. "They're too young to understand."

"Are they? They understand their mama's dead."

Garrett flinched.

Roland persisted. "They need a woman in their lives. Especially Sadie."

Garrett hung his head. "I know, but how can I? There isn't a day that I don't think of Eva, but they were so young. Soon they won't remember their mother. I don't want that to happen."

"They won't forget." Roland wished he was certain of his words. "You won't let them."

His big brother, burly enough to heft logs against the circular saw, trembled. "I don't know what to do."

"Let's start by having a talk with Isaac and Sadie."

"You really think they did that?"

"They were the only ones who could have snatched it out of the stove."

Garrett shook his head. "But send it to New York? How and why? Isaac wouldn't even be able to read it, least of all figure out how to send it to a newspaper. And why New York?"

"Eva was always talking about New York. Remember?

How she wanted to go there? She made it sound like the shiniest, brightest city in the world."

"I would have taken her."

Roland ignored the jab. If he hadn't been so certain that the future was in this part of the world, Eva might have stayed with him. Instead, she'd leaped at Garrett's promise. "The point is that your children sent that fake advertisement to a real newspaper."

"They wouldn't know how."

"Someone must have helped them. I'd guess Mrs. Calloway, since they spend so much time with her and she happens to agree that they need a mother."

Garrett heaved a sigh. "I still don't believe it."

"There's only one way to find out. Ask."

Chapter Six

Pearl waited beneath a borrowed umbrella for Alfred Farmingham to unlock the door to the schoolhouse. He had arrived at the boardinghouse just as breakfast was served, and Mrs. Calloway had set a place for him at the crowded table. Judging from his corpulent figure, he didn't miss many meals. He had introduced himself as a councilman from Saugatuck, the town upriver, appointed to show her the school building.

Before breakfast, Amanda had offered to join her, but the moment she'd heard Isaac and Sadie would be spending the day with Mrs. Calloway, she'd changed her mind. Fiona and Louise also declined, apparently having decided overnight to forgive Garrett for his misleading advertisement.

"I've asked Roland Decker to find employment for all of you," Pearl told them.

Fiona had shrugged. "Maybe I won't be needing work."

Louise had sighed. "I wonder if there's a bookstore or library in town."

Pearl doubted it. From what she'd seen last night, not even a church steeple graced the tiny village. Nor could she spot the school. She'd soon found out why.

The wood-framed structure was small, a single room, she suspected, and not in town. Instead, it was located along a sandy, rutted road in a rare wooded area. Moss peeked out between shingles on the roof and the windows could use a good cleaning.

If not for the persistent drizzle and chill that heralded the upcoming change of seasons, the walk would have been a pleasant one. The narrow road, little better than a pathway, meandered along the river before cutting up over a rise and intersecting with another pathway that, as Mr. Farmingham indicated, led to Saugatuck to the south, and Goshorn Lake, and eventually Holland, to the north.

"Here we are." Mr. Farmingham pushed open the door and waited for her to climb the single step and walk inside. "As you can see, the desks are fairly new."

Pearl could see nothing of the sort. The benches and tables were worn, with initials and other doodling scratched into the surface. She ran a hand along one and it wobbled. The teacher's desk looked sturdier, if small. A woodstove filled the front right corner. An uneven chalkboard had been hung on the front wall. Grimy windows lined each side of the single room. A cupboard stood in the back left corner, while pegs lined the wall on the back right. One room. No luxuries. This was nothing like the schools she had attended in New York.

"This new school was built in '55." Mr. Farmingham swept an arm wide, as if boasting over it.

"Fifteen years ago?"

"Practically new. Why, I nailed shingles on the roof myself."

Pearl could not imagine the rotund man scaling a ladder, least of all climbing onto a pitched roof. She walked between the desks and found most of the tables sturdy. Likewise, the benches felt secure.

"The teacher's desk has drawers," he pointed out.

Pearl walked behind the desk. Sure enough. It was a proper desk with three drawers. She tugged out the top one. Empty. Same with the others. "Where are the supplies?"

"In the cupboard, I assume."

"And the primers?"

"The same, providing the children didn't take them home last year."

"Home? Why would they take them home?" Neither Roland nor Garrett had mentioned anything about that last night.

The councilman shrugged. "Some folks figured it was part of their tuition."

Pearl's jaw dropped. "They must pay to attend?" She would have no students.

"Not anymore. Not since our illustrious state congress decided all students could attend without charge."

"That's a good thing, isn't it?"

Mr. Farmingham scowled. "Considering they took our money, saying the state could do a better job, and then didn't send back half of it, no. It's not a good thing."

Pearl's mouth grew dry. "If you can't pay my salary, I'd appreciate knowing that now so I can make other plans."

"Now don't go getting yourself into a dander. Of course we can pay your salary. Just don't go asking for anything else, if you know what I mean."

Pearl had a sinking feeling. Without basic supplies, teaching would be difficult if not impossible. "How many children will be in each grade?"

"Let me see. There's the Bailey boys from Saugatuck. Three. Add in the two Wardman girls. The Clapps from Goshorn makes seven, and then the Deckers make nine."

"Only nine? What ages?"

"Make that twelve. I forgot about the Norstrands out on the farm. They'd probably send the three youngest, all girls, maybe the boys after harvest."

Twelve or possibly more. She could handle that. "What ages?"

Mr. Farmingham shrugged. "All ten or less, I'd say."

"There aren't any children older than ten in the area?"

"They're working, Miss Lawson. Like I said, after harvest, you might see some of them."

"And when would that be?"

"About November."

November. Until then she would just have the little ones. Arithmetic didn't require books, but she must have primers for reading and writing. She headed for the cupboard. "I need primers, even old ones. Surely the last teacher left them here somewhere."

Pearl opened the door to the large cupboard. Inside were tiny pieces of chalk, slates and primers in a dreadful state of disrepair. She lifted a book. It was waterlogged. She tested the chalk. Wet.

"What happened?" She thrust a moldy volume at Mr. Farmingham.

"I—I don't know." He backed away. "I don't oversee the school. That's Mr. Stockton's responsibility."

Stockton. She'd heard that name before. She searched her memory. Ah, yes, Roland's boss was named Stockton. "Very well, then. I will speak with Mr. Stockton."

Farmingham blanched. "You can't do that."

"Why not?"

"Because he's not here."

"What do you mean? Doesn't he own the general store?"

Farmingham mopped his brow. "He owns the whole town of Singapore, but he's not here."

"Then where is he?"

"In Chicago."

Well then, she'd reach the man through Roland Decker. Pearl dropped the ruined primer on the nearest desk.

"These must be destroyed. Mr. Stockton will have to replace them."

Farmingham wiped his round pink face. "He isn't going to be happy."

Whoever this Mr. Stockton was, he inspired fear even in a councilman from another town. Pearl didn't have political aspirations. She had children who needed to learn.

"Happy or not, he will supply primers." Even if it meant nagging Roland within an inch of his life.

Roland reached the top of the dune after Holmes. Thinking the older man would not be able to manage the deep sand, he had hung back. Holmes proved an intrepid hiker, scaling the dune faster than Roland could on a good day.

Today was not ideal. Last night's rain had calmed to an annoying drizzle. Though they wielded umbrellas, the chill sank into the bones. From the top of this tallest of the dunes, he'd expected to see Lake Michigan's rolling waves, but the mists shrouded them. Likewise it prevented seeing how far the dunes extended, which he'd hoped to impress upon the investor. This sand would not run out anytime soon, making his glassworks the perfect answer for Singapore's future.

"Can't see much today," Holmes noted.

"Imagine that three more dunes, nearly as large, stand between us and the water. They stretch for miles north and south of the river mouth. The supply is virtually unlimited."

"You own this property?"

That was the problem. "I know who does." Stockton. "And he might be eager to sell under the proper circumstances. I do own riverfront property large enough for the glassworks."

"But no supply source."

"As I said, the owner of this property would be willing to deal." Roland could feel the investor's interest slip away.

"You're certain of this."

"I know the man personally." He forced a casual smile. "He is a businessman first. Once he sees the advantages, he'll sell the sand if not the property."

Holmes grunted, unimpressed. "If this is as good a deal as you're making out, why hasn't he developed this glassworks already?"

"His interests and investments are in timber."

Holmes grunted again. "I believe I've seen enough. Let's head back to town."

Roland followed the man down the dune. Without Holmes's investment, Roland couldn't afford to build the factory. Without the factory, he couldn't convince Stockton to sell the sand. He'd tried already. Stockton wouldn't sell until he saw progress. Then he wanted a cut of the profits in addition to the cost of the sand. Roland had run through the figures a hundred times, and it always came out in his favor as long as he could secure the capital at the right rate of interest to build the glassworks. No one here or in Holland would invest. They'd all laughed him out of their offices. Holmes was his best chance. If he turned down Roland, the dream would slip away.

"How did your supper with the ladies go last night?" Holmes asked when they reached the bottom of the dune.

"Fine." Roland didn't want to discuss that debacle, especially with a man who held matrimony in the highest regard.

"They are a lively bunch, especially Miss O'Keefe. She does speak her mind."

"Not as much as Miss Lawson."

Holmes gave him a strange look. "The schoolteacher?"

Roland nodded.

"I didn't think she was responding to the advertisement."

"She's not, but that didn't stop her from taking charge. She expects me to find them all employment."

Holmes guffawed. "Now that's a woman worth her salt."

"She's interfering."

"She's looking after the other three, like a hen looks after her chicks."

Roland didn't relish the comparison, for it reminded him that she had gone to the children first. What if Garrett took his advice and then considered Pearl the best prospect for a wife? Even though Roland didn't care to marry, he didn't want his brother marrying her.

Holmes must have read his mind, for he asked, "Did your brother settle on any of them?"

"No." Roland squirmed. "It seems he didn't place the advertisement after all."

"He didn't? Then who did?"

"We're pretty sure his children did, though they won't admit it." All their persuading and threatening had produced only tears.

Holmes guffawed. "From the mouths of babes."

"They're six and seven years old. They couldn't have placed an advertisement on their own."

"True."

"My guess is the woman who looks after them took the lead."

"But that's not the point, is it?" Holmes's eyes twinkled in spite of the dismal gray light. "They want a mother and found a way to take matters into their own hands."

Roland sighed. "But now there are three women expecting a husband, and one groom determined not to marry. What if Isaac and Sadie like one of the women?" Pearl came to mind again. "What then?"

"Then they'll convince their father." Holmes clapped him on the shoulder. "Wait and see. Everything will work out. They'll get their new mother."

That's what had kept Roland awake all night.

A bell tinkled when Pearl pushed open the mercantile door. She'd been surprised to discover the store occupied the ground floor of the building that the Deckers called home. At first she couldn't figure out why she hadn't seen that last night. Then she realized Roland had approached the building from the rear, perhaps on purpose.

Regardless, she must secure primers from Mr. Stockton, and Roland would know where to find the man. For all she knew, he had spoken to Mr. Stockton in Chicago before embarking for Singapore on the *Milwaukee*.

The door slipped shut. No one rushed to meet her or to even greet her. She surveyed the goods on display. All were utilitarian, from basic foodstuffs to durable fabric in a few plain colors, ready-made Kentucky jeans and an assortment of tools and cooking implements that would serve in a shack or over the open fire.

A long counter ran in front of the smaller items: soap, jars of medicines, tonics, perfumes, tobacco and the like. An account book presided over the center with a small display of candy sticks and drops to one side. No one manned the counter.

Curious. If Roland was in back, he should have come out at the sound of the bell.

She tapped the tip of the umbrella on the floor, and the last of the precipitation slipped off. "Hello?"

No answer. If anything, the quiet was more pervasive, no small feat considering the numbing howl of the sawmill.

"Is anyone here?"

The question met the same lack of response.

Perhaps she should check outside. He might be unloading supplies from one of the ships in port. She turned and caught her reflection in a mirror hung next to a display of hats. Hers was askew, probably from that umbrella. She took a moment to straighten it and was just replacing the last pin when the bell jingled, signaling a new arrival.

She had to step back to see the front door. By then, the businessman, Mr. Holmes, was entering the store.

"Let me know what he says to the plan," the man said.

Roland appeared next, shaking the rain from his umbrella. "You can be sure I will. Don't worry. Stockton will approve the plan wholeheartedly."

Stockton. There was that name again. Regardless of Roland's plan, her business must come first. On the other hand, she shouldn't interrupt their conversation, like Fiona would. She spotted a bench near the stove and sank onto it. Considering the chilly day, a warm stove sounded wonderful. She extended her cold hands, but no heat emanated from it.

"...like to speak with the leaders up in Holland," Mr. Holmes was saying.

They must have moved closer.

Pearl slid across the bench in order to be out of earshot. She did not eavesdrop. She'd learned that lesson the hard way in the orphanage when she thought the Chatsworths had chosen her. Instead, it was Amanda.

"I'll go with you," Roland replied.

Surely they'd seen her. She glanced back, but they were in discussion near the counter, both facing away from her. Pearl covered her ears with her gloved hands, but it made no difference.

"No need, son. I understand the *Lily Sue* is headed that way in the morning. No sense taking you away from your business again."

"Charlie can man the store while I'm gone."

"That lad? He doesn't look older than twelve."

"Fourteen." Roland said it as if proud of the boy. "I had three jobs by that age."

"Yet you got your learning. That's most important."

Pearl could almost hear Roland bristle.

"He knows his letters and can add up a full page of numbers in seconds." Roland's defensive reply set off Pearl.

She couldn't help herself. She shot to her feet. "I suppose you think that's enough, that a boy of fourteen can't learn anything more in school."

Roland whipped around, but his initial surprise soon turned to annoyance. "Endless schooling might be all well and good in New York City, but on the frontier, a boy can't afford to waste time in primary school."

"Waste time! Education is never a waste of time." She stomped a foot and would have stuck a finger into Mr. Know-It-All's chest if not for Mr. Holmes's chuckle.

Roland shifted his attention to the businessman. "You agree with Pearl, er, Miss Lawson?"

Mr. Holmes had a kindly face. Pearl had noticed that on the ship. How he fit into Singapore was still unclear, but his opinion seemed to matter a great deal to Roland.

Holmes shook his head. "As a matter of fact, you both have a point. Education is valuable, as Miss Lawson indicated, but sometimes a family can't afford to send their children to school, especially once they're old enough to earn an income."

Pearl felt her cheeks heat. She'd been so focused on what was best for the boy that she'd forgotten about the cost to the family. Mr. Farmingham had tried to tell her that in a roundabout way. The farm came first. A family struggling to make ends meet needed every income they could get. Other than the little ones, she could expect only girls in her class. Even though tuition was no longer required, she couldn't expect the families to purchase new primers. She needed Mr. Stockton to step up.

"Can I help you find something?" Roland asked her.

This was her chance. "I'm looking for Mr. Stockton."

Mr. Holmes peered at her. "You, too?"

Roland, on the other hand, looked irritated. "Why would you need to speak to Mr. Stockton?"

"Mr. Farmingham told me that Mr. Stockton is the head of the school committee."

Roland gave her a quizzical look. "Is there something wrong with the school?"

"Indeed there is. I need books, especially primers."

"There aren't any primers?" Mr. Holmes exclaimed.

"They're ruined. Waterlogged and moldy."

"How?" Roland snapped.

"Apparently the roof leaks and has been soaking the books all summer. I picked up one, and it fell apart in my hands. School begins in less than two weeks, and I need books, even if they're not primers." On the way here she had thought of one other possible source, thanks to Louise's musing this morning. "Is there a library or a private collector that would be willing to lend us books until new ones can be ordered?"

Now Roland looked amused. "You aren't in the city. This is a lumber town. There aren't any libraries here, and no one has a book collection, at least not one fit for children."

"Does Holland have a library?" Mr. Holmes interjected. "If so, I could approach them with your request."

Roland shrugged. "I don't know."

"It's worth looking into." Mr. Holmes turned to her. "I'll let you know what I find out."

"Thank you." She smiled her gratitude.

Roland looked skeptical. "You can try, but I wouldn't count on it. Holland is, well, they're Dutch."

"As if that makes any difference," Pearl snapped.

"You do want books in English, don't you?"

She felt her cheeks heat. "They don't teach English?"

"Come now, Decker," Mr. Holmes said, "I'm sure there are plenty of books in the English language in Holland. If not, they can be procured."

Roland grinned at her. "I could order some primers for you."

"I'll take that order back with me to Chicago and send the primers back on the next boat," Mr. Holmes offered. "You shouldn't have to go too long without them."

Pearl felt ill. Roland hadn't said anything about Mr. Stockton or anyone else picking up the cost. He must think she would purchase them, but she couldn't begin to afford enough books for a dozen children. Not unless he accepted credit. Even then, it would take some time to repay.

"A reasonable solution," Roland said. "How many do you need?"

Pearl did not want to discuss the cost in front of Mr. Holmes. Later, after he was gone, she would ask Roland to ply Mr. Stockton to donate them.

She forced a smile. "I will have to compile a list."

"Good." Roland's eyes gleamed as if he was already calculating his profit. "We'll put the order together when Mr. Holmes and I return from Holland on Saturday."

"You're confident in the lad, then," Holmes said.

"Absolutely. He can handle the store."

Pearl saw a chance to earn a little of the cost of the primers. "If you need an adult to watch the store, I would be glad to do so."

Roland looked skeptical, but Mr. Holmes beamed.

"The perfect solution. Why don't you two run over the procedures the rest of the day? I'll see you at supper." The man shook Roland's hand, bid Pearl farewell and departed.

That left her alone with Roland and the absent Charlie, who might very well have been listening to the entire conversation. The very thought of working side by side with Roland heated her cheeks. To be so close to him made her head spin. Truly, she was behaving more like a schoolgirl than a woman of twenty-one. This had to stop. She examined one of the waterproof coats and tried to get her emotions under control. Still, she could not help but notice the boyish grin on his face. Maybe he wanted to work with her, too. She replaced the coat, but it slid off the table and onto the dirty floor. Oh dear, her clumsiness was ruining the merchandise. If he made her pay for it...

She grabbed for the coat.

"Let me get that." Roland leaned over at the same time she did.

Their arms brushed, and she jumped back at the sensation his touch caused.

He stood and tried to brush the dirt off the coat with only moderate success. His smile vanished.

She had ruined the merchandise. Now she would never get this job watching the store. If he insisted she pay for the coat, she couldn't ever afford new primers.

Chapter Seven

"I don't need your help." The statement came out more harshly than Roland had planned. Judging by Pearl's pained glance at the dusty coat, she must have thought he was chastising her for letting it slip onto the floor. "I meant your offer to watch the store. Charlie can handle it. He took over when I went to Chicago."

Still, her wounded expression did not change.

He inwardly groaned. He hadn't meant to hurt her feelings. That was the trouble with women. You had to tread carefully, or they'd shatter like bone china. Speaking of which, he'd better keep her away from anything fragile.

He motioned her toward the front door. "You must have a great deal to do to get the school ready."

She did not budge. "I do, but I couldn't find so much as a bucket or scrub brush in the building."

Roland had a tough time believing that. Surely someone had cleaned the school building last year. He searched his memory for anything Garrett might have said, but came up empty.

She continued, "No soap. The water pump needs priming and the privy is in deplorable condition, not to mention the leaking roof. One woman will not get that building ready in time for school."

"Perhaps your lady friends could help." That would at least get them away from him for a week or two.

"You think that would solve everything, don't you?"

He hated that she could read his mind. Even Eva hadn't done that. She never seemed to guess what he wanted, and he sure didn't see where she'd been headed. Marry Garrett! What did his brother have that he didn't?

At Pearl's curious glance, he reined in the memories and focused on the present. "I'm merely trying to help you find a solution. You need help, and they are available."

"They cannot repair the roof and privy."

She had a point.

"I'll talk to my brother. Garrett will be able to round up some men to take care of that."

Her gaze narrowed. "You could help."

He could, but he had plans involving a certain investor. "I will be in Holland tomorrow and most of Saturday, if not longer."

"Of course." Her mouth twisted into a triumphant smirk. "And I will be assisting your customers. You had best show me how the accounts work and anything else I need to know."

This was not turning out the way he'd planned. "You don't need to know how the store operates because you won't be working here."

Charlie's thin voice broke into their debate. "Excuse me, Mr. Decker, but I can't work tomorrow."

"Why?" Roland choked on the untimely news.

"I told Mr. Farmingham that I'd help fix the schoolhouse roof."

Pearl smiled and, if possible, stood even taller than her already unusual height. "My offer still stands."

Roland raked a hand through his hair. That was the last

thing he wanted. That big-headed politician from upriver must have gotten to Charlie while Roland was talking to Holmes. Someone had to fix the schoolhouse roof, but why tomorrow?

"You could stay here," Pearl suggested.

Roland made a quick decision. Future plans were more important than the present business. How much disaster could happen in one day?

"All right." Roland held up his hands in surrender. "I know when I've been bested. Go ahead, Charlie. Miss Pearl will watch the store tomorrow, but I expect you back here Saturday."

The scrawny lad's grin split his freckled face. "Thanks, Mr. Roland. I'll go tell Mr. Garrett. Mr. Farmingham said he was gonna talk to him next."

Roland had to give Farmingham credit. The man knew precisely whom to volunteer for the job. Unfortunately, that meant he'd have to spend this afternoon shoulder-to-shoulder with Pearl Lawson. Even worse, he looked forward to it.

The tension escalated once Charlie left. If the store had been busy, Pearl might not have noticed, but no one stopped in and no one browsed. She was alone with Roland. A lock of his dark hair drooped over his eye, and he raked it back with his left hand. Was he left-handed? She'd considered how to deal with that issue in the classroom. Her instructor insisted the child must be broken of the habit, but Amanda favored her left hand and she had no difficulties learning or writing.

Roland cleared his throat. "I suppose we should begin. The sooner I go through everything, the sooner you can head home."

"Home?" Pearl lifted an eyebrow. Was that a slip of the tongue? Roland had made it perfectly clear that he wanted all of them to disappear. She had hoped his brother would fall for Amanda, but he had turned out as pigheaded as Roland. This fortuitous circumstance gave her an opportunity to change the brothers' minds. Once she and Amanda finished with the store tomorrow, both of them would see what a fine asset Amanda would be. "I assure you that I have no intention of returning to New York."

"No, of course not. You're the schoolteacher, after all." He cleared his throat and straightened the already straight candy jars. "You would like to see your friends safely returned to their families, though."

"Amanda stays with me. As for Fiona and Louise, that is their choice. If this morning is any indication, though, they seem intent on winning over your brother."

"You do speak your mind." The old grin was back. "Garrett could use a wife, but he doesn't want to admit it."

"Apparently a common malady in these parts."

He gave her a peculiar look, but she was not going to explain that the brothers were more alike than they thought. They shared a stubborn streak and an inability to recognize the opportunities right in front of them.

"Shall we address the accounts first?" she suggested.

He looked relieved by the change in direction. "First you need to familiarize yourself with the merchandise." He held out an arm. "Allow me to give you a tour."

She was not going to touch him. That had proven too disconcerting thus far, so she nodded and motioned him forward. "Show the way."

Instead of leading her, he placed his hand ever so gently at the small of her back. The touch sent shivers up her spine, but it was not altogether uncomfortable. In fact, as his hand remained there, she found the sensation somewhat...pleasant. No man had ever escorted her in such a protective, yet endearing manner, as if claiming her as his own. Her? A man like Roland Decker wouldn't claim someone like her.

She hazarded a glance.

He grinned like a schoolboy.

Impossible. Yet his hand remained as he showed her the dry goods. He said something about pricing, but she couldn't hear above the thunder in her ears. Surely she was wrong. He had stated quite clearly that he would not marry. Then why the gentle touch of his hand, the leaning close when he spoke?

He must feel the same as she did. That thought nearly left her speechless, and Pearl Lawson was *never* unable to speak.

"Most men take their meals at the boardinghouse, the hotel or the saloons." His silky voice flowed over her like a cool river in summertime as he led her past the barrels of flour, cornmeal and other dried foodstuffs. "The Elders, the Calloways and some of the folks from upriver, or on the farm, would be most likely to come in for food provisions."

She liked how he said that, as if they were setting off on a grand journey. "Like pioneers."

"Hmm?" He peered at her. "I guess you're right. In a way they are pioneers, first on the land." He drew in a deep breath. "Appealing thought, to stake first claim to property."

"Thinking of heading west?" She held her breath, hardly daring to believe he would share her dream.

He shrugged. "Just thinking about how much easier it would be to claim land out on the vast plains."

"Or the far west. I hear San Francisco is booming." She held her breath.

"San Francisco? I suppose, but it's already a city. I aim to make Singapore into the San Francisco of the east."

"It's not on the ocean."

He laughed. "It's on the next best thing—Lake Michigan, the Great Lakes, which eventually drain into the ocean."

"Over a gigantic waterfall," she pointed out.

"A small matter, considering the canal and system of locks built around it. A regular feat of engineering." His gaze focused far away. "One day Singapore will send its resources through that canal to Europe. People will want to come here like they now visit San Francisco."

She couldn't help but look out the window at the dreary landscape shrouded in fog. The dozen buildings could not compete with any town she'd ever known, least of all the golden city of San Francisco. Roland was a dreamer.

But then he smiled at her, and his hand drew her imperceptibly closer. "I knew from the first time we met that you would understand."

She could not breathe, could not think, could not stop looking at the curve of his lips and her reflection in his eye. What if he got even closer? What if he wanted to kiss her? Her. Pearl Lawson. Her heart practically leaped out of her chest.

"Mr. Decker?"

The feminine voice made Pearl jump. She hastily withdrew from Roland. A woman with honey-gold hair looked from Roland to Pearl and back again. She was not elegantly dressed, but her gown marked her as either skilled with the needle or a bit more prosperous than most in this timber frontier. Pearl expected condemnation, but the woman's expression reflected compassion and an eagerness to meet her.

"Mrs. Wardman." Roland stepped toward the customer. "What can I get you this fine day?"

The woman held out her basket. "A half pound of sugar and five pounds of flour."

He took the basket and headed across the store to the counter.

The woman turned again to Pearl. "You must be new in town. I'm Debra Wardman. Please call me Debra. My husband's a sawyer up at the Saugatuck mill."

Pearl swallowed. "I'm Pearl Lawson, the new schoolteacher."

"Welcome." If she wondered what Roland and Pearl had been doing so close to each other, she had the grace not to say anything. "My two girls will be pleased to meet you. They didn't much care for Mr. Grich. He was so somber that I think he frightened them, but he did teach them to read. They're eight and eleven and love books."

"I look forward to meeting them."

Pearl felt a twinge of regret that she didn't even have primers yet. She had hoped that Mr. Stockton would provide them and in the swirl of talk about the store and the men going to Holland, she had neglected to ask Roland to speak with his boss about the matter. She would remedy that as soon as he was done filling Mrs. Wardman's order.

"When does school begin?" Debra asked.

"The first of September."

"Angela and Beth will be there." Debra reached out to clasp Pearl's hand. "There are so few women in this area. I do hope we will be friends."

"Me, too." Pearl's heart swelled at the gesture. Although she had more than her fill of female companionship at present, in time Fiona and Louise might leave. If all worked as she hoped, Amanda would marry. Pearl could use a friend. "Do you live here?"

Debra shook her head. "We live upriver in Saugatuck."

Of course. She had said her husband worked in the mill there. Pearl tried to hide her disappointment. "Is it a long walk?"

"Not far, but you don't want to walk." She glanced at

Roland. "Have Mr. Decker bring you by boat. And congratulations."

"Congratulations?"

Debra blushed. "You and Mr. Decker."

Pearl's eyes widened when she realized what Debra thought. She must have heard about the advertisement and the women's arrival. After seeing Roland with his arm around her waist, she had assumed they were courting. She opened her mouth to correct the mistake, but nothing came out.

Roland called out, asking if Debra wanted brown or refined sugar.

Debra left to deal with her order.

Pearl turned away and fanned her face. My, oh my, did she need some cooling off. Her cheeks must be glowing like the sky at sunset. Her and Roland? Though the thought had crossed her mind, hearing it said aloud made her feel ridiculous. He had made it clear that he was not going to wed. She could not marry, or she would lose her job. All such thoughts were just daydreams and nothing more.

"Pearl," Roland called out. "Let me show you where I keep the scale."

Business. That's what she needed to concentrate on. Romantic notions needed to disappear, or someone like Debra Wardman might say just enough to get Pearl removed from her teaching position.

Roland had no idea what Debra Wardman was saying to Pearl, but he couldn't mistake the latter's high color. Thankfully, Mrs. Wardman was not one to pass on rumors or create gossip. Her husband worked at the Saugatuck mill when he wasn't on one of Stockton's lumbering crews upriver. They had two girls who would be in Pearl's school. That must be what they were talking about. He hoped.

Women could get to talking and go on for hours. With each passing moment, his irritation grew. Hadn't Pearl insisted on manning the store tomorrow? This was the perfect opportunity to learn, yet she stood there chattering away with the customer.

That's why he called her over, not to show her where he kept the scale. A woman of her intelligence would figure that out.

"Weigh the empty container first," he instructed. "If they're not buying a full sack, they'll bring something to hold the foodstuff. Today we'll add the flour until it reaches five pounds plus the weight of the container."

He expected a sharp retort about simple arithmetic, but Pearl looked distracted, her thoughts far away. Color still dotted her cheeks, making her irresistible. Moments ago he'd nearly broken his pledge when he got too close. She'd looked so vulnerable, so unlike her usual prickly self that he couldn't resist.

Thankfully Mrs. Wardman had arrived before he'd made that mistake.

"Pearl?" He drew her attention back to procedure.

Her color rose even higher, and Mrs. Wardman smiled in such a way that he suspected she misunderstood the relationship between Pearl and him.

"Miss Lawson is going to watch the store for me tomorrow while I travel to Holland," he explained.

Mrs. Wardman's grin didn't go away.

"I need to instruct her."

"Of course." But her gaze darted between Pearl and him.

Now *he* felt overheated. "Strictly business."

Pearl finally responded, echoing his words with an emphatic nod.

"What else could it be?" Mrs. Wardman said, but that smile still hung on.

Roland gave up trying to convince her and turned back to the matter at hand. "Once you have the weight of the flour, look up the cost per pound on the list." He opened his book that detailed all the products in the store with their wholesale cost and retail price. He pointed to the retail price for wheat flour to ensure she got the correct figure. "Multiply that by five."

Pearl nodded.

"I assume you can do simple calculations."

That brought out the old Pearl. "I should hope so, since I will be teaching arithmetic."

Roland relaxed and moved on. "Keep track of accounts in this ledger. There's a page for each account, in alphabetical order by last name. If someone pays, it's usually in company money. Sometimes in government currency. Most will put their purchases on account. Those who work for Stockton get a portion of their wage in store credit."

"I see." She looked pained but thankfully said no more.

"On account?" he asked Mrs. Wardman.

She nodded, and the transaction was soon completed.

"Stop by anytime," the woman said to Pearl. "Our house is the one with the bridal veil bushes in front."

For some reason, Pearl flushed again, though she bid Mrs. Wardman a warm farewell.

Once the door had closed behind her, Roland turned to Pearl. "That went well."

She glared back. "If you intend to confirm rumors."

"What rumors?"

"If you can't figure it out, I don't see why I should tell you."

Women. This was exactly the sort of response that had driven him crazy with Eva. He wasn't about to start down that road with Pearl, so he finished explaining where to find prices for the rest of the goods and how to log cash sales.

"Now you know the basics about the store's operation. You can sell anything on the price list, but don't go into the stockroom." He did not need a woman fiddling around in there.

"What if someone asks for something not on display?"

"Take their order."

Her irritation had eased while he outlined procedures. As long as he kept things strictly on business, they got along. The moment it drifted across the line, their relationship faltered. That was fine with him. He didn't need the complication that a woman brought.

"That should be enough to get you through the day," he declared. "Anything else can wait until I return."

She nodded, as if she understood, but then rolled right into the unexpected. "When do you expect Mr. Stockton?"

"Mr. Stockton? Why should you care?"

"Would he show up tomorrow?"

Ah, she was worried that his boss would find her in charge and ask where he was. Roland closed the ledger and tucked it back under the counter. "He went north looking for future business opportunities."

"Oh. Mr. Farmingham said he was in Chicago."

"That's where he lives and where his business empire is centered, but he's not there now. Don't worry. He won't stop in tomorrow."

Instead of easing her concerns, his reassurances deepened her frown. "Then when do you expect to see him?"

"Why the sudden interest in Mr. Stockton?"

"Because of the school. Mr. Farmingham said that Mr. Stockton oversaw operations."

Roland wasn't aware of that. He thought the township officials were in charge, but it didn't surprise him that Stockton had gotten involved. "From what Charlie said, it sounds like everything is being taken care of. The men are going to fix up the building, and I'm sure your friends will help you clean it."

She drew up to full height. "That will not replace the primers."

Roland groaned. Not the primers again. "Mr. Holmes and I will see if there are any in Holland."

"We need new primers."

"I can order them. You heard Mr. Holmes offer to take the order to Chicago with him."

The fire never left her eyes. "And who will pay for them?"

Roland was no fool. That's why she was asking all those questions, albeit in a roundabout way. "I'll tell you right now that Mr. Stockton will not pay for primers."

She did not flinch. He respected that in her. She would make a fine businesswoman since she refused to back down to anyone. He would relish seeing her face down Stockton, but it wasn't likely to happen. Not this month or next. Stockton would spend the ice-free months north and stop by to check on operations on his way to Chicago for the winter.

"A donation, then," she said. "Surely Mr. Stockton values educating the next generation. It can only help his business."

Roland stifled a grin at her idealistic vision. Stockton cared only about profit. Once the timber was gone, he would move on. Thus the trip north, where the forests were still thick. Stockton didn't care about primers. If Pearl was going to the trouble of suggesting libraries and donations, Farmingham must have refused to pay. The parents around here sure wouldn't take on an extra expense.

He started to explain, but Pearl looked so certain of her plan that he couldn't dash her hopes. Somehow he'd find primers or at least some books. Since Holmes took an interest in education, Roland could score extra points if he scrounged up the necessary materials.

"We'll find something in Holland," he assured her.

She didn't look like she put much stock in that source.

He added, "If not, we'll find a way to buy them."

"We?"

His use of the plural had brought the flush back to her cheeks. He liked it.

"Yes, we."

Her gaze softened. "Thank you."

Her words whispered into his heart. He sure wished he had time for marriage, but his plans had to come first.

Chapter Eight

Pearl hummed as she washed the shelves in the general store. "I don't think these have been touched in months."

"Maybe years." Amanda sighed from the rear of the store. "I've been cleaning for hours."

"Only since seven o'clock this morning. It's not even noon yet."

"It does smell better, though. That lavender soap makes everything so much nicer. Oh my!" Amanda gasped. "Look at these."

"Look at what?" Doubtless Pearl's friend had found another reason to stop working.

"What pretty little teacups."

"Teacups?" Pearl couldn't imagine why Roland would have teacups in stock. She hadn't found one pretty item in the entire store.

"An entire tea set."

Pearl joined her friend, who was peering into a crate by the door to the stockroom. "I don't think we're supposed to touch those."

That didn't stop Amanda. She lifted a tiny porcelain cup. "It's a child's tea set. How sweet." She drew in her breath. "Maybe it's not for sale. Maybe it was ordered for someone." Amanda bit her lip. "Could you check the books?"

That felt a lot like snooping. "No, I won't. We are here to help out, not meddle."

"I'm not meddling." Amanda pouted. "I just wondered… It would be so touching if the set was for Sadie. Maybe she has a birthday." Her eyes lit up. "We could celebrate. I-it might…well, her father might think differently about us if we got her a little gift."

Though there were a lot of ifs in that train of thought, Amanda could well have struck upon a way to impress the reluctant bachelor. The quickest way to his heart might be through his children.

"I'll look." Since no one had stopped in the store after the early morning rush, she could devote a moment to looking through the ledgers. "But only if you put the teacup back exactly where you found it." She did not want Roland to think they'd been looking through the crates.

By the time she reached the counter, the bell tinkled, and one of the mill workers entered.

"Where's Mr. Roland?"

Pearl assumed her most businesslike posture. "He was called out of town and left me in charge."

"He done took Charlie with him?"

"Charlie is helping repair the schoolhouse. How may I help you?"

"Need a hat. The wind done snatched it right off my head and plunked it into the river. Sank before we could get to it."

Pearl led him to the display of hats. "Make sure it fits snug, since the band tends to loosen over time."

He tried every one. "They're all too small. Don't ya got any more? Mr. Roland usually has some out back."

Pearl hesitated. Roland had told her not to go into the stockroom, least of all get anything out of there, but a customer's needs must come first. She caught Amanda's gaze. "Will you check the stockroom?"

Her friend hurried through the back door, and Pearl turned her attention back to her customer. "We'll know soon enough."

"Thank ye much, ma'am. A man can't stand ta work outdoors without a hat."

"No, indeed." Pearl scanned the list of goods, looking for additional hats, but she could only locate the ones on display.

Amanda returned with an armload of hats. "Will one of these work?"

It didn't take long for the man to find one that fit perfectly, a sharp black leather hat with a brown leather hatband. "Put it on my account."

Pearl took his name and located the account, but she had no idea what price to put for the hat. It was different from the ones on display and she couldn't locate any other listing.

"What's it cost?" the man asked.

Pearl bit her lower lip. "I'm not certain. Mr. Decker doesn't have the cost in his price list."

"Well now, I can't go takin' it if I can't afford it."

That was the problem. "May I see the hat?"

He handed it over. She examined it and decided it most closely matched a hat that Roland sold for two dollars. When the man agreed to the price, she wrote the transaction on his account and asked him to sign. He marked an X.

"Thank ye, ma'am." He plopped the hat on his head and left.

She'd seen enough illiteracy that it shouldn't have bothered her. After all, many who worked with their hands did so because they'd never learned to read and write. There was no dishonor in good hard labor, but the next generation must reach for more.

She closed the book. "I'm going to change that."

"Change what?" Amanda asked.

"It might be too late for the parents, but the children will learn to read and write."

"There you go again trying to change the world."

"For the better." Pearl firmly believed that.

"Will you at least let the children play? They can't take constant education."

Naturally Amanda would think that. She had not excelled at studies, preferring to chatter away with friends or watch whichever boy she'd found handsome that week.

"They will have a chance to exert themselves out of doors."

Amanda leaned against the counter and laughed. "You're always so serious."

"Serious got me out of the orphanage."

Amanda's high spirits deflated. "I'm sorry. If I could have stayed with you, I would have."

"No, you wouldn't have. I wouldn't have allowed it." Pearl felt awful for bringing up the past. Amanda had always carried a burden of guilt because she'd been chosen whereas Pearl had not. "It all worked out for the best. Now, let's get back to finding that tea set."

As she'd expected, that pushed Amanda's attention in a more positive direction. Her eyes sparkled. "Guess what else I found in the stockroom."

"I can't imagine."

"A new rag doll. Just like Sadie's except with both eyes and all its hair. She must have a birthday soon." Amanda paused and bit her lip. "It won't work, though."

"What won't work?"

"She'll never take a new doll over her old one."

Pearl thought back to her Dollie, long gone. Miss Hornswoggle, the director of the orphanage, had taken it from her, saying she was too old for dolls. The director had carried it to the parlor, a room that was off-limits to the children unless they were sent to meet prospective parents. Doubtless her doll ended up in the parlor stove, for she never saw it again.

No other doll or toy had replaced that loss in her heart. "You're probably right."

"Maybe the tea set will make her smile," Amanda said hopefully. "I must get her something." She glanced around the store. "There's nothing here for children."

"You already promised to make her a dress. And a matching one for her doll."

Amanda's eyes lit up. "Of course! Now I just need to know when her birthday is. You could ask Roland."

"I am not asking him."

"Why not?" Amanda had perfected pouting. "He would know, and you are so good at getting people to tell you things."

Pearl was nothing of the sort. "You could ask Garrett."

Amanda blanched. "I could never."

"You might ask Mrs. Calloway."

"Of course. She would know. She watches the children almost every day. She also has a sewing machine. Can you believe it? She told me I could use it any time I wanted. Now all I need is fabric. Did Roland point out the cloth he said we could have?"

Pearl had forgotten about that offer. "No, but it must be here somewhere, probably in the stockroom. Look for a bin of scraps."

Amanda was already gone.

Pearl leaned against the counter, envisioning Roland giving Sadie the tea set. The solemn little girl might smile. Maybe she would even speak. At the very least, her eyes would light up. She hadn't figured Roland for the thoughtful type. Though Garrett might have ordered the tea set, from what she'd heard last night, that was doubtful. He didn't appear willing to part with a single penny for something unnecessary. The rag doll was more likely his gift.

Roland saw the value in something pretty. That's why he'd offered the fabric. He knew a little girl needed something to make her feel special.

Pearl choked back a tear. At the orphanage, she always received the plainest frocks. The pretty girls got the pretty dresses. Pearl didn't begrudge Amanda. She deserved a family and every good thing in life. Her parents had truly died. They did not abandon her like Pearl's parents had. Just once Pearl wondered what it would feel like to be Cinderella at the ball instead of the ugly stepsister. She closed her eyes and imagined walking down the center of the ballroom with all those present amazed by her beauty.

Just once.

One time to think that someone would actually care about her, might even love her.

"I found it!" Amanda's exclamation shattered the fantasy.

Pearl opened her eyes and stared at the ledger. No balls or fine dresses for Pearl Lawson. She would teach school and give hope to the next generation.

Roland stepped into his store and stopped short. "What happened in here?"

After yesterday's meeting, he'd been so concerned about the place that he decided not to wait for a return boat and set off for Singapore on foot along the cart path between the towns. After ten miles of horseflies and blistering sun that turned into mosquitoes and muggy moonlight, he had simply noted that the store was still intact with the door locked before heading upstairs to yank his boots off and sink into bed.

He had not expected to open up in the morning and see his store turned upside down.

Charlie shrugged, hands in pockets like always. "Looks good to me."

"Did you stop in like I asked?"

"Nope. Too busy up at the schoolhouse. By the way, I gotta finish up there today. Miss Lawson said she'd mind the store again."

Roland fumed. Miss Lawson would not set foot in his store except as a customer. Maybe not even then.

He had only been gone a day. The place was…tidy. And clean. And… He sniffed. It smelled like…soap? And some flowery scent.

He sneezed. Flowers always made him sneeze. He pulled out a handkerchief and pressed it to his nose.

"Open the windows and doors," he ordered Charlie as his eyes watered.

"I gotta go to the schoolhouse."

"They can wait long enough for you to open some windows." Roland had to bang on the window casing to loosen the window from the frame. He should ask his brother to help him wax them, but time always got away. Now that the big sawmill was back running full steam, Garrett wouldn't get many days off.

"Never mind, Charlie. I'll help Mr. Decker."

Pearl's voice made Roland whip around.

There she stood in the same dull brown dress that she'd worn every day except when he'd met her aboard ship. Oddly enough, the plain color made her features shine more intensely. The chestnut hair looked dark so early in the morning, but her emerald-green eyes stood out.

She dropped her bag on the counter and headed for the window Charlie had been trying to open. "Though I can't imagine why anyone would want the windows open on such a cool morning. It smells like rain."

Roland sneezed. "It smells like flowers."

"Lavender," she said with evident pride. "Mrs. Calloway gave us a bar of the loveliest soap."

"I—I—" He sneezed again. "I sneeze around flowers."

Pearl pushed open the window while Charlie scooted out of the store. "You poor dear."

Something in the way she said it irritated him even more. He did not need a mother. "You were only supposed to watch the store, not overhaul it."

Was that a smile or a smirk on her face?

"We needed to do something."

"We?" This was getting worse and worse. How many people had been messing with his store?

"Amanda and I. We decided to spruce up a bit. The dirt on the shelves was a quarter-inch thick."

"You're exaggerating." He hefted open the next window and breathed in the fresh air. Without a strong wind, it would take hours for the scent to leave the store.

"Maybe, but dust does not display your merchandise to best advantage."

"This store is for the lumberjacks and mill workers. They don't care about pretty displays and flowery scents." He sneezed again.

"Mrs. Wardman isn't a mill worker or a lumberjack."

He hated when she was right, even if only a little. "Few of the workers are married. Those who are often don't have their families here. Mrs. Wardman is an exception. You will find little female companionship here. I suggest you make the most of those you do meet."

"I have every intention of doing so, but that is not my point. A little tidiness goes a long way, even with the men. Why, we couldn't find a proper-size hat for the gentleman who came in yesterday."

Roland frowned. "Then you didn't sell him one?" He

hated to lose any business, even though the man would likely be back today.

"Of course I did. We found one that fit in back."

Roland choked, and this time it wasn't the floral scent that did it. "You did what?"

She didn't even blink. "Found a hat that fit."

"I told you not to go in the stockroom."

"You would rather lose a customer?"

"He would be back today. You could have told him to wait."

"And subject him to the heat of the sun?" She clucked her tongue like the schoolmarm she was. "He could not have worked all afternoon without a hat."

She might be right. In fact she probably was right, but she had directly disobeyed orders. He strode to the counter and hauled out the ledger. "Who was it? You tell me exactly what you sold him, and I will mark it down."

"No need." She fluttered her hand in his direction and headed for the next window. "I already entered the sale on his account."

Roland scanned the general ledger and then flipped to the accounts. So she had. The price might even be reasonable. Maybe. "Which hat did you sell him?"

"The black one."

His ears began to ring. "The black leather hat? With the tan hatband?" The words came out strangled, probably because of the pinching in his chest. That hat cost double what she'd charged. It wasn't just that he hadn't made any profit, but he'd lost money.

"That's the one." She cheerily hopped off to the next window.

He fisted his hands, wanting to punch something. He should never have let her talk him in to putting her in charge. It would have been better to close the store.

"I told you not to go into the stockroom." Each word came out like a rap on a drum.

Her smile vanished as she drew near. "Is something wrong?"

"Something wrong?" He swallowed in a vain attempt to calm himself. She didn't know what she'd done, but she also hadn't followed his orders. On the other hand, she had the best of motives. She'd wanted to help the customer, except her help had actually been harmful. He groaned. The damage was done, and nothing could change that. He couldn't very well charge the man the true price after the fact. He could only ensure it never happened again.

"Go help out at the school. You are not needed here today." Or any day.

She didn't move, and he made the mistake of looking at her. Her lip didn't quiver, like Eva's would have. She hadn't burst into tears, but her disappointment was still obvious.

"I thought I was helping." She shoved back her shoulders. "If I charged him incorrectly, I will pay the difference."

Now he felt like an insensitive oaf. If she couldn't afford primers or a change of clothing, she surely couldn't pay for the hat.

"Don't worry about it."

The disappointment returned. "I will make this up to you. I promise."

He should say something, but what? He couldn't lie. He could only stress that this was not her problem. "Don't. Just leave."

This time her lip did quiver for a second before she reined it in. Color dotted her cheeks. She straightened her spine, spun around and strode out of the store.

He *was* an insensitive clod.

* * *

What a self-serving, arrogant man! Pearl stomped past the big sawmill and up the sandy road that led to the schoolhouse. The river bubbled and swirled beside her. On another morning, she might have paused to enjoy its deep color and the way the light danced across the surface. Today she barely noticed it.

He hadn't thanked her for cleaning the store. He'd complained about the scent.

He hadn't thanked her for waiting on his customers and ensuring they left the store with the proper merchandise. He'd accused her of selling the wrong item at the wrong price.

He hadn't appreciated one bit of the work she had done without a penny's compensation. She had stepped in so he could go to Holland and perhaps procure books for her classroom. He not only didn't mention finding any, but she also doubted he'd even looked.

If she was prone to tears, they would have been streaming down her cheeks by now. Instead she was mad. Livid. That man did not have one kind or gracious bone in his body.

Be ye not unequally yoked together with unbelievers, the Bible counseled. If she'd needed any confirmation that Roland Decker was not the man for her, she'd just received it. From now on, she would confine her comings and goings to the school, the boardinghouse and church services. As for the latter, tomorrow was Sunday and she had yet to locate the church.

She climbed the hill that rose steadily from the river's bank. This area must have been dunes also, before the forest took over. She was glad the lumbermen had left this patch of woods. Perhaps the aspen and poplar were too small to tempt them.

Near the top of the hill, men hammered new shingles

onto the schoolhouse roof. Charlie called out when he spotted her.

"Look at all the work we've done." He practically beamed with pride.

Pearl smiled at the boy's enthusiasm. "It looks sturdy enough to outlast a blizzard."

"Or a tornado," he added.

She couldn't imagine tornadoes in such a place, but she supposed anything was possible. Certainly a windstorm could damage a roof.

The burly man beside Charlie turned to glance at her. Garrett Decker. At least he was willing to help when his brother was not.

"Thank you, Mr. Decker."

He nodded curtly and pounded in another nail.

Pearl waited until he finished. "Might you tell me where the church is located in Singapore?" Roland had mentioned that his brother was a Bible-reading man.

Garrett looked back at her again. "If you mean a building, there isn't one."

"What? How can a town have three saloons and no churches?"

He grunted. "My thoughts exactly, but that's the way it is. We gather together in the parlor of the boardinghouse and take turns reading from the Bible or reading one of the sermons from Mr. Calloway's book of sermons."

Pearl tried to wrap her mind around this. She admired their initiative, but the boardinghouse parlor was small. "You need a proper church and a proper preacher."

He stopped hammering again. "You go ahead and tell that to Mr. Stockton. See how far you get."

"But he won't be back here until November or December."

"That's right."

"How are we supposed to build a church and find a

preacher that late in the year? Winter will be upon us soon."

"Probably already have snow."

Everything Pearl had imagined about this place had been completely wrong. This wasn't a tidy little town with picket fences and friendly storekeepers. It was a frontier company town with little sign of advancement.

"Well, then," she said, more to herself than anyone else, "if no one else will do anything, it's up to me."

She would find someplace for a proper church, even if it meant using the schoolhouse.

Chapter Nine

Over the course of the following week, the schoolhouse shaped up nicely. To Pearl's surprise, Fiona and Louise did pitch in to clean up the place. By Friday, her three workers headed off on other ventures. Louise left with book in hand for a "nature tour" of the nearby dune. Fiona disappeared with Mrs. Calloway into the kitchen. Amanda wanted to finish the dress and matching doll dress for Sadie, having learned that the little girl's birthday was on Sunday.

Pearl stood alone inside the school and surveyed the progress. In addition to the thorough scrubbing and the repaired roof and privy, a new blackboard hung at the front of the room. Even the woodstove looked fresh after a good cleaning. The slates had been scrubbed, and Mr. Farmingham delivered dozens of sticks of new chalk. If only she had books. A globe or map would be helpful, too, but that might come later.

Roland burst through the door carrying a large pail in one hand and a roll of oil cloth under the other arm.

"A gift." He set the pail on her desk with that sheepish little-boy expression that melted her resolve. "Can you forgive me for not thanking you appropriately for your help with the store?"

She hesitated. "What did you bring?"

"Paint. For the walls."

Though she and the ladies had attempted to clean the plaster, they couldn't do much to remove the years of grimy fingerprints and the soot from the woodstove. Paint would make a huge difference.

"You have paint here?" She'd seen little evidence of it except for the boardinghouse porch railing and some trim at the hotel.

"I can mix up as much as you want, as long as it's white."

She had to laugh. "White will be perfect. It'll brighten up the place."

"Then am I forgiven?"

In the days since their falling-out at the store, she had found it impossible to stay angry with him. He'd carried a sleepy Sadie home after Sunday's church service. She'd spotted him tossing a ball with Isaac. It didn't hurt that Mrs. Calloway gave her recommendation of him each and every day, but those boyish grins of his did her in.

He perched on one of the student tables waiting for her answer.

She ran a finger around the rim of the pail. She tried to scowl, but she just couldn't do it. The laugh that had been building burst out. "All right, I accept your apology."

He reached into his inner jacket pocket, pulled out two paintbrushes and extended them toward her, bouquet style. "For you."

She stifled a smile. He might figure he was back on solid ground with her, but she wasn't ready to let him off completely. "Do you always treat the ladies this way?"

"Only the ones I like."

"Oh, so now you're playing favorite with the teacher."

His grin broadened. "You'll give me a passing grade?"

Their teasing repartee made her laugh, but she had to feign a scowl or he'd think he could get away with bad behavior. "You will need to do more than offer me a gift that requires labor."

"Ah, labor." He slipped off his jacket and rolled up his shirtsleeves. "I am at your service. Just point the way."

"You? Paint?" She surveyed his fine suit. "You're not dressed properly."

"You seem to think I'll get paint on my suit."

"I have no doubt you will."

"Would you care to put that to a test, Miss Lawson?"

She stood a little taller. "Is that a challenge, Mr. Decker?"

"I'm willing to claim that I can paint that section of the wall without getting one drop of paint on my clothing." He pointed to a two-foot strip from ceiling to floor.

"Prove it."

He held up a finger. "I'm not finished. I suggest that I can do this work better and faster than you. I will paint the strip on this side of the window, and you paint on that side."

She eyed the two sections. "They are equal in size, but how do I know you won't flick a drop of paint on my skirt?"

"Moi?" He made an elaborate bow. "My lady's suggestion offends me."

"All the French and fancy manners in the world won't convince me."

"Very well, then, if any paint should end up on the other person by virtue of nefarious means—"

"Meaning you put it on me."

"Or you on me. As I said, if any paint should end up on our persons from the competitor, the offending party shall be disqualified."

"Fair. But what will I win when I defeat you?"

"Confident, are you?"

"I'll have you know that I whitewashed many a wall in the—" She caught herself just in time. Roland did not need to know that she'd grown up in an orphanage and that much of her last years there had been spent toiling. "I've whitewashed many a wall in the past."

He must have caught the change in her tone, though, for he sobered. "Very well, Miss Lawson. If you win, I will provide sufficient primers for your students."

She drew in her breath. "You will?" This was the answer to her prayers.

The grin returned. "Now the only question is what prize I will receive when I win."

"You aren't going to win." He couldn't. She needed those primers.

"Ah, but in the unthinkable event that I do best you, I must receive a prize."

She searched her scattered thoughts. She had nothing to offer him. Other than her Bible and clothing, she owned nothing. Even her schoolbooks had been borrowed and long ago returned. "I don't have anything you'd want."

"Perhaps you do." He touched a finger to her chin and tipped up her face so she looked right in his eyes.

The thrill of his touch left her breathless. His gaze had softened, the teasing gone. She moved her lips to ask what that was.

He smiled. "A token for a gentleman." He brushed a finger across her lips, making his intent perfectly clear.

She felt the flush clear to the roots of her hair. "Mr. Decker!"

"Roland. A friendly gesture. That's all."

He made it sound so unimportant, and perhaps it was for him. Not for her. Certainly not for her.

But she needed those primers and had nothing else to

offer. If she won, she need never give him the kiss he desired. She straightened her shoulders and stuck out her hand. "Very well, Roland. You have a deal."

Roland felt her hesitation. He had asked too much. He might have requested a walk on the lakeshore instead, but her nearness made him giddy enough to ask for more.

When she'd stiffened and stuck out her hand to shake on the deal, he knew he couldn't force a kiss any more than he'd been able to force Eva to love him. Gifts brought gratitude, but not love. He had no idea what would win over a woman's heart, but he could afford to be patient. If what Pearl said was true, she couldn't consider marriage for the year of her teaching contract.

Maybe courting didn't count. He intended to find out.

He also did not intend to lose this competition. What had possessed him to offer to buy the primers? That would take a chunk of money out of his glassworks project, money he'd set aside from his wages since coming to Singapore. At first he'd intended to save enough to leave the town and his brother's family behind. Now he could not let Eva's death mean nothing. For the sake of her children, he had to make Singapore into the vibrant town he had once promised her it would become.

"Who is going to judge us?" Pearl asked.

Roland pulled his attention back to the present and the spunky lady beside him. She had stuck a handkerchief into the neck of her dress like a napkin.

He pointed to the handkerchief. "That counts as clothing, too."

"A handkerchief is not clothing, as you well know."

"No gentleman would leave the house without one."

The corners of her mouth teased upward. "Do you consider yourself a gentleman?"

"Ouch!" He mocked being struck in the heart. "You've wounded me."

"Very well, Mr. Decker." She whipped off the handkerchief and shoved it into her apron pocket. "No handkerchief."

"And the apron counts as clothing."

"Agreed."

"Then shall we begin?"

She crossed her arms. "Not until we have a fair and impartial judge. Amanda, perhaps."

"Your friend. I nominate my brother."

"Completely biased."

"Charlie, then."

"He's watching the store," she pointed out.

"Perhaps Miss Fiona, then." He couldn't resist the jab that generated the expected reaction.

"Also biased. Louise would be fair, but we'd have to retrieve her from somewhere on the dunes."

"I don't know her well enough to agree or disagree."

She tapped a finger on the handle of her paintbrush. "Then I fear we are at an impasse. If the town had a minister—"

"But we don't." Movement outside caught his attention. A man, lean and old enough to be Pearl's father. The man nailed the traditional moon symbol on the privy door. Roland grinned. "That's it! Mr. Calloway."

"He is not a minister."

"He reads the sermons on Sunday." He felt her resolve slipping so he tacked on another incentive. "Garrett says he sat in on the discussion leading to hiring you as teacher. He cares about the school."

As he'd suspected, she acquiesced. "But it'll take time to find him and bring him here—if Mrs. Calloway doesn't have him busy fixing something at the boardinghouse."

"Have no fear." He strode past Pearl and stuck his head out the door. "Ernie!"

Calloway looked up, hammer still in hand. "What d'ya need?"

"Would you mind judging a little competition?"

Pearl must have snuck up behind him because she chimed in, "If Mrs. Calloway doesn't need you."

Ernie touched a finger to the brim of his worn hat. "Nice ta see ya here, miss. The missus is always needin' me fer this and that, but I don't see what a bit o' friendly competition won't keep me overlong."

His grin revealed crooked teeth and a genuine affection for his fellow townsmen. Aside from Roland, he was the one Singapore resident who most wanted the town to grow. At one time he'd dreamed of buying the inappropriately named Astor House and turning it into a true reflection of its namesake, but the hotel's owner refused to sell.

"Thank you, Mr. Calloway." Pearl beamed at the man in an obvious attempt to sway his goodwill. "It's for the school and the children."

"Well now, can't rightly turn down anything that'll help out the young'uns."

Roland felt his advantage slipping away quickly. "Or it might benefit the town." He couldn't exactly say how winning a kiss from Pearl would benefit the town, except perhaps by keeping her here for more than a single school year.

"Well, then, let's get on with it," Ernie said, tucking his hammer into a loop sewn onto his leather belt.

As general handyman around the boardinghouse, he carried tools with him all day. Roland had seen him with screwdrivers and wrenches tucked in that belt of his.

Roland brought him inside and explained the competition.

"And when I win," Pearl pointed out, "Roland, er, Mr. Decker, will supply primers for all the students."

"Well now, ain't that the mark of a generous soul." Ernie turned to him. "And what do you git if'n you win?"

The deal that had seemed so reasonable moments before now sounded crass spoken aloud. Still, Roland knew how to charm even the crotchetiest man, and Ernie was far from dour. The old man still brought his wife wildflowers every Friday morning from spring until the first frost of autumn.

"The lady will take a stroll along the lakeshore with me."

Pearl lifted an eyebrow, and he was pleased to see a corner of her mouth tick upward. Seeing as her color didn't heighten, she must have approved of the change in terms. Besides, the romance of the lakeshore might lead to the very thing he'd first proposed.

"And you are to judge who finishes first," he continued, "and disqualify anyone who splatters paint on the other person."

"All righty, then. Are ye ready?"

Roland spread out the oil cloth on the floor and then set the pail of paint midway between their patches of wall. He dipped his brush. Pearl dipped hers.

"Go!" Ernie yelled.

Roland brushed furiously, dipping as quickly and cleanly as possible. No splatters. No drips. That was the deal. He glanced out of the corner of his eye and was surprised to see Pearl was keeping up. Moreover it appeared she was doing a good job. She did have experience painting walls.

"Yer ahead, Miss Pearl," Ernie urged, "but only by an inch. Hurry!"

"You're supposed to be impartial," Roland pointed out.

"Tain't right fer a man ta go against a lady."

Had Roland caught Pearl smiling? He paused long enough to check, and she took advantage, gaining another inch on him.

"Stop that, Ernie. You're distracting me."

The old man chuckled. "Seems ta me that I ain't the one distractin' you."

That brought out the color in Pearl's cheeks, but she didn't say a word. Instead, she tucked her tongue between her lips and concentrated on the painting. My, oh my, that gal could concentrate when she needed to. If she taught school the way she painted, those children were going to come out of the school year able to recite every one of Shakespeare's sonnets from memory.

"'Let me not to the marriage of true minds admit impediments,'" Roland said, quoting from the sonnet that he had often recited to Eva.

Pearl paused. "You know Shakespeare?"

"As do you, apparently."

She blushed. "I borrowed a book of sonnets from the library."

"And memorized them all, no doubt."

She shook her head. "Only a few, but I recognize that one."

"My favorite." Though he had not spoken it aloud since that horrible day.

"You will have to recite it all to me one day."

A bittersweet ache settled into his heart. That would be too much like what he'd done with Eva. He had been so serious with her, wanted to marry her, to make a life together. He had recklessly spent money on hothouse flowers, confections and baubles. She had accepted each gift until the day she returned them with the announcement she was going to marry his brother. His brother!

"Are you all right?" Pearl was peering at him with concern.

He pasted on a grin. "Better than all right. I intend to recite that poem to you on our lakeshore stroll."

Ernie cleared his throat. "Not if'n ye don't stop talkin' an' start paintin'."

Roland finally noticed how far ahead Pearl had gotten while he'd been stuck in memories of the past. He loaded his brush full of paint and slapped it on the wall. The paint splattered, landing on his shirtsleeve.

"Done!" Ernie declared. "Miss Pearl's the winner."

Roland tightened his grip on the paintbrush. Eva had cost him again. Would it never end? He stood back to criticize Pearl's paint job, but she had completed the work expertly. Moreover, not a single drop of paint had landed on her clothing.

"Congratulations," he said stiffly.

Her eyes widened. "Your shirt! It's ruined."

That, too. "It's nothing."

He swiped the brush against the wall, finishing the job, but she caught his arm.

"Hold still a moment." Pearl dabbed at the speck of paint with her handkerchief.

"Don't," he said, more worried about her losing a handkerchief than his shirt. "The color of the paint matches the shirt. Moreover, my jacket will hide it."

"I know, but…" Her voice trailed off, and her eyes glistened.

Something tugged at his heart. Perhaps it was the vulnerability visible beneath the surface or the gentleness of her touch. Whatever it was, it hurt. It ached fiercely, for it unearthed the feelings he'd managed to bury for years.

"I would like that walk," she said softly.

He stared. "You would?"

She nodded slowly. "Tell me about the town and your plans."

It was happening all over again. This time would he

win, or would Garrett walk in again with his two children and steal her away? A cautious man would walk away. Roland had never lived life cautiously.

Chapter Ten

"*You* are buying schoolbooks?" Roland's brother stared at him from the other side of the store counter. "You? The man who has been saving every penny for that crazy dream of yours?"

"My dream is not crazy. The glassworks will save this town."

"Maybe it doesn't need saving," Garrett grumbled. "Maybe it's fine the way it is."

"The timber won't last forever."

"Then we move on. Things change."

"Since when did you start accepting change?"

"Since it was forced on me." Garrett's scowl made it perfectly clear that Roland was responsible for that forced change.

He was. But that was in the past. They had to move forward. "You might just pack up and leave, but I happen to believe in this town. With the right opportunities, it can boom."

Garrett clearly didn't share his belief. "That doesn't explain why you're buying primers."

"Education is the foundation for the future. I want educated workers at my glassworks." Roland was beginning to sound like Holmes, who had promised an answer a week ago. Still no word.

"Humph. Sounds to me like you're sweet on the new teacher."

Though Roland felt the blood rush to his face, he kept his composure. "Maybe I care about Isaac and Sadie."

"Are you saying I don't?" Garrett leaned over the counter, his hands curling into fists.

Roland tensed. It had always been like this between them. Even as boys, they'd battled over the smallest things. Who could throw the ball farther. Who got the best grade in arithmetic. Who got the most mashed potatoes at dinner. Everything had been a competition. Even Eva. Garrett always won the physical battles, while Roland bested his brother at anything that required wits. Except Eva.

Maybe it was time to stop competing.

That thought triggered the memory of Pearl's triumphant win. He owed her, but he didn't know how he was going to pay for the books. If he hadn't suggested the competition... He grinned. Her delight was worth any cost. Hopefully Holmes would come through with the funding, and Roland wouldn't have to delay the glassworks another year.

"I don't need your help with my children." Garrett slammed a fist down on the counter.

Roland jumped. "Fine. Pay for their books, but the other children will need primers, too."

"How do you suddenly know so much about schooling? You were never interested before."

"Pearl told me what each grade would need. Once we went over the likely students, it didn't take long to come up with an order. It'll go out on today's mail boat."

Garrett studied Roland as if inspecting an unusual insect.

Roland waited.

Garrett's shoulders relaxed. "You called her Pearl." He grinned. "Kind of wish you'd take one of those other ladies off my hands."

Roland hadn't failed to notice their devoted attention to the children. Every evening Isaac told them what Miss Fiona or Miss Amanda or Miss Louise had done for them over at the boardinghouse. "Hasn't one struck your fancy yet?"

"I told you I'm not marrying."

"Hmm."

"Hmm, what?"

"Did you or did you not just tell me that change is inevitable?"

Garrett peered at him trying to figure out his angle. "Yes."

"And you are perfectly capable of taking care of your children without any help whatsoever?"

Garrett wasn't as quick-witted as Roland, but he figured out where this conversation was headed. "No, and that's final. I will not marry some stranger just because my children want a new mother."

"Don't you think they deserve a mother?"

Garrett glared at him. "I think you deserve to have your head dunked in a horse trough."

In an instant he was over the counter, but Roland was faster. Like boys, they raced through the store and out onto the boardwalk, laughing. There was nothing like a good wrestle to bring them together.

Roland stopped in his tracks, and Garrett crashed into him.

"Ladies."

Garrett snatched his hat off his head. Roland straightened his coat.

Pearl and Amanda stood in front of them. The latter

carried a package wrapped in brown paper and tied with a blue hair ribbon.

Amanda held it out. "For Sadie."

"For her birthday," Pearl added when her friend said nothing more.

Roland spotted his brother blinking back tears and staring at the ground. Garrett had a weak spot for his children, thus the new doll and child's tea set Roland had ordered. Garrett had chosen to give her the doll while Roland would give the tea set. He puzzled how the ladies had managed to discover it was Sadie's birthday this weekend until he recalled how much time the children spent with the Calloways. No doubt Mrs. Mabel Calloway spilled that little fact.

Regardless, Garrett still had not taken the gift.

Color dotted Amanda's cheeks. "Please take it. I wanted her to have the dress in time for school. And I made a matching one for her doll."

If that didn't crack Garrett's heart, nothing would. Still, the man didn't budge.

Roland accepted the gift from Amanda and handed it to his brother, who still didn't look at the woman who had gone to great lengths to make his daughter a present.

Roland cleared his throat and glared at Garrett before turning back to the ladies. "Since my brother appears to have lost his tongue, I will thank you for him, Miss Amanda."

She blushed. "I hope the dress fits her." Amanda bit her lip and held Roland's gaze. "Let me know if it doesn't."

That's when he noticed her eyes were an unusual shade of violet. Like Eva's.

"Until later, then," Pearl said.

Roland nodded. "Until later."

Garrett dug into the sand with the toe of his boot.

Once the ladies were out of earshot, Roland turned on his brother. "Why were you so rude? Miss Amanda made your daughter a gift."

Garrett's jaw was set. "She's not Eva."

Roland shivered. His brother had seen it, too, but he couldn't let something so insignificant stand in the way of a potential match. "Of course she isn't. Any resemblance is no excuse for bad manners."

"I'm not getting married, especially to someone who looks like Eva."

That narrowed the field, but Roland couldn't help wondering if his brother had thrown away the perfect match over something unimportant.

To Pearl, the two brothers looked like boys who'd been caught doing something they shouldn't have. Garrett wouldn't look them in the eye, even when Amanda had handed him the gift, and Roland kept mopping his neck and smiling too broadly to make up for his brother's lack of gratitude.

"Sadie's father doesn't like me." Amanda sighed once they'd headed back to the boardinghouse.

"I'm sure there's another explanation. It looked to me like we interrupted a heated discussion."

"Whatever about? Jake and I never quarreled, and we were children. They're grown men."

"You were five and six years old," Pearl pointed out. "If you did quarrel, you were too young to remember it, especially after..."

"Especially after the accident. It's all right. I can talk about it now."

"I'm glad." Pearl no longer had to pretend it didn't happen, as if Amanda had ended up in the orphanage due to some huge mistake instead of the train accident that claimed her parents' lives and sent her brother first to an uncle in Missouri and then, after he ran away, into thin air.

"Surely your brother would have returned to New York if he was looking for you."

Amanda halted in front of the boardinghouse. "He must not have been able to, or he tried but I was already gone to the Chatsworths'."

Pearl shook her head. They'd been over this part a dozen times. "He didn't appear while I was still there. By then, a dozen years must have passed. He probably didn't know where to look. When your uncle moved on, there wasn't anyone left who knew where you were."

"Uncle Griffin never knew where I was."

"How can you be sure?" From what Pearl recalled, Amanda was only five at the time of the accident and seven when her grandmother passed from typhoid. Most children that age wouldn't have any idea where to find family. "You said you never met your uncle."

"He moved before Grandmother died."

The how and when didn't matter. Amanda was alone in the world except for a brother who might still be alive somewhere. She could cling to that hope, but not Pearl. Her parents would never come back for her.

"Perhaps it's time to set the past aside and move forward with your life." Pearl had voiced that opinion often enough, but since arriving in Singapore that path had never seemed clearer. "If Jake is still alive—"

"He is. I know it."

"If he's still living, you have no way to find him. He might live anywhere, even in the Western territories."

"Or here."

Pearl had never heard her friend sound so certain. "Why would you think that?"

"It's as good a place as any, and Mrs. Calloway says there are at least two men named Jake who work upriver cutting down trees. She says they're young enough to be my brother." Amanda bit her lip. "Do you think Mr. Decker would take me upriver to search?"

If one of those men turned out to be Amanda's brother,

it would be an enormous coincidence. Pearl couldn't dash her friend's hopes, no matter how faint. So she smiled encouragingly. "I'm sure making that dress for his daughter helped soften his heart, though I must admit that he certainly isn't very vocal about his feelings."

"Not that Mr. Decker." Amanda picked at the lace edging her sleeve. "The other one."

"Roland?" It came out before she could stop herself.

"Why not? He is so kind and so thoughtful. And handsome." Amanda giggled. "Don't you think so? From the moment I first woke from that swoon and saw him bending over me, I couldn't stop thinking of him. At first I thought you might have fancied him, but then you reminded me that you can't marry and don't want to marry. I do. And with Roland Decker, I wouldn't face any competition." She spun in a circle like a little girl, her arms held out. "I'm in love!"

Pearl felt ill. She had said all that and the part about not being able to marry was true, but that was almost two weeks ago. So much had changed. That silly painting competition and the way he'd tried to steal a kiss from her, for one. His promise to walk with her on the shore was another. She turned away so Amanda didn't see her dismay.

"That is all right, isn't it?" Amanda touched her arm. "You seem upset."

"No. Not at all. I simply forgot that I, uh, had business. I'd intended to ask at the store when I might expect the primers. Tell Mrs. Calloway I might be a few minutes late for supper."

Before Amanda could stop her, Pearl took off at a brisk walk.

Roland headed back to the store after a long walk on the dunes to settle himself from a tense midday encounter with his brother. The whole weekend had been a disaster. The happiness of Sadie's birthday crumbled when she adored Roland's tea set and rejected Garrett's gift of a new rag doll. When Garrett tried to take away her old doll, Sadie had insisted that Miss Amanda would fix it. The pretty new matching dresses only confirmed that the brunette had more than enough skills to complete the task. Garrett had taken out his frustrations on Roland, and Monday hadn't brought any letup. Roland had to get away to clear his temper before returning to the store.

The walk, and the thought of spotting Pearl again, had done him good.

"Crate from Chicago for you," Charlie called out as he wheeled the handcart to the rear of the mercantile. "Came in on the mail boat."

"The mail boat's here?" Roland darted for the back entrance and the order he needed to send out on that boat. He couldn't face Pearl's wrath if her primers didn't arrive in short order, and the next mail boat wouldn't arrive for at least a week.

"It's come and gone."

Roland halted with his hand on the door handle. Missed the boat again. Pearl would not be pleased, but there wasn't much he could do about it now. Best get to work. Miffed at himself, he pulled open the door.

"Don't you wanna look in the crate?" Charlie asked.

Roland blew out his breath. It was probably something he'd ordered ages ago or something Stockton had had shipped up from the emporium, thinking it would sell well here. He headed back and noticed that "Holmes Enterprises" was stenciled on the side of the crate.

What would Holmes have sent him in a crate? Roland was waiting for a letter, not something big enough to require a crate.

"Fetch a crowbar," he told Charlie. "Let's find out."

The boy took off at lightning speed and returned almost as quickly. His eyes sparkled. No doubt he dreamed of baseball bats or some new contraption. Charlie had always been fascinated with machinery. It was a wonder Roland had been able to talk him in to working at the store rather than the mill, but he couldn't stand the idea of risking the fatherless boy's life. His ma depended on him. So Roland had made up a position in the store and paid Charlie the same wage he would have gotten at the mill. Stockton wouldn't like it, but then Stockton wasn't paying the wage. Roland was.

"Hurry, hurry," Charlie said, hovering over the crate.

Roland had to put his weight into prying off the lid. At last it came free. Charlie was ready to dive into the straw, but Roland held him back. "Maybe it's one of those mannequins that ladies use when putting together their dresses."

As expected, Charlie's nose wrinkled before he found a reason to counter that speculation. "Nope. It's too heavy for that. It's gotta be a machine."

"A sewing machine, perhaps."

"It'd better not be."

Roland had to chuckle at the dismay painted across the lad's face. "Go ahead. Pull off the straw, and let's see what we have."

It didn't take Charlie long. First he pulled out a sheet of paper and handed it to Roland. Then he came up with a book.

"It's schoolbooks." The lad tossed the book back in the crate. "Lousy old schoolbooks."

Roland looked closer. "Primers." Not sparkling-new but in good condition. "Holmes kept his promise." That was a good sign if the man decided to invest. He hadn't given Roland an answer before heading home, saying he needed to check some figures and mull it over. Maybe this sheet of paper was his answer. Or an invoice.

Roland unfolded the paper. It looked like an invoice except the detail noted used primers and the cost was zero. What a relief! He wouldn't have to spend money he didn't have, and Pearl could start school with books. At the bottom of the invoice, Holmes had scrawled a note. Roland stared at the illegible handwriting. He turned it this way and that. It couldn't say what he thought it said. It made no sense. But he couldn't decipher any other meaning.

If Roland wanted Holmes to invest, he first needed to find a church building in Singapore.

Chapter Eleven

"Why don't you use that empty worker cabin?" Mrs. Calloway asked someone in the parlor.

Pearl paused outside the room. She didn't want to eavesdrop, but she couldn't help but overhear her landlady's loud voice. Moreover, the question piqued her curiosity. For Mrs. Calloway to entertain a visitor during the breakfast hour, it must be urgent. Based on her suggestion, someone must be coming to town, and it wasn't a worker. Had that Chicago businessman returned? That made no sense. He had stayed at the hotel last time. Why would he need a cabin now? Unless he'd brought family. Maybe she'd have more students in her classroom tomorrow for the first day of school.

Roland's voice broke into her thoughts. "Think Stockton will go for it?"

Pearl's spine tingled. Roland was here? At this hour?

"Can't see why not," Ernie Calloway said. "Ain't usin' the place for anything."

Pearl held her breath. It must be a family arriving, someone who intended to stay.

"Psst!" The whisper came from Fiona, who was standing in the hallway opposite Pearl. She motioned for Pearl to follow her into the dining room.

Though Pearl wanted to know who was due to arrive, she couldn't eavesdrop now that she'd been discovered. She slipped into the dining room, where Amanda and Louise were eating breakfast.

Fiona closed the door. "Did you hear what they're discussing?"

"Only that they want to use a worker cabin for someone."

Fiona shook her head. "Not someone. Something. A church."

Pearl's heart leaped. Roland had come to the Calloways looking for a place to start a church. Until this moment, she hadn't been certain if he was a believer or not.

"A church in Singapore," she breathed.

"An answer to prayer." Amanda beamed as she buttered a biscuit. "Isn't it wonderful?"

For a second Pearl wondered if her love-struck friend had convinced Roland to look for a church building, but that was not in Amanda's nature. She could barely speak to an eligible man. She certainly wouldn't have demanded anything, and that was exactly what it would have taken based on Pearl's experiences with Roland.

"About time," Fiona said. "If I'm going to make my home here, there has to be a church."

Now, Fiona was one who would have insisted a man do something for her.

"Did you suggest it?" Pearl queried.

Fiona hemmed and hawed before answering. "I might have said something to Mr. Decker about it not being right holding services in a boardinghouse."

Then Fiona *was* behind it. "I'm surprised Roland listened. He doesn't heed my suggestions."

"Not that brother," Fiona scoffed. "Why would I bother with him? I'm after Garrett. He's the eldest and most suited to my temperament."

Meaning she could boss him around. Pearl would have figured Fiona to lean toward the suave Roland, but apparently she preferred the strong, silent types. That didn't bode well for Amanda, though. With Fiona on the attack and Amanda setting her sights on Roland, Pearl would never see her friend properly matched.

She threw up her hands. It was all too much. "I need to go to the school to get ready for tomorrow."

Amanda looked up at her. "Aren't you going to eat breakfast?"

"I'm not hungry." Not with Roland across the hall in the parlor.

"But you will be. I know you. You always eat breakfast."

With the three ladies watching her, Pearl felt compelled to force something down. She poured a cup of tea and nibbled on a biscuit.

Amanda handed her a pot of strawberry preserves. "They're delicious, and the butter is freshly churned."

Pearl assuaged her friend's concerns by spreading both on the biscuit, but she still wasn't hungry. After drinking the tea and forcing the biscuit down her throat, she rose and excused herself.

"I will join you when I'm finished," Amanda said.

"Oh!" Louise looked up from the book she was reading. "Amanda said you need something to read to the students tomorrow. I have *Little Women* if you would like to borrow it."

"Thank you. That would do nicely." Though it would not help her teach them letters. Pearl hoped those primers came in soon.

"And *Jane Eyre*," Louise added.

Pearl fought a pang and avoided Amanda's doubtless stricken look. The heroine's orphaned beginnings too closely matched their own situation. "Perhaps later."

She slipped out of the dining room and glanced into the parlor as she passed. The Calloways and Roland were still in deep discussion. None of them noticed her departure. Well, she couldn't very well interrupt to ask when he expected the primers. She would have to talk to him at the store later.

Her hand was still on the doorknob when Roland's voice rolled out of the parlor.

"I know exactly who to ask. Her attention to detail and beauty make her the perfect fit. Together we'll make this church a reality."

For the briefest moment she hoped he meant her, but no one had ever accused her of paying attention to fine details or creating anything beautiful. He must have meant Amanda, who had created those darling dresses for Sadie and her doll.

She stepped through the door and closed it behind her, trying to ignore the disappointment. Why couldn't she learn to sew or create beautiful things? Why did every piece of needlework turn into a snarled mess? Her fine hair fell out of its pins constantly. She couldn't make this old brown dress look like a fancy traveling suit or a ball gown. She couldn't compare to the other ladies, so why did she think she could ever attract the attention of a man like Roland? Best to give it up and accept the life God had given her.

Roland saw Pearl walk away from the boardinghouse, but between Ernie and Mabel Calloway's suggestions, he couldn't get away until she had passed the big sawmill.

Since the howl of the saws made it impossible for her to hear him, he raced after her.

She had a long stride and had reached the river path before he caught up to her.

"A moment, please," he gasped, out of breath.

She jumped and whirled around. "Oh. Roland. You startled me."

He braced his hands on his knees until he could catch his breath. "Whew, you set a brisk pace."

Her lips curved into a smile, and he discovered just how much he liked pleasing her.

"I have something to ask you." He waved toward town.

Her smile vanished. "I won't let you out of your promise."

He had to grin. "Of course not. That's not what I need to talk to you about, though I have news on that front. But first, I stopped by the boardinghouse this morning to ask the Calloways where we might set up a church building."

"That would be a blessing for the men."

And for his project, but she didn't need to know that. "They suggested the vacant worker's cabin, but it'll need some work. I was wondering if you would like to help."

"Me?" Her surprise seemed out of place.

"You did a wonderful job setting up the school."

"It was already a school."

"This is a single-room cabin. I'll get Garrett and some of the men to remove the bunks and make benches. Do you think that will work?"

She nodded slowly. "Wouldn't it be easier to use the school?"

He didn't want to get into the controversy that might start, since the school belonged to three communities, one of which had its own church. "I think it's best to stay in town, don't you? Easier for the men and for visitors."

"You have a point. If we make it too difficult, they might not attend."

"Precisely. So you will help?"

Her brow furrowed. "I still don't know why you need me."

"To figure out how it should be set up and tell me what all is needed." Since she still hesitated, he added, "You are the fastest painter in town."

She laughed. "When will I have time? School begins tomorrow."

"I'm busy in the daytime also. Could you spare an hour in the evening and some time on Saturday?"

Her smile turned teasing. "And what do I receive for this assistance?"

"Why, the joy of starting a church. And that walk along the shore."

"I'd like that." She drew in a deep breath, as if pulling herself from a blissful dream. "But at the moment I need to prepare the classroom for tomorrow."

"That reminds me. I have a surprise for you."

"What?"

He wanted to see her reaction when she opened the crate. "I'll bring it up to the schoolhouse later this morning."

She looked like she was going to insist he tell her what it was, but in the end she laughed and shook her head. "I don't know why I let you talk me into things."

"Because I'm utterly charming."

With a final laugh, she headed off to the school, her back straight and her step sure. Pearl Lawson was an impressive woman, and he was sure glad she'd agreed to work with him on the new church. She would be able to fill in all the details that he would miss, so when Holmes visited he'd be impressed enough to invest in the glassworks.

Roland was full of surprises. After delivering a crate filled with primers for every grade level and helping her place them in order inside the now-dry cupboards, he asked her to walk with him to the worker cabin that was to become the new church. Since she could do little more until she met her students tomorrow, she agreed, locking the door with the key Mr. Farmingham had given her.

"Do you think someone will steal the primers?" Roland asked with a bit of incredulity.

"Mr. Farmingham thinks it more likely critters would get inside and tear things apart."

"Such as bears?"

"I should hope not." The idea of finding a bear in the school made her shiver. "I was thinking more of raccoons."

"Last I heard, raccoons couldn't reach high enough to open a door."

He had a point, but then why had Mr. Farmingham insisted she lock the door? "Are there really bears around here?"

"They've been seen."

She didn't want to admit she feared encountering one. Better to dwell on the project at hand.

"Which cabin is going to become the church?" she asked as they descended the path and turned toward town.

Though the undergrowth was lush after a summer's growth, they could see around the bend of the river to the sawmill and closest buildings.

"The farthest one from the waterfront."

"The longest walk, then." She huffed out her breath, annoyed that this too was impractical. "I'd hoped it would be near the big mill."

"Why? The men don't work Sundays except during peak logging. This is closer to the other worker housing."

She hadn't considered that. There was a lot Roland knew about Singapore that she didn't. "You seem to think the town will grow, but other than this stand of young trees near the school, I don't see much timber."

He got that dreamy look she'd seen on the *Milwaukee.* "They're cutting upriver, but you're right. Eventually there won't be enough left to make cutting and floating it downriver worth the cost. They'll move north. That's why we need new industry."

"Like what?"

"Like a glassworks."

"A glassworks," she repeated, not quite understanding what he meant. "Why that?"

"What makes up glass?" He picked up a handful of sand from the path and let it trickle through his fingers. "Silica. Sand. Look at it all." He swept his hands toward the dunes.

"I see what you mean."

"With the river and the lake, it's the perfect location. Singapore can change from lumber to glass and continue to grow."

She couldn't help but get caught up with his vision. "And a church will become the bedrock of the community."

He blinked, as if startled by that statement, but then the old grin returned. "And the school. We want educated workers."

Did he mean that, or was he saying it simply to get on her good side? She wasn't certain. He had gotten her primers, though.

"Thank you for buying the primers."

He looked a little flushed, even uncomfortable. They stepped onto the boardwalk. "Actually, I didn't buy them."

"You didn't?"

"Do you remember Mr. Holmes?"

She nodded.

"He sent them." He looked sheepish. "I can still order new ones if you want."

He didn't say as much in words, but he clearly hoped she wouldn't ask him to do so. If he was planning to build a new enterprise, he would need every dollar he had. And her students would need the jobs a glassworks could provide.

"These will do," she stated, "but you will have to provide a different reward."

The sparkle returned to his eyes. "Name it."

What could she ask? To spend time with her? To stay away from the others? That wasn't fair when she couldn't consider marriage.

She pursed her lips and came to a conclusion. "That walk on the shore would be nice."

He brightened. "My pleasure."

The way he said it sent her stomach fluttering. Walking alone with a gentleman on the lakeshore was a risk. People would talk. Amanda would be crushed. But she wanted it. Oh, how she wanted that time with him.

"Perhaps you might tell me more about the town and your plans."

He beamed. "I can't wait, but we'll need to, at least for a little while. We're here."

They stopped in front of a weathered little cabin at the farthest reaches of town. There were gaps in the wood siding and the shingles looked less watertight than the old ones on the school. But it was a building.

He opened the unlocked door. "Shall we go inside?"

She was half-afraid of what they'd find in the dark space. "You first."

He laughed. "No bears. I promise."

But he went in first. She followed and let her eyes adjust to the lower light. The room was filled with bunks from floor to ceiling. There was only enough room to walk between them. Dust motes danced in the light from the two windows and door.

"It must sleep a dozen men," she exclaimed.

"I imagine so, but it hasn't been used in years, not since before the big sawmill burned down."

That explained why that mill looked newer than the other one.

"Think it will do?" he asked.

"Once we get rid of the bunks." But the place gave her the chills. She shivered.

He placed an arm around her waist, sending her stomach fluttering again. She really should have eaten more breakfast.

"Which way should the benches face?" he asked.

She tried to concentrate. "The cabin is wider than it is deep. It's opposite a church, but we'll make do. Put the pulpit at that end." She pointed toward the lake. "The morning light will be better there. The benches will face the preacher. And we should whitewash the walls." Detailing what needed to be done took her mind off the musty smell and dank interior.

Nevertheless, she was grateful to step into the sun again when they finished the assessment.

Roland placed a hand on the small of her back as he helped her down the large step. My, she could get used to that attention.

"Thank you, Pearl." He gazed into her eyes. "I wish we could take that walk right now, but the day is getting late."

She broke from his riveting gaze to see that he was correct. The sun hung just above the dunes. They'd spent more time going over the plans than she'd thought. But she hated for him to leave.

"Perhaps we could walk to the top of the dune," she suggested, unwilling to end this time together.

His smile spoke of regret, and he removed his hand from her waist. "The children will want their supper, and I'm the cook."

She'd never considered who cooked their meals. Alas, cooking was one thing she could not do. Yet another strike against her.

She mustered a smile. "We can't keep them waiting."

"Especially not when tomorrow is their first day of school."

He lifted her hand to his lips and kissed it, as if she was a lady. He then tucked that hand around his arm. "Shall I escort you home, miss?"

Home. The old longing to one day have her own home returned with terrible fierceness. Even better if it was with Roland.

The walk to the boardinghouse was far too short. When they drew near, Pearl couldn't help but notice that Amanda, Fiona and Louise were gathered on the long porch. Louise was reading, as usual, but Fiona spotted Pearl and Roland at once. Whatever she'd been saying died on her lips. She rose and strode to the railing, as if to make sure she was truly seeing Pearl being escorted by Roland. Her lips twisted into a frown.

Triumph surged through Pearl with the same elation that she'd felt when she'd bested Roland at painting. Yes. She, Pearl Lawson, was being escorted by the handsomest man in town.

She put on her best smile to confirm this was no accident.

Then she saw Amanda drop her needlework, her eyes and mouth round with shock. She blinked once, twice, and then fled into the boardinghouse.

Pearl's heart sank. How careless she'd been with her dearest friend.

"Why did Amanda run off?" Roland asked.

Pearl extricated her hand from his arm. "A misunderstanding. One I must endeavor to clear up."

Chapter Twelve

"Don't you care at all?" Amanda sobbed into the pillow.

Pearl stood helplessly at the door to their room, feeling every bit of shame due her. She hadn't once thought of Amanda's feelings. She hadn't even told her friend how she really felt about Roland. If she had, then Amanda wouldn't be suffering now.

"I'm sorry. I should have told you." She set Amanda's embroidery on top of the bureau.

"Yes, you should have." Amanda lifted her tearstained face. "I thought we were friends. I thought we were the best of friends. How could you keep something like that from me when...when you knew how I felt about him?"

Pearl had no excuse. "I'm sorry. I botched it terribly, but I didn't think—"

"You didn't think I had a chance with him." The tears flowed again, and Amanda hid her face in the soggy pillow. "You already knew he liked you and would reject me. Just like Hugh." Her sobs increased in intensity.

Pearl opened the bureau drawer and pulled out a clean handkerchief. She sat down beside Amanda, who scooted to the other side of the bed.

Pearl held out the handkerchief. "At least take this."

"I—I don't want anything from you." Amanda collapsed onto the pillow again. "Traitor."

"I was wrong. I thought, well, I thought any connection between us was all in my imagination."

Amanda lifted her face and protested, "You can't even marry anyway."

Pearl grimaced. "I know, and I told him that. He said he didn't want to marry, either."

"Then why was he holding your hand?"

"He was simply escorting me back to the boardinghouse." Even Pearl knew that wasn't entirely true.

She didn't fool Amanda. "That doesn't explain the way he looked at you, and the way you looked at him."

Pearl felt no better than the fly buzzing inside the window, desperate to get out. She sympathized with the poor insect, but neither of them could escape the trap they'd gotten themselves into without the help of someone with greater powers. For Pearl, that meant turning to God. She knew what to do—love Amanda as herself—but she would have to give up claim to Roland, for her friend was right. This dalliance could come to nothing.

She sighed. "I will not spend any more time alone with Roland." That hurt, but Pearl must accept whatever came to pass, even if Amanda and Roland fell in love.

"You would do that for me?" Tears glistened on Amanda's long, dark lashes.

Pearl managed a nod.

Amanda threw her arms around her. "You're the best friend I've ever had, and I don't want to lose you over some silly man."

Pearl hugged her friend, but secretly she hoped this meant Amanda would relinquish her hope of catching Roland's attention. "It is silly, isn't it?"

Amanda looked her in the eyes. "I know you'll be perfectly happy teaching school."

Pearl felt her heart sink before Amanda finished.

"And I—" Amanda clasped Pearl's hands, her eyes sparkling. "I will make him a wonderful wife."

Roland whistled as he carted the whitewash to the cabin that was fast becoming a church. In the course of a week, the bunks had been removed and benches built. Garrett was still working on the pulpit, but it was shaping up. Saturday, he and Pearl would paint the walls. They ought to be plastered, but that would take too long. He needed Holmes's approval so the glassworks project could get underway.

"Why don't you wait until Saturday to haul that over to the cabin?" Garrett had asked as Roland loaded the cart.

"I have time today."

The weather was also exceptionally calm for a September day, and Roland hoped to convince Pearl to take that long-delayed walk along the shore. The timing was perfect. He'd waited until he spotted her walking back from the school. He would offer to show her the progress on the church, since he was heading that way to drop off the whitewash. Sometime during their time together, he'd slip in the suggestion that they stroll the shoreline.

The thought of her hand in his had occupied his thoughts all day. In fact, he'd been trying to figure out how to approach her all week. She always seemed to have others surrounding her. At the boardinghouse, her friend Amanda clung close as a burr. At Sunday's church service, the parents surrounded her with unending questions. Isaac and Sadie walked with her back and forth to school. He'd had no opportunity to speak with her alone.

Over the week he'd learned her patterns. She left for the school just as the sun lightened the eastern sky and returned shortly after the sawmill's steam whistle signaled the end of the work day. Today was the first day she'd returned from school alone, since Isaac and Sadie had come back to town with the Wardmans.

He wheeled the cart directly in her path, forcing her to stop.

"Miss Pearl. It's good to see you."

She looked toward the boardinghouse. "And you, Mr. Decker."

Her stiff reply surprised him, but then she might be responding in kind since he'd begun the conversation somewhat formally. "You look lovely today."

At last she looked at him. Unfortunately in disgust.

"I am exhausted, and my dress needs cleaning."

She still wore that bland brown dress. Its only saving grace was the way it made her green eyes stand out.

"I wasn't referring to your clothing." He offered a broad smile to lift her mood. "You provide the beauty."

She rolled her eyes. "I have much to do tonight, and Mrs. Calloway would appreciate my assistance."

He was getting the distinct impression she didn't want to see him. "At least allow me to escort you to the boardinghouse."

Even that seemed to make her uncomfortable. She glanced around, as if looking for someone, and then sighed. "You are clearly delivering something. I don't want to keep you."

That was his opening. "I'm bringing the paint to the new church. I thought you might like to see the progress."

A battle played out on her face. She wanted to see the church, but something was keeping her from agreeing.

"Perhaps Amanda would like to see it, too."

He didn't want Amanda with them. "I thought, considering the fine weather, that it might be the perfect afternoon for our stroll on the lakeshore."

She visibly stiffened. "That wouldn't be…a good idea." Her eyes darted everywhere but at him.

What was going on? "Have I done something to offend you?"

"No." She swallowed but looked over his shoulder. "Not at all."

"Then why are you acting this way?"

She shook her head. "I'm sorry, Mr. Decker, but I need to return to the boardinghouse."

"I thought we were on a first-name basis." He widened his smile in an attempt to draw her in. "If you can't see the church today, I hope you'll be there Saturday to paint. We wouldn't want Singapore's best painter to miss out."

"We will be there."

We? His heart sank. Of course there would be others. Garrett said he'd help, but Pearl seemed to wield those friends of hers like a shield. Perhaps she was just exhausted. Perhaps whatever was weighing her down now would be gone by Saturday. "I look forward to it."

"I'll see you Saturday, then." For the briefest moment she looked directly at him with almost a wistful look. Then she left the boardwalk and skirted around his cart. Once past, she turned back briefly. "Thank you for taking such interest in the new church."

Then she hurried away.

Pearl dropped her books and papers on the bed and collapsed to her knees. It had taken every ounce of will to walk away from Roland. She wanted to see the church. She wanted that stroll along the lakeshore, but she had promised Amanda. She must stay away from Roland until Amanda lost interest. But would that ever happen?

Lord, help me.

She buried her face in her hands and felt the sting of a tear of frustration.

The week had been long. The children were exuberant, to say the least, and she'd soon discovered that her experiences in the orphanage and her education had not fully prepared her for the realities of teaching. Instead of attentive young minds, the children bounced from their seats at the slightest sound. Giggles, whispers and out-and-out defiance had turned each day into a struggle. She could not rely on the older children to keep still while she worked with the younger ones. If she didn't figure out something soon, none of them would learn a thing.

A week ago she would have asked Roland for advice, but now she couldn't spend any time alone with him. If Amanda had seen the little chat today, she would get upset all over again. She needed a friend who understood children. Mrs. Wardman came to mind, but she lived all the way over in Saugatuck and did not attend church services here.

It felt like her world was crumbling.

She heard the door open and close softly. Then she felt Amanda sink to the floor beside her and wrap an arm around her shoulders.

"What happened?" her friend whispered.

Pearl could not mention the encounter with Roland, so she began with school. "I'm a terrible teacher."

"I don't believe that for a minute. You were always trying to educate us at the orphanage. Remember your little classroom?" Amanda held out a handkerchief, but Pearl hadn't let one tear fall.

"They were better behaved. These children are... energetic."

Amanda laughed. "Of course they are. They've been climbing trees and swimming and fishing all summer long. They probably don't want the fun to end."

"I hadn't considered that." She sighed. "That's why I'm an awful teacher."

Amanda rose and patted the bed. "The floor is terribly hard. Let's sit while you tell me everything."

Pearl sat beside her friend and heaved a big sigh. "They're noisy and won't listen. When I work with the older children, the little ones run around. When I work with the little ones, the older children create havoc. I don't know what to do."

"It sounds like you could use help."

"With only ten children? If I can't handle ten children, what sort of teacher am I?"

"A good one." Amanda hugged her. "You helped me learn to read." She paused, pensive. "Are Isaac and Sadie causing problems, too?"

"Honestly, they are the only children who behave." She sighed. "But in comparison, they seem almost too quiet and somber."

Amanda echoed the sigh. "I know what you mean. Sadie barely says a thing and almost never smiles. Isaac acts like he has to look after his sister, but he's too young for that. You don't think their father is ignoring them, do you?"

Pearl had wondered about that. Garrett Decker always looked terribly serious and melancholy. It was understandable, but it might be affecting the children. "Maybe I should have a talk with him. But to be honest, that fills me with dread."

Amanda squeezed her around the shoulders. "I know what you mean. He's intimidating with that scowl of his."

Was that it? Was that what drew Amanda to the younger brother rather than the older? "He has suffered a terrible loss."

Amanda bowed her head. "I know. It's affected Isaac and Sadie, too, but they really seem to want a new mother. They hang on every word Mrs. Calloway says, and they love to play games. I've spent hours and hours playing jacks and marbles with them."

Pearl should have realized that her friend had spent her free time with the children. Amanda was naturally drawn to the innocent and vulnerable—whether a child or a pet.

"A pet!" Pearl exclaimed. "Do they have a dog or cat?"

"I don't think so. At least they never mentioned a pet. Surely they would have said something."

"And there wasn't a dog or cat at the house when we visited. Perhaps a pet would be helpful."

Amanda stared at her. "Somehow I doubt their father would allow it."

"Then maybe we could have one at school. It would give the children something to care for and would teach them responsibility."

"And what would you do with it at night? You can't leave it alone in the school, and we can't bring it here."

Pearl scrambled to figure it out. "Perhaps the children could take turns bringing the kitten home at night."

"A kitten! Then you've decided."

"I saw a mama cat with kittens on my walks to and from school. We could raise one of the litter at school."

"*We* will." Amanda beamed. "It might just bring Sadie out of her shell."

Pearl didn't miss the emphasis. "Are you volunteering to help out with the project?"

Amanda nodded vigorously. "The Chatsworths had three cats. I know all about them. When you're working with one group of children, I can show the rest how to care for a kitten."

"That just might solve my classroom problem." Or it would make it worse. "Now all we have to do is catch one of the kittens without mama cat shredding us with her claws."

Amanda glowed. "Let's ask Roland to help. I know he will since it's for his niece and nephew."

God had answered her prayer. She would spend time with Roland, but so would Amanda, who would do all in her power to attract him. Pearl could only watch as her dearest friend took away the man who dominated her thoughts.

Chapter Thirteen

So many people showed up to paint the church on Saturday that they finished before lunch. Pearl stood outside the small cabin breathing in the fresh lake breeze. A chill was in the air, though the sun shone brightly. Soon autumn would be upon them and then winter. All those kittens would need a warm home by then. The last time she'd passed the mewing family, she'd counted three. The black-and-white one captured her heart, but she would like another's opinion.

Garrett Decker had joined the rest preparing the church, but he was a tough man to single out, for there were always men around him, not to mention Fiona and Louise. The two women made a show of painting, donning smocks and carrying a paintbrush. Fiona's never saw paint. She offered her artistic opinion of every feature in the room. Some ideas had merit, but they hadn't the time or the funds to attempt them. Louise painted a tiny portion of a bench near the prospective groom, who didn't appear to notice her. Both helped out at the boardinghouse in exchange for a portion of their room and board, but that could not last forever. Pearl must press Roland again to find them employment.

She pushed out a breath, which the breeze carried away in an instant.

"Tired?" Roland walked up, wiping his hands on a rag soaked in mineral spirits.

"Not a bit."

His very presence unnerved her. She'd promised Amanda to steer clear of him. That meant she hadn't been able to ask if he'd found positions for Fiona and Louise. This was her chance. She could do it if she kept her gaze fixed on the low dune separating the town from the lake. One look at him would send her thoughts spinning again. "You could answer a question for me."

"Fire ahead." He handed her the rag. "To get rid of any paint on your hands."

"Of course." She rubbed at the few spots while formulating precisely how to approach the topic. "I asked you to help Fiona and Louise find employment."

"I thought they worked for the Calloways."

"In exchange for a portion of their room and board. Soon they will need more." The roar of the waves could not drown out the roar in her ears.

"There isn't any place else except the saloons."

"Unacceptable."

"Have you asked Fiona?"

His question carried such mirth that she had to glance at him. What a mistake! A lock of his dark hair brushed across his forehead, nearly falling into his eye. Those eyes, blue as the lake on a sunny day, took her breath away. She couldn't think. She could barely remember his question.

"No," she breathed out. "Have you?"

He laughed. "That's what I love about you, Pearl. You can turn anything in a different direction."

Loved? About her? The pressure on her chest was greater than any stays she'd ever attempted to wear. "Me?" She really ought to look away, but she couldn't.

"Yes, you." His smile eased into that lazy one she'd grown to appreciate. "I enjoy sparring with you." Those eyes of his twinkled. "I enjoy any time spent with you."

Pearl drew in a shaky breath and finally managed to look away. The wind whipped sand off the tops of the dunes like snow in a blizzard. Snow. That brought to mind the other project she had in mind. They must act before winter.

"Have you seen the litter of kittens living under the rotten old dinghy?"

He drew in his breath so sharply that she had to see if he'd suffered a cut or some other misfortune. His complexion had paled, but he, too, stared straight ahead at the dune, all trace of a smile gone.

"Kittens?" He had to clear his voice.

What a peculiar reaction, as if he was terrified of them. "Yes, a litter of three from what I can determine. They will need homes by the time the snow falls."

"Of course." He visibly relaxed. "I should have realized that was what concerned you."

"You don't think I should care about their welfare?"

His chuckle sounded forced. "They'll find shelter inside a sawmill or warehouse with the rest of the strays."

"The sawmill? Isn't that a rather dangerous place for a kitten?"

His expression pinched. "I suppose it is."

"Have you ever taken one into your store?"

"Are you mad? And have them getting into the flour and the biscuits and everything else?"

"I suppose you have a point." But it wasn't looking good for her plan if Roland opposed kittens. "Perhaps one of them might stay upstairs."

"No, no and no."

"The children would love a kitten," she pointed out. "It would be a great way to learn how to take care of something." She saw him waver just a bit and seized the advantage. "Especially after they've cared for one at school. It might take their minds off…other things."

His jaw still worked. "That decision belongs to my brother."

"It's his house, then."

"It's his family."

She would get no further. Though the thought of the wee kittens in a dangerous sawmill bothered her, she might spare one at least.

"There you are!" Amanda exclaimed, her cheeks bright red and her eyes unnaturally bright.

Pearl inwardly groaned. Once again it must appear to Amanda that Pearl had broken her promise. "I asked him if they would take one of the kittens."

As she'd hoped, the mention of kittens changed Amanda's focus. "Will you help us? Sadie is so excited at the prospect. When I mentioned it, she smiled."

Pearl noted Roland's surprise at this news, but he also cast Amanda a look of admiration. Oh, dear, what if he *did* fall for her?

"She did?" He grinned. "Well, if that isn't something. Miss Amanda, you have a way with children."

She blushed even more furiously. "Why, thank you. I'm especially fond of Sadie and Isaac."

Pearl couldn't bear to watch or listen to her friend's pointed efforts. She edged away, but the breeze carried every word in her direction.

"Will you help us catch one of the kittens?" Amanda hung painfully close to Roland.

"You'll have to ask my brother's permission first. He's been dead-set against having any animals in the house."

"Can't you ask him? Pretty please? He…well, he scares me."

Roland laughed. "Don't let that crusty exterior frighten

you. He's gentle as a lamb inside, especially when it comes to his children. Go ahead. I guarantee he'll agree."

Pearl knew her friend wouldn't ask Garrett Decker anything.

Amanda's next words bore that out. "Won't you go with me? I get all tongue-tied when I'm nervous, and you could be such a help."

If Pearl hadn't given Amanda explicit permission to pursue Roland, she would think her friend a minx. As it was, she could only cringe.

Roland, on the other hand, laughed. "I will if Pearl joins us. Three will make the case better than two, especially since it's for the school."

Pearl looked up in surprise, only to see Roland grinning at her in triumph. Her heart soared. In spite of Amanda's best efforts, he had chosen her.

Roland would never have been able to convince his brother if the ladies hadn't been standing there. Pearl made a perfect case for the educational benefits of adopting a kitten and explained that the litter would reside at the schoolhouse until the weather got too cold. The others chimed in their agreement. Garrett had been too overwhelmed to protest, but Roland could tell that he didn't think much of the plan.

On the walk to the abandoned skiff, Roland avoided his brother. That boat brought back painful memories for both of them. Roland had begged Garrett to let him burn it or sink it. Garrett had refused. Roland figured his brother wanted to make him suffer. He deserved it, so he took the punishment like a man and didn't ask again.

Now Pearl kneeled beside Sadie in front of the rotting skiff. The nest of kittens, which had apparently been abandoned by their mother, squirmed under the protection of the overturned hull. Though Roland hung off to one side, he could make out three, maybe four, mewing kittens.

"Which one do you want?" Pearl asked Sadie.

The little girl pointed to a black-and-white one that stood in front of her howling its displeasure. Naturally she had to pick the loudest one. Garrett was going to be furious. Pearl, on the other hand, took it all in stride. She showed Sadie how to stroke the little one's head and pick it up while avoiding the prickly claws.

"What will you name her?"

Sadie looked to her father.

He growled under his breath. "Whatever you want."

The little girl buried her face against the soft fur. "Cocoa."

Her voice was so soft that Roland almost didn't hear the name, but then Pearl confirmed it. His stomach churned. Eva's favorite drink had been hot chocolate, which she called cocoa. Garrett's strained expression showed he understood the significance, too.

Roland turned away from the abandoned skiff with its horrible memories and the kitten that would now remind him of that awful day every time he saw it.

"Are you all right?" Amanda said softly.

Though she was a pretty girl, her hovering had begun to drive him mad. He could not explain what had happened. Not to her.

He rubbed his stomach. "A bit of dyspepsia."

"Mrs. Calloway might have something."

He attempted to shrug away her attention. "I have what I need at the store."

His brother's loud voice interrupted the conversation. "Pick a different name."

Sadie wavered, her lip quivering.

Amanda abandoned him and ran to the little girl's side, dropping to her knees to embrace her.

Pearl faced off against Garrett. "Cocoa is the kitten's name. Sadie chose it."

Garrett's face grew red. "It's my house and my daughter. You have no say."

"Of course I don't." Pearl didn't flinch one bit. "This is your daughter's kitten. Her wishes should be most important."

My, she was fine when standing her ground. Roland couldn't help but grin. If this debate escalated into an argument, he figured she could outlast Garrett any day. One day she would make a fine wife. That thought sobered him. His brother needed a wife for the sake of those children, but not Pearl. Something else simmered inside her. A restlessness. She had dreams, just like him. Could their dreams fit together?

He shook off the thought. The glassworks came first, and she had the school.

"You said that creature would stay at the school." Garrett fisted his hands, though he had no one to fight.

"Cocoa will stay with us at the school until cold weather," Pearl confirmed.

Amanda whispered something in Sadie's ear. The girl set down the kitten and wrapped her arms around Amanda.

Roland glanced at his brother, who was frowning. Garrett and Amanda might work if he could convince Garrett to give her a chance. If he could, then maybe that woman would stop hounding him.

Pearl donned her good dress for the first services in the new church. The russet-colored gown wasn't fancy compared to Fiona's elegant attire, but its simple lines accented her figure. It was also considerably warmer than her everyday gown, as she'd discovered while traveling.

Today's wind promised a taste of autumn, making this gown the perfect choice.

At last the church was ready. The paint had been too sticky last Sunday, but Mr. Calloway assured them everything was set now. He'd even donned an old frock coat in the style popular before the war and plunked a faded old top hat onto his balding head.

Mabel Calloway chuckled, but her eyes glowed at the sight of him. "He hasn't been this excited since we first set eyes on Singapore."

Pearl had heard the story many times of their being hired away from a hotel way upriver and coming down by boat in the rushing spring waters. They'd almost been crushed by logs and tossed upside down by the current. When she'd set foot on dry land, she'd vowed never to step into a boat again.

"I'm here 'til the good Lord takes me home," she would then say.

Pearl had grown fond of the Calloways over the weeks, until they'd become like family. They treated their four female guests like daughters. When Pearl went to pay the next month's rent, Mabel had brushed it off, saying Amanda did so much around the place that rent wasn't necessary. Though Pearl hadn't succeeded in paying rent, she did put the money on their account at the mercantile, a fact that did not escape Mabel, who blustered and scolded her when she found out.

At Roland's suggestion, Louise had secured employment reading to Mrs. Elder, the elderly woman who with her husband had stepped off the *Milwaukee* ahead of Pearl. Fiona had joined a fellow from the mill who played piano and together they offered a nickel concert on Saturday evenings at the lumber warehouse. They would travel to Saugatuck next Saturday to play at the community hall.

Fiona's skill carried over to Sunday services, and Pearl had to admit her soprano could have graced a New York stage. Today her voice rang over the congregation with such uplifting tones that it felt as if they were standing on heaven's shores.

When the service ended, the congregation lingered to discuss every inch of the renovations and every aspect of the service. Pearl slipped past the children racing around the boardwalk and took to the sand. Her feet sank into it, but she hiked on alone to the top of the dune. The wind tugged at her skirts and pulled the lake into great, rolling breakers. The freshness of the air and the brilliance of the sunshine reminded her that summer was almost over. Autumn arrived this week and with it the promise of winter.

Everything was beginning to fall into place here. With Amanda's help, teaching had become manageable. The kittens proved a blessing, as the children learned how to care for them and begged to play with them. She and the other ladies had settled into the boardinghouse. If not for Amanda's continued attraction to Roland, life might be perfect.

Lord, help me to accept this, to set aside my selfish desires for the sake of my friend.

It was a noble prayer, but she didn't feel any better. Words aside, her heart still called out to Roland. Every minute in his presence was torture. Rehashing each moment of Amanda's encounters with him made her stomach churn like the lake below. The wind whipped at her hat, testing the ribbons tied beneath her chin. She wrapped her arms around her midsection and squeezed shut her eyes.

"The view is beautiful from here."

Roland! She gasped and turned in the direction of his voice, half expecting to find Amanda at his side. She was not.

Pearl looked back at the view. "The lake is wild."

Roland reached her side though he did not touch her. "It makes me want to run down the dune and splash into the water like a boy."

"I can see you doing that."

He laughed. "I see that smile trying to peek out. Why are you cross with me?"

"I'm not cross."

"Then why the silence and going out of your way to avoid me?"

Had she been that obvious? She drew in a deep breath, uncertain how much to tell him. "I am not in the market for a husband."

"And I am not looking for a wife."

"Perhaps you should tell Amanda that. Oops!" She clapped a gloved hand to her mouth. She hadn't intended to say one word about her friend.

But he didn't look surprised. "I thought she would have given up by now. I've done everything in my power to discourage her."

Pearl looked at him sideways. "Including telling her you will not marry?"

"Not in so many words."

"Then her hope will continue."

This time he heaved a sigh. "I don't suppose I can avoid this."

"Not if you want to be kind."

He raked a hand through his hair. "I suppose you're right." That grin returned. "You usually are."

"Right?"

"Correct."

They both burst out in laughter. Perhaps it was the relief of knowing he did not love Amanda, but Pearl laughed so hard she had to bend over to catch her breath.

He touched her shoulder. "I do have news I want to share with you."

That sounded serious. Pearl swallowed the laughter and blotted her eyes. "News of what?"

He looked so solemn that she half feared he was about to tell her he would leave Singapore.

"I received word from Mr. Holmes, the investor who traveled with us on the *Milwaukee*." A grin split his face. "He's pledged a substantial sum toward the glassworks."

"He has?"

She could see the spark in his eye, the anticipation and eagerness to begin. "It's going to become a reality. Singapore will grow from a sleepy little lumbering town into a vibrant city with a school building all its own and a real church."

"With a steeple."

"And a bell tower on the school, too."

She got so caught up in his excitement that they ended up arm-in-arm, dancing around in a circle like two children who'd discovered buried treasure.

"It will be wonderful!" she cried out. "I can see it now."

"It will." He hugged her.

The masculine scents of soap and spruce intoxicated her. She could feel the beating of his heart and drew close like a moth to flame. In that instant, they were one. With perfect clarity she saw the meshing of their lives.

"Thank you for believing in me." Only his voice had grown ragged.

It stirred something deep inside. She could barely breathe, couldn't help but notice that his lips were inches from hers, that his stormy blue eyes had darkened.

"Pearl," he breathed, leaning closer.

His lips brushed hers, ever so lightly. She wanted more. Oh, she wanted more. She closed her eyes and let herself slip into bliss, waiting for his return.

Below them, a strangled cry was followed by the exclamation "Traitor!"

Pearl jerked from the reverie and spun to look toward town.

Amanda stood not ten feet away, her hands pressed to her mouth.

Chapter Fourteen

"You promised," Amanda cried out for what seemed like the hundredth time.

Pearl's head throbbed. They'd missed Sunday dinner and sequestered themselves in their room. While Amanda sobbed and accused, Pearl attempted to fend off the indefensible. She *had* promised, and in the moment of testing had fallen far short.

"I failed. I let you down."

"You stole him!"

Pearl squeezed the bridge of her nose and closed her eyes. "He outright told me he does not want to marry."

"It didn't look like he wasn't interested." Amanda's protests had slowed, though her tears hadn't. "He kissed you."

"I might have appeared like that—"

"It was more than appearance."

"It might have appeared like that," Pearl said again, this time with emphasis, "but we were simply sharing a moment of excitement. He received funding to start his glassworks."

"Glassworks?"

"A factory for making glass. Roland has great plans for Singapore."

Amanda's brow pinched. "What's wrong with the store? It's right below their lodgings and perfectly situated for looking after the children."

"Sadie and Isaac are not Roland's children. Perhaps he wants to begin life on his own."

"With a wife!" That ushered in yet another round of sobs. "Just like Hugh."

Pearl sat on the bed and wrapped an arm around Amanda's shoulders. "No wife. I assure you. He was very clear about that."

Amanda wiped her eyes. "Then why the kiss?"

"It was more like congratulations." Yet, it hadn't felt that way. Her lips still tingled from the brush of his. "I told him I could not marry. That's when he insisted he was not looking for a wife."

Amanda heaved a sigh. "Why do I always choose the wrong man?"

Pearl wondered the same. Amanda was drawn to the dashing gentleman rather than the steadfast type who would make the best husband. She kissed the top of her friend's head. "I don't know why we do that. Roland Decker would only break both our hearts."

"Then you don't want to marry him, either?"

What did she want? Pearl searched her jumbled feelings. For too long she'd kept them to herself. Amanda deserved the truth. "I'll admit that I'm attracted to him. It shouldn't be that way, but it is. I've tried everything to counter it, but somehow he always manages to find me alone. Then I'm lost." She shook her head. "I'm sorry. I should have had better self-control."

Amanda watched her solemnly. Then her shoulders dropped. "I think I always knew that you felt something for him. I'm the one who should be sorry. I tried to take him away from you, just like Lena took Hugh from me." She nibbled on her lower lip. "I'm so sorry. I shouldn't have done that." She swiped her eyes with her sleeve. "You're my dearest friend. How could I do that to you?"

Pearl hugged Amanda close. "You followed your heart with abandon. I could never fault you for that. In fact, I admire that about you."

"You do?"

"Sometimes I wish I wasn't so cautious."

"And I wish I was more like you. If only I weighed the options more carefully, I wouldn't get so disappointed."

Pearl forced a smile. "Who knows? Perhaps in time things would work out between you and Roland. You needed to know, though, that he said he doesn't want to marry now."

"I understand." Amanda sighed. "We missed dinner, didn't we?"

"I imagine Mrs. Calloway saved us something in the warming oven." Pearl stood. "Shall we find out?"

Amanda smiled. "Once I wash my face and fix my hair."

Pearl had to laugh. Only Amanda would worry about her appearance when no one was likely to see her. After all, Roland wouldn't be waiting in the kitchen or parlor or even on the front porch. After today's scene, he wasn't likely to wait for either of them. She smoothed her now-wrinkled skirts. That promised walk would never happen.

"That new schoolteacher," Garrett mumbled between bites of ham and potatoes, "she seems to be doing a decent job."

"Pearl. Pearl Lawson." The memory of her kiss still went to Roland's head. He'd expected her to turn away, to slap him, or at least to chew him out. Instead, she'd leaned closer, eager to continue. If it hadn't been for her friend's untimely arrival, they would have gone far past the limits he'd set for himself.

He ought to thank Amanda Porter. Ought to, but he couldn't. Not while the disappointment gnawed at him. Perhaps once he got the steam tractor moved up from the mill to his property, he'd be so busy clearing the land that these unending thoughts of Pearl would go away.

"Miss Lawson," Isaac chimed in.

Sadie kicked the rungs of her chair. "She's nice."

That any words came out of her mouth had to be credited to Pearl. She'd been both diligent and compassionate, from what he could make out from the children's reports.

"Miss Porter, too," Isaac added.

Roland looked up from his plate of food. "Miss Porter is helping out at school?"

Sadie nodded vigorously. "She takes care of Cocoa and Dandelion and Freckles."

Roland could guess which name went with which kitten. Cocoa was black-and-white. Dandelion must be the fuzzy white one, while Freckles had brown and black spots.

Garrett frowned. "Is she there every day?"

Roland glanced at his brother, who was at last taking more interest in his children's schooling and well-being. Maybe it had to do with the new schoolteacher and church, but he hoped it had to do with Amanda Porter. She clearly loved children, and her temperament might work for Garrett. They were both quiet.

Isaac's head bobbed up and down. "She teaches us how to feed the kittens and brush them."

"And pick off the fleas?" Garrett grumbled. "I hold her responsible for the fact that we'll have to house one of them."

Sadie blinked back tears and stared down at her plate, once again retreating into silence.

Roland shook his head. Not only had Pearl, not Amanda, been the one to insist that Sadie have a kitten, but Garrett was also ignoring his daughter's deep need to love something. "Isaac. Sadie. Why don't you take your dishes to the kitchen? I'll clean up later."

Both children slipped off their chairs and grabbed their plates.

"They're not done," Garrett snapped.

The children froze.

Roland wondered what had his brother so upset that he was taking it out on his son and daughter. Garrett didn't mean to hurt them. He loved those children. Perhaps too much. He wouldn't let them go near the river. The docks were off-limits. He'd impressed on Isaac that it was his responsibility to stick to his sister like a burr to a sweater. He wasn't eight years old yet. They had precious little time just to be children.

Roland got up. "Come with me. I'll speak with your father."

He led them downstairs to the small kitchen in the back of the building.

"Do we have to stop eating, Uncle Roland?" Isaac asked, dead serious.

"No. Eat here and then play nearby." He left them somewhat more cheered, but his temper was building. By the time he climbed the stairs, he was ready to explode.

He burst through the door. "Why do you always have to be so harsh with them?"

Garrett tensed. "What right do you have to tell me how to raise my children? It's your fault they're motherless."

Roland's throat constricted even though it was an old argument. The guilt never went away, but he'd thought they might learn to live with it. "I can't change what happened."

"No, you can't."

"But we have to let it go. You have to move on." Roland

would get back to his point no matter how much Garrett wanted to drag him back to the past.

The vein on Garrett's temple throbbed. "I am moving on, as you put it."

"Those children need a mother."

Garrett stood and slammed his fist down on the table. "They need their father and no one else."

"You must admit they've changed since the ladies arrived." His brother wavered, and Roland seized the opportunity. "Sadie is talking again. Isaac enjoys school. They love spending time at the boardinghouse because of Miss Amanda." He would tick off a hundred examples, but his brother stopped him.

"Why do you keep talking about Amanda when it's Pearl who's made the difference? She's a strong woman who won't stand for nonsense."

Roland felt the knife slip between his ribs. Either Garrett was deliberately goading him, or he had noticed Pearl the way he had. He swallowed. "A good trait in a schoolmarm."

"Better in a wife and mother."

Roland couldn't help but think of Eva. She'd been demanding, always thinking happiness was just a stone's throw away. He would never have considered her strong. In comparison, Amanda came closer to Garrett's late wife. Maybe that's why Garrett dismissed her in favor of Pearl.

"Pearl can't marry. It's part of her contract."

That didn't sway Garrett. "There's not a woman in the world that wouldn't trade a job for marriage."

Roland fisted his hands. "Not Pearl. She honors her word. She wouldn't abandon the children, even for marriage."

Then he noticed Garrett trying to hide a grin. This must be another of his brother's tricks. Garrett wasn't sweet on Pearl. He was trying to make Roland admit that he was.

Roland called his bluff. "You missed the mark, this time, brother. I'm not running after any woman, even Pearl Lawson."

Garrett laughed. "We'll see about that, little brother."

In the following weeks, Pearl watched the growing piles of brick and stout wooden beams with a mix of admiration and apprehension. Roland had staked his future on this glassworks, but how would it take root in a small town centered on lumbering? Where would he get the workers, for one? When he'd talked about it, she'd envisioned it happening years from now, when the oldest students had finished their schooling. The truth hadn't even sunk in when he told her the investment monies had come in. This accumulation of building materials meant his glassworks would soon become a reality.

When she and Amanda stepped from the boarding-house in the gray light of dawn the second week of October, she was surprised to hear the growl of a steam engine added to the whine of the big sawmill. Judging from the smoke and steam rising above the mill roof, whatever was going on was taking place upriver.

She pulled her shawl tight around her shoulders. Autumn's chill had set in. The leaves, such as they were in this barren landscape, were turning. Most were gold, but one vibrant maple shone its oranges and reds just below the schoolhouse.

"Let's press leaves today," she suggested to her friend. "It looks like the rains have ended. The children will enjoy going out of doors."

"I'll take half the class while you teach the other half."

This division of students worked, though it usually took some adjustment to keep the troublemakers apart.

"Brrr!" Amanda shivered. "It's chilly this morning. I'm glad I wore a scarf."

Pearl didn't own a scarf or a winter coat. She would have to spend precious savings on them or suffer on her trips to and from the schoolhouse. Already the soles of her shoes were wearing thin. She'd stuffed newspaper inside and prayed they wouldn't wear through until after winter.

"I hope Jake isn't out in this cold." Amanda sighed.

"I'm sure your brother has plenty of warm clothes wherever he is."

Lately Pearl had spent more and more time consoling Amanda about her brother. Apparently with Roland beyond reach, she'd turned her attention back to her lifelong quest. Pearl had hoped her friend would warm to Garrett, but neither party had shown the slightest movement toward the other. They sat on opposite sides of the church and never spoke. Amanda wouldn't even look at him. Romance could never hope to bud if they wouldn't talk.

Fiona, on the other hand, didn't shy away from Garrett, though he looked like a cornered fox every time she approached. Louise spent more and more time with Mrs. Elder until announcing Saturday that she was moving in to help care for the elderly couple. That meant one less lady in pursuit of the suitor, or at least within sight of him.

Pearl sighed. At this rate, Amanda would never find her match.

"Why the heavy sigh?" Amanda asked.

Pearl shook her head. "Just thinking of the future."

As they rounded the mill, the shouts of men and growl of machinery grew louder.

"What is it?" Amanda asked.

"I suspect it's the new glassworks."

"Oh."

Any mention of Roland or his project made Amanda clam up. Seeing him must still sting.

Pearl skirted along the river with Amanda on her heels. The water raced past after the recent rains. With each step, the din grew louder. A tree crashed down. The work was definitely closer than she'd first thought. When they rounded the last curve before the cutoff to the school-house, the catastrophe came into full view.

Lumbermen toppled trees and sawed off the branches. The steam tractor from the mill hauled logs into a pile and tore up stumps, all while turning the forest floor into a rutted mess. A pile of branches and limbs rose high in the air. And Roland supervised it all. He darted from spot to spot, directing the men, oblivious to her presence and to the fact that he was clearing the land directly below the school. Given the sandy soil and steep slope, a good gully-washer could send the whole building toppling down the hill.

Amanda stared. "What are they doing?"

What indeed. Pearl's blood boiled.

"Stop!" she cried out, waving her arms.

Naturally no one heard. How could they over the ear-splitting growl of machinery?

She spotted Roland talking to two of the lumbermen who were tugging a giant crosscut saw through the large spruce tree. Not that tree! The children loved its cones. They'd made wreaths from them to give their parents for Christmas. Now Roland was ruining it and everything else. How could she teach school with that racket? The kittens must be terrified. And two more men prepared to cut down her maple.

"Stop!" Pearl raced toward the lumbermen. She had to halt this before they destroyed everything.

The men set the saw against the trunk.

She picked up her skirts and ran. Mud oozed through the thin soles. A stick jabbed the arch of her foot. She hopped but didn't stop. Pearl threw herself against the tree, arms outspread.

"Stop at once!" she cried.

The surprised lumberjacks dropped the saw and stood up.

The din lessened bit by bit, and gradually she realized the work had stopped. The men all stood staring at her. Only one moved, and his long strides covered the distance between them in no time.

Roland halted in front of her. "What are you doing?"

Chapter Fifteen

❧

"What are *you* doing?" The feisty schoolteacher shot Roland's question right back at him. She waved at the work underway. "You're destroying everything."

Ordinarily Roland would find her flashing eyes and spirited reaction appealing, but at the moment she was slowing down progress.

"I'm clearing the land for the new glassworks, so if you will get out of the way, my men can get back to work." Work for which he was paying a good wage.

"But you're cutting down the trees."

"That's what clearing the land means."

After their talks, that should have been obvious. Yet she crossed her arms and glared.

"Not my maple." She waved a hand in the air. "Isn't it bad enough that you're killing the spruce?"

Her misplaced defense of the trees was amusing. He couldn't keep his lips from inching upward. "This is not Central Park or any park at all. It's a lumber town. That means stands of timber are destined for the sawmill to be turned into lumber. How else did you think fine houses got built?"

Her lips pressed into a straight line. "I am not a simpleton, Mr. Decker. This is not a lumbering venture, and these logs are not destined for fine homes."

"As a matter of fact, they are. We do not waste timber. These logs will go to the mill." He turned to the foreman, Sawyer Evans. "Resume work."

"Oh, no, you don't." Pearl flung herself between Roland and Evans. "This can't continue."

"It can and will." He nodded at Evans, who stepped away.

She stomped her foot. "Did you ever once consider what effect this will have on the children? They made wreaths using the cones from that spruce. We were going to press maple leaves today. You've ruined everything. I can't bring them into this…this wasteland." She'd gotten so wound up that she was sputtering.

"Press leaves? I thought you were teaching them to read and write and add."

Her jaw locked, and she stood on tiptoe to glare inches from his face. "I am, but tell me how I'm supposed to teach anything with this racket?"

He hadn't considered that. "Surely with the windows and door closed—"

"Have you checked to see that the noise is bearable?"

"How can I check the sound level from inside the schoolhouse when it's locked and I don't have a key?" he countered, stepping back. As a rule, he didn't back away from a fight, but her presence had an unnerving effect on him. Instead of getting angry, he wanted to hold her and calm her down and tell her that they could work together, but she would insist he shut down his operation, which was not possible. "We can check now, if you wish."

Her arms crossed again, and the frown deepened. "It doesn't matter. The moment the children see all this activity, they won't be able to concentrate on the lessons."

She might have a point, but he wasn't about to let her

know that. "Maybe for a day or two, but they'll soon lose interest."

She considered that a moment before coming back with another concern. "And how do you intend to ensure their safety?"

"Their safety?" This completely puzzled him. Anyone could wander into the sawmill, which was much more dangerous.

"From falling trees and whatnot."

He stifled a chuckle, not very successfully judging by the flash of her eyes. "I assure you that my men can fell a tree in the proper direction—away from the school. Your school is in no danger."

"And when they walk here in the morning and leave in the afternoon?"

Roland's head ached. "We are well clear of the roads. There's no reason for the children to go near our operation. Simply tell them to stay on the roads." Roland noticed the men were still watching and listening to every word. He gave her a smile intended to calm her down. "Now, don't you fret. We won't be any bother to your students or classroom."

Instead of simmering down, she stiffened. Red dotted her cheeks, and she looked like she was about to spit out something extremely unpleasant. What had he said? He was just trying to calm her down. Instead, he was about to face her wrath.

"Pearl? Shouldn't we go to the school?" Amanda had edged near, and her halting question managed to deflate Pearl's ire. "The children will start arriving soon."

"Yes, I suppose we should." But Pearl said that to Roland, not Amanda. "We must ensure the children's safety, not to mention drying their tears when they see their beloved spruce and maple trees fall."

With that, Pearl stomped off with Amanda on her heels.

"Everything all right, boss?" asked Evans.

Roland watched Pearl's retreating figure. "Yes. Everything is just fine."

But it wouldn't be. Knowing Pearl, this was just the beginning.

"He is sadly mistaken if he thinks he is going to jeopardize our school," Pearl huffed as she readied the classroom.

She'd left Amanda outside to guide the students past the mayhem, so her words weren't heard by anyone but the kittens, who wove around her legs, eager for the milk they received each morning. Today, Sadie and Isaac had been charged with bringing some. She hoped they didn't forget, what with their uncle's rush to destroy the last patch of woods near Singapore.

Had she been too harsh with him? With all the windows and doors closed, the racket was muffled enough so she could be heard, but the construction activity would prove a terrible distraction, especially to the boys. Roland might think one or two days would dampen their interest, but spelling and addition tables could not compete with machinery and crashing trees. Already the spruce had been toppled. The maple would soon follow.

Once the property was cleared, those piles of brick and wooden beams would be assembled into a formidable factory just down the slope from their school. Surely the towns could not approve of the glasswork's location so close to the school. Then again, Singapore appeared to have no government, and she'd heard no protests from Mr. Farmingham or anyone in Saugatuck. Regardless, in one fell swoop she would lose all the progress she'd made settling the children down enough to focus on learning.

By the end of the school day, her fears had been realized. Once the children left for home and Amanda returned to the now-empty classroom, Pearl had come to a conclusion.

"We must find another place to hold classes until this construction ends."

Amanda picked up Dandelion, whom the children called Dandy, and stroked his white fur. "But where?"

"The new church would do. I can't see any objections."

"The children from Saugatuck and Goshorn Lake would have to walk farther."

"True." Pearl breathed out in frustration. Most of her students hailed from outside Singapore. Though the distance wasn't far, it would entail a longer walk. The days were growing shorter, and soon they would have to walk in the dark. She would have to dismiss them earlier and start later if they moved to the church building. "It can't be helped. The students will never learn a thing with all that commotion going on."

"Oh, Pearl, they were just excited today. Every new thing does that. They'll come around. Give it time. Soon enough the noise will lessen and the construction will seem ordinary."

Cocoa pawed at her skirt, begging to be picked up. Pearl bent down to gather the little ball of fur. "Soon it will be time to send these little ones to their winter homes." She stroked Cocoa's cheeks until she purred. "Why can't things go along smoothly?"

"Didn't Jesus say that in this life we would have trouble?"

"True." Pearl set the kitten down. "Trouble is a given, but it doesn't mean lying down and accepting it without a fight. This is not for my comfort. This is for the sake of those precious children. I will not accept defeat without trying. We will ask if we can use the church, at least until the noise dies down."

"Who do we ask?"

That was the problem. "Since Mr. Stockton isn't here, I will have to ask Roland."

After today's outburst, he wasn't likely to listen, least of all agree. She must somehow convince him that this change would be to his advantage.

"More sawmill workers?" Roland stared at his brother, who met him in the store at the end of the work day.

"That's what the cable says." Garrett spread it out on the counter. "Postman brought it down from Holland this afternoon."

Roland read the short message again.

Two dozen workers coming. Stop. Ready all housing. Stop. Stockton

That meant both mills would run at full capacity. The store would be busier than ever, cutting into his time on the construction site. That also meant closing the church and reinstalling the bunks. Pearl would not be pleased. That church meant a lot to her. He'd seen the glow in her eyes that first Sunday and the way she sang with abandon, as if in the actual presence of God. He'd felt both unworthy and irresistibly drawn to her. After today's argument, heaping on the news that the church must be dismantled would drive an even bigger wedge between them.

"Why bring in more workers now?" Roland grumbled. "That usually happens in the spring."

Garrett shrugged. "Must have a lot of logs heading our way."

That much was obvious. Handling the rest would not be pleasant. He groaned and rubbed his throbbing temples. Ever since arguing with Pearl this morning, his head ached.

"Pearl is going to hate me."

Garrett grinned. "Glad I'm not in your shoes, but maybe she'll pay me a little more attention." He cuffed Roland on the shoulder.

"Don't pin your hopes in that quarter."

"Why? Don't you think I'm a good enough catch for a schoolteacher?"

"I think she doesn't want to marry."

"Could've fooled me a few Sundays ago up on the dune."

Roland groaned. Had all of Singapore seen that ill-advised kiss? He'd gotten carried away in the moment. That was all.

"Uncle Roland? Can I have a licorice?" a small voice asked.

Isaac stood politely on the other side of the counter with Sadie by his side. How long had they been there? Had they heard the whole conversation? Roland swallowed hard. That wasn't the sort of thing he and Garrett should be discussing in front of children.

"If your father agrees."

"All right, but only one." Garrett lifted the lid off the jar of licorice and let Isaac take one.

Roland leaned over the counter and caught his niece's eye. "What would you like?"

"She doesn't know," Isaac said.

"Why don't we let your sister answer," Roland suggested. He'd noticed Isaac taking the lead far too much. His niece needed to stand on her own. Like Pearl. His gut twisted. She was going to hate him.

Sadie didn't answer. Isaac shrugged and headed through the back to the kitchen. Sadie eyed all the jars of candy, peering intently at each one before moving on to the next. It seemed to take forever. Finally she lifted her big blue eyes up to him.

"What would Cocoa want?"

"The kitten? Cats don't eat candy."

"They don't?"

He shook his head. "That's why you bring her milk." Soon they would need meat, yet another expense his brother had placed on his shoulders. Garrett insisted that since Roland had encouraged Sadie to take a kitten, he was responsible for feeding and taking care of the cat.

"Then I want a milk candy," she exclaimed.

The bell on the door tinkled.

Roland looked up and groaned.

Pearl Lawson strode toward him with purpose, an artificially buoyant smile pasted on her face. Something was up, and he was sure he wouldn't like it.

"Good evening, Roland. Garrett. Sadie, what a pleasure to see you."

"Hello, Miss Lawson."

Roland handed Sadie a caramel, hoping it would suffice. "Go play with your brother. I think Miss Lawson wants to talk to the grown-ups."

She skipped away, humming a tune that sounded vaguely familiar.

Pearl watched her, a genuine smile curving her lips. "Isn't it wonderful how far she's come? She even remembers the hymns from last Sunday."

The hymns. That was it.

"Is there a problem with Isaac or Sadie in school?" Garrett asked.

"Not at all." Again that forced smile. "I've simply been thinking about our situation, and I've come to a conclusion."

Roland inwardly groaned.

"Situation?" Garrett asked in spite of Roland's gestures not to say anything.

"The fact that the construction is disrupting the classroom."

Garrett turned on him. "Is that true?"

"It, uh, well, the tractor and timbering might prove a bit fascinating to some of the boys," Roland admitted.

"Not to mention the noise," Pearl said. "We can barely hear each other."

"You said it wouldn't bother the school," Garrett said.

Roland couldn't very well back out of that statement now, not with Pearl providing evidence to the contrary. "It won't last long."

"Humph." She made it perfectly clear that she didn't believe him. "Precisely how long is 'not long?'"

"It depends on the weather. A week or two, perhaps."

"One or two weeks too long."

"I agree with Pearl." In fact Garrett had rounded the counter to stand next to her.

If he hadn't just talked about winning her over, Roland wouldn't find the gesture so distasteful. Surely Garrett didn't really have designs on Pearl. He couldn't.

"Mind you," Pearl was saying, "I do respect your plan for the future of Singapore, and I understand the need to build before winter sets in."

Roland let out the breath he hadn't realized he'd been holding. She understood! The elation drove away the pain in his head. The door opened again, but he couldn't miss what Pearl said next.

"I have found a solution." She looked at Garrett and then him. "The church is not in use during the week. We can hold classes there until the most disruptive work is completed."

"Then what Angela and Beth told me is true." Mrs. Wardman stepped close. "The woods are being torn down."

"For a glassworks," Roland countered. "Jobs for the future." It had sounded fine when paraded before Holmes, but with two women staring at him, it sounded like the spiel from a circus pitchman.

"And our school?" Mrs. Wardman asked.

He thought he caught his brother chuckling.

Roland cleared his throat. "It's a temporary situation."

"I've thought of a solution," Pearl interjected. "Just until the worst of the commotion is done. We can use the new church here."

"Oh, I'd heard that you have a church now. What a blessing that must be. It would make a fine building, but isn't it in town?"

Pearl turned from Roland to answer Mrs. Wardman's questions. With every word, Roland felt worse. He was going to have to break the news to them that the church was not available, but they wouldn't stop talking long enough for him to say it.

Garrett chuckled and clapped him on the shoulder. "Let me know how it works out."

Then the coward made an excuse about checking on the children and left Roland to fend for himself against two women who would soon want to tar and feather him.

Chapter Sixteen

"They're closing the church." Pearl dropped her books on the parlor tea table and removed her gloves while making the announcement to Fiona and Amanda. She was still steaming mad. After all the work they'd done to turn the cabin into a church, Roland was shutting it down. The moment he'd announced it, she'd shouted a few angry words and stomped from the store.

Amanda set down her embroidery. "Why would they do that?"

Pearl opened her mouth to inform them of his treachery, but Fiona spoke up first.

"Because they need the housing." Fiona paused from writing a letter.

"They what?" This sounded like just the sort of excuse Roland would make. "Where did you hear that?"

"Sawyer Evans mentioned it when I asked about heat for the warehouse on Saturday."

"Sawyer Evans?" The name sounded familiar, but Pearl couldn't place it.

"He plays a fine fiddle and is working on that new construction project of Roland Decker's."

Of course. It always came back to Roland. She'd heard

him mention Mr. Evans by name this morning. "What do they need to house? Building supplies?"

Fiona eyed her more intently. "They need to house incoming workers. That is the cabin's purpose."

Pearl recalled the bunks that had filled the room. Roland had said it hadn't been used in ages. Why the sudden need? The answer didn't take long to surmise. "I suppose the new construction would need extra workers."

Fiona resumed writing. "I wouldn't know about that. Sawyer said they're mill workers and lumberjacks. They're expecting a huge raft of logs from upriver within a week or so."

"Logs?" Shame swept through Pearl. She hadn't waited for Roland to explain. She'd leaped to a conclusion and shouted something awful at him before storming away. The memory of her words burned. Why had she assumed the worst? She hadn't given him a chance to explain. She hadn't listened to what he had to tell her. She had thought only of her own situation.

Fiona's lips curved into a smug smile. "Ah. Had a falling-out with Roland, did you?" She glanced at Amanda. "All the better for someone else."

Someone more worthy. Fiona might as well have said it. It was true. Amanda was more worthy. She loved with abandon, sometimes foolishly, but always with her whole heart. Pearl held back until she was certain of the other.

She sank into a chair. Much as she hated to admit it, Fiona was right. Pearl might well have destroyed her last chance for any sort of relationship with Roland. Even friendship was out of the question after the way she'd stormed in, accusing him. When he learned that she'd talked Debra Wardman into rallying the parents Friday morning, he would never speak to her again.

Amanda lightly touched her shoulder. "Could you help me gather our laundry from the line and bring it upstairs?"

Even in the depths of her misery, Pearl recognized her friend's kind and gentle spirit. No doubt there wasn't any laundry on the line or certainly not enough to require assistance. Amanda saw her distress and was giving her a reason to escape further questions and comments from Fiona.

"Let me bring my books to the room first. Then I'll meet you outside."

As she'd suspected the laundry consisted of two night-gowns and a couple of unmentionables. One woman could easily carry them, but Amanda laid the gowns in Pearl's arms and carried the rest herself.

Amanda hesitated at the kitchen door. "I should iron them, but I can do that later."

Pearl could hear Mrs. Calloway chopping something inside. Her stomach rumbled. Supper was still an hour away. She fingered the stiff cotton. Amanda had quietly taken care of all the laundry and mending while Pearl fussed on and on about the school. "I prefer mine fresh from the line." She stuck her nose in the dried garments to emphasize the point.

Amanda laughed. "No, you don't. No one likes a stiff, wrinkly nightgown."

"Then I will help you after supper."

Amanda looked aghast. "Don't you remember what happened the last time you wanted to press the clothes?"

"How could I forget?" In spite of the day's exhausting emotions that had ended with gloom, Pearl laughed. "I burned Miss Hornswoggle's red petticoat."

"And spent a week scrubbing the kitchen stoves and ovens as punishment."

Even now Pearl could smell the rancid grease that had coated the surfaces. "I doubt they'd been cleaned since the orphanage opened."

"There's a basket in the pantry where we can leave the

laundry until later. You worry about teaching school, and I'll take care of the ironing."

Pearl stopped her friend. "I can't let you do that. You've been doing too much for me. You help with the classroom by day and do laundry and whatnot every other spare moment. I should be helping instead of reading and making plans that come to nothing." Such as a life with Roland.

Amanda simply smiled. "You have given me a home."

"In a boardinghouse."

"With my dearest friend. I've made friends here, friends I've come to love." Her eyes glistened. "Thank you."

"Sometimes I wonder if I should have dragged you away from the Chatsworths."

"Oh, yes." Amanda shuddered. "I can't bear to think of still living there."

"Even when Fiona tries to maneuver ahead of you?"

"Don't let Fiona get to you. She likes to think she has the upper hand with Garrett, but I don't think she does."

Pearl pulled her thoughts around to what most concerned Amanda. "Has he warmed up to you?"

Amanda shook her head. "He's still grieving. You can see it every Sunday in the way he tears up while singing the hymns and how close he holds his children."

Pearl hadn't noticed those little details. Her friend was quite perceptive. "But his brother seems to think he should remarry."

"For the children's sake."

"You disagree?"

Amanda shook her head. "They do need a mother, but he's not ready." She sighed. "He must have loved his late wife very much."

Pearl tried to recall the few words Roland had spoken about her. They hadn't struck her as much as his reaction. "I've noticed. Roland doesn't like to talk about her."

"I think it was tragic."

"That would make sense, then." But Pearl suspected there was much more behind that situation.

"You like Roland, don't you?"

Pearl forced a laugh. "After today it wouldn't matter what I thought. I said some awful things to him, that he was inconsiderate and selfish." The last word caught in her throat. She was the one who'd acted selfishly. "It's a good thing my teaching contract forbids marriage."

"A contract doesn't mean anything. If you fall in love, you would stop teaching." She led Pearl into the pantry while Mrs. Calloway hummed and worked away in the kitchen. "You can't tell me you haven't wondered what it would be like to marry Roland."

Pearl felt the heat rising and deposited the nightgowns in the basket on top of Amanda's bundle of dry clothing. "What I have or haven't thought is irrelevant."

Naturally Amanda saw through her attempt to deflect the question. "He suits you far more than he would have suited me."

A lump formed in Pearl's throat. "How did I ever deserve such a gracious friend as you?"

"You took care of me when I'd lost hope. You wouldn't let me give up, even when I thought no one would ever love me."

"At one time or another all of us thought that." It was a hazard of the orphanage. Some of the children had reacted by retreating. Others had lashed out. Pearl had tried to unite them all under the banner of hope, and they'd all found families—except her.

Amanda squeezed her arm. "Don't give up on what you want. All this turmoil will work out for the best."

Pearl forced a smile. "I know God has a place set aside for me. I thought it was Singapore, but maybe I was wrong."

"Maybe you were right, just not in the way you expected." Amanda squeezed her hand, and Pearl could feel excitement trying to burst forth.

She stared at her friend. Despite the dim light, Amanda nearly bubbled over. "What happened?"

"It's so wonderful," Amanda said, gushing. "I can't believe it."

"Garrett asked to court you?"

"No, silly. He won't say two words to me."

"Then what could possibly have you so excited?"

"It's Jake." Amanda trembled with joy. "Fiona said that that Sawyer Evans told her the lumber crews are headed downriver with the load of logs."

"And what does Jake have to do with that?"

"Mr. Evans confirmed that one of the men is around my age with the same dark hair and goes by the name Jake. It has to be him. It has to be my brother."

Pearl wasn't convinced. Worse, Amanda's excitement and anticipation meant she'd be crushed if this Jake didn't turn out to be her brother. "Don't get your hopes up."

"You sound like Mrs. Calloway, but I must believe it's him. It has to be."

Pearl sighed. Amanda's joy could get crushed. Pearl could not believe her friend's missing brother would end up in such an obscure place. Possible, yes, but not likely.

"When are they expected to arrive?"

"Fiona said they have to finish cutting and then ride the logs down the river. The first should arrive in a week or so, and then the others will follow."

That gave Pearl time to settle the school problem before having to console Amanda. The rally would take place the day after tomorrow, but she was no longer certain of her course.

"Did you hear what they're planning?" Garrett asked over the midday meal at the store counter.

Roland looked up from his soup and grabbed another chunk of the fresh bread Fiona O'Keefe had dropped off this morning. Either she'd turned into a decent baker or had convinced Mrs. Calloway to send a loaf to them. "What who is planning?"

"The women."

The bread stuck in Roland's throat. He took another gulp of coffee to wash it down. "You'd better tell me what's going on."

"Miss O'Keefe told me that the mothers are rallying tomorrow morning at your work site."

"Rallying?"

"To shut you down." Garrett didn't seem to take any pleasure in delivering the news.

Still, Roland had a tough time believing it. "How would Fiona O'Keefe know what the mothers are planning? She doesn't have any children."

"She stays at the boardinghouse with Miss Lawson."

Roland gnawed on that. Fiona could easily learn about any plans there. Though Pearl didn't appear to spend time with Fiona, Mrs. Calloway was free with her tongue. Any news that crossed the threshold would soon spread to the boarders. Yes, it was entirely possible.

"Maybe she's spreading rumors," Roland suggested. Fiona had cause, after all, considering she was doing her best to win over Garrett. Sharing a tidbit that affected his children would be one way to garner his goodwill. Moreover, she had delivered bread this morning precisely when Garrett was sending the children off to school and Roland was already at the store. "There might not be a grain of truth to it."

He hated to think Pearl would deliberately shut down the glassworks when she had so eagerly embraced his plan a few weeks ago. Yes, she hadn't taken the news of the church's closing well, but he was only asking for a week or so to clear the land.

Garrett dashed all hope of a rumor. "Your foreman confirmed it. Since they can't use the church, they want you to wait until next summer to build."

"Next summer! That's seven, no, eight months away. I can't wait that long. Holmes won't stand for it."

"What are you going to do?"

Roland set down the bread, no longer hungry. "Stop them."

"How?"

Roland blew out a breath. He had no idea how, but he knew who stood at the center of this storm. "Is there any other building available?"

"Not once the workers arrive. And you know Stockton won't stand for you pitching tents this time of year."

"I know. I know." But the comment got him thinking. "Do we have a tent big enough for a school?"

"You're going to put school children in a tent?" Garrett stared at him incredulously. "I don't want Isaac and Sadie in a tent come November."

Roland groaned. "No, of course not." He drummed his fingers on the countertop. "How bad is the noise inside the school? Did Isaac say anything to you?"

"No." Garrett frowned. "He doesn't tell me things like he used to."

Roland suspected Garrett was still sour over the children's role in placing the advertisement. Mrs. Calloway had confirmed that Roland's speculation was correct and tried to shoulder the entire blame, but Garrett still held his son and daughter partly responsible.

Rather than start another fight on the subject, Roland chose a different explanation. "Isaac is growing up. He wants to stand on his own."

Garrett blew out his breath. "I suppose you're right, but I can't help wondering what's going through his head."

Roland certainly didn't have answers. More important now was figuring out a way to stop Pearl's crusade.

"I can't believe the noise is that disruptive," he mused. "I told Pearl the worst would only last a week or two. Once the workers begin arriving, we'll have to halt construction anyway. Why would she get the parents riled up now?"

Garrett grinned. "I knew you were sweet on her. Never thought I'd see the day Roland Decker fell hard for a woman."

Roland bit his tongue before pointing out he'd fallen for Eva before she chose Garrett. His brother didn't know the depth of Roland's feelings for Eva and the blow her departure had struck. Garrett thought they'd happened to see each other at various social functions like the theater, soirees and whatnot, and from that developed a friendship. Neither Roland nor Eva had ever shared the truth.

The blow that had severed his relationship with Garrett had come later, on the day Eva died. Roland could not risk a disastrous relationship again. Family had to come first.

He held Garrett's gaze, trying to look convincing. "I am not sweet on a woman who causes trouble wherever she goes."

"And brings out your better side."

"Now you're hitting low."

"The truth hurts."

Garrett's grin was beginning to irritate Roland. "If you think you're so wise, tell me how to convince Pearl to call off this nonsense."

"Who am I to tell you how to handle a woman? Aren't you the dashing man about town?"

"That's not saying much in Singapore."

"Forget Singapore. I heard the stories of you in Chicago. Eva told me you could charm any woman, that you had a different woman on your arm each night."

Roland gritted his teeth. That wasn't true—Eva had been the one and only woman on his arm for months before she met Garrett. But it was safer to project the image of the man about town charming the ladies. That had allayed any suspicions. "Unlike you."

"Eva was the only woman for me. Ever." Garrett made that point a little too firmly. "None of those New York women will ever convince me to marry." He grabbed another chunk of bread as the mill whistle blew. "Back to work."

"Convenient excuse," Roland called out to his brother's retreating back.

Garrett waved off the barb with a laugh.

Roland considered his brother's words. Garrett had reminded Roland of his chief asset. Unfortunately, Pearl Lawson was completely unaffected by charm.

Pearl had hoped Debra Wardman would come to fetch her daughters after school. A sleepless night thinking and praying had left her more confused than ever about the rally. There had to be a way to satisfy both the students' needs and Roland's project, but she couldn't see it. She'd hoped Debra would be able to spot an answer.

Amanda helped the youngest girl, Beth, into her coat.

Pearl handed the older girl her bonnet. "I thought your mother would be here by now."

"It's baking day," Angela solemnly informed her. "Mama can't go anywhere on baking day. We're to walk home with the Baileys."

Amanda finished buttoning Beth's coat. "You'd better hurry, then. They're already walking away."

Pearl followed the girls out the front door. "I'd hoped to speak with your mother about tomorrow morning."

"Oh! I forgot. Mama said to tell you that everything's all set. They'll be here at seven thirty."

"Hurry now." Amanda grabbed both girls' hands and walked them toward the brothers, who had already reached the edge of the newly cleared land.

"Goodbye, Miss Lawson," the girls said in unison.

Their smiles and waves touched Pearl's heart. Angela was a whiz with arithmetic, and Beth could recite the alphabet backward and forward. Writing out the letters was more of a problem, but she would learn in time. Pearl hugged her arms. She would do anything for her students, even if it meant delaying Roland's dream just a bit.

She glanced at the construction site, which had been unusually quiet that day. Though the sun shone through the remaining trees, it didn't warm her. She shivered. Winter was on its way. Construction should have pressed on at a torrid pace from dawn until dark, but the tractor sat idle, and she spotted only a handful of men piling branches into the huge pile to be burned.

"Pearl!"

That cheerful call could only come from one man, the very one she did not care to see. By now he must have gotten wind of what was going on. By breakfast, both Fiona and Mrs. Calloway knew about the rally, doubtless from one of the parents or through the mill.

Roland's grin gave her pause. Maybe he didn't know yet. As impossible as that seemed, it was even more unlikely that he'd be waving at her like an old friend if he did know.

She mustered a smile in return. "Roland." She rubbed her arms. "It's chilly today."

He appeared surprised, and considering he was dressed in his usual rolled-up shirtsleeves, he probably hadn't realized the chill had set in. "A fine October day. Won't be many more like this. Would you care to take a stroll along the river?"

A few days ago, Pearl would have leaped at the chance to spend time alone with Roland, but everything was so confusing now. With the rally in the morning, this walk would not offer anything close to romance.

"I need to take care of the kittens and close up." She hoped the excuse would put him off gently.

"I'll wait."

She opened her mouth to protest, but Amanda returned after seeing the Wardman girls safely to their escort.

"Go along," Amanda said. "I'll feed the kittens and close the schoolhouse. We do need to send those kittens to their winter homes soon, though." She smiled at Roland. "Sadie will be so glad. She adores Cocoa."

To Pearl's amusement, he looked less than thrilled by the idea of a cat underfoot.

"I'll tell my brother."

Amanda hurried into the school and returned with Pearl's shawl and hat. "Now you two go on. I'll take care of everything."

Pearl shot her friend a glare for this bit of matchmaking, but Amanda ignored the hint.

"You should enjoy every moment of good weather," her friend suggested.

Pearl grumbled as she plopped the hat on her head and tied the ribbons under her chin.

"May I?" Roland took her shawl from Amanda and held it up. The light shone through where the weave had thinned or broken. "This won't keep you warm."

Pearl snatched it from his hands. "I'm aware of that."

He tilted his head in that charmingly boyish way. "We have a few women's coats in stock. I can give you an excellent price."

Pearl wrapped the shawl around her shoulders and held her response until Amanda slipped back into the school.

"Perhaps I will stop by sometime to try them on." She had hesitated this long because of the cost.

Roland seemed to read her mind. "There's one in the back room that would fit."

"My arms are longer than those of most women due to my height."

He nodded. "Exactly why this cloak would work. It won't fit anyone else in the area. I've had it in stock for years. If you wouldn't mind a somewhat outdated style, I can sell it to you at cost."

Cost! That was exactly what she needed. She was about to thank him when a thought crossed her mind. "What would you expect in return?"

He blinked, looking genuinely surprised.

She felt awful. He might have come here today with the finest of intentions, and she'd judged and condemned him before he'd done one thing wrong. "I'm sorry. Sometimes I speak before I think. It's just that, well, we parted on rather bad terms yesterday."

"True, but I've been considering options that could solve both our problems."

"You have?" For some reason she'd never expected that a man of Roland's influence and stature would change his plans to suit her. Now she felt really awful. In the morning, the parents would gather on his construction site and rally to halt his project. While he'd worked to help her, she'd made plans to hurt him. She lowered her gaze.

"That's why I came here today. Shall we walk?" He extended his arm.

She couldn't take it. She'd made a mess of things, as he would find out soon enough. "To the river?"

He dropped his arm and waved her in that direction. "To the river."

They walked in silence for a while. She waited for him to explain those options. When he made no move, she nudged.

"What did you come up with?"

"Let me first explain what I considered and why each proved unsuitable. As you know, Mr. Stockton ordered all the worker housing fit out. We're expecting the first mill workers next week. Then the lumberjacks will trickle in when the logs arrive from upriver."

Then Fiona had been right. Pearl sighed.

"Thus the church had to go." She could spare him that much.

"For now." Again that sheepish smile. "I wish it didn't have to be that way, but he owns the cabins."

"Perhaps we can use the school for services. It won't attract all the workers, but it is something."

"Garrett and I have been talking about that. Until the warehouse fills with lumber, we could use it."

"And after the cold sets in?"

He nodded. "The schoolhouse would be a great help."

Since he kept talking about the school building, she hoped that meant he'd decided on his own to halt construction, at least during school hours. "Then we will continue classes at the schoolhouse?"

This time he blew out a breath. "I couldn't find another building that would work."

"And your construction?"

They'd reached the river. The current boiled, surprising considering the recent lack of rain. She had spotted storm clouds on occasion, but they'd all passed by without a drop of rain. The riverbank hosted a fringe of willows and red dogwood that would soon lose the rest of their summer leaves. Across the wide expanse, a low, swampy area filled with reeds crowded the shore before the big bend leading to Singapore. Behind the swamp rose the dunes, blocking all view of the lake as well as the breezes that likely blew there.

Roland had crossed his arms. He stared at the opposite shore, every muscle in his face tense.

Pearl shivered. She would not like this answer.

He began slowly. "After tomorrow and Saturday, the last of the trees will be cut. Once the logs start to arrive, construction will halt since every man will be needed in the mills. You will have your quiet school."

But at what cost? She opened her mouth but could not find the right words.

He sprinted away from her. "I have to get away from this place."

Though he waited for her after striding up the path, he was not at peace. The emotions playing out on his face spoke of deep distress and agitation. What wasn't he telling her?

She picked up her skirts to climb, but the loose soil gave way under her feet. He extended a hand and helped her up the bank.

She brushed off her skirts. "Thank you."

He seemed not to hear her, instead taking off down the path. Something terrible had happened, something that turned his buoyant temperament to melancholy, and she could not put her finger on what it was. Unless something had happened to his project. Unless her insistence on delay meant he'd lost funding.

She hurried to catch up to him. "Tell me I haven't caused you problems."

He stopped, his stare vacant. "I need to leave this place."

The breath caught in her throat. She had crushed his dream, and he was leaving Singapore.

Chapter Seventeen

Pearl managed to stop the rally before costing Roland any delay. She and Amanda arrived early, in the darkness of predawn, and told the arriving parents that he had promised to diminish the noise. Though they were met with grumbles from those who had walked far or postponed work on the harvest, confrontation was averted.

The steam tractor started up before the parents left, and she suspected more than one didn't believe her assurances about the noise, but there was no time to address the issue. Each parent had brought his or her children, so school had to begin early. Before entering the schoolhouse, she scanned the clearing for Roland. He wasn't there.

A small part of her was irritated that he'd stayed away at this key moment. The larger part feared he had already left town. Though Amanda insisted he couldn't have meant he would leave Singapore, Pearl wasn't so certain. His bleak expression yesterday weighed heavily in her thoughts. He looked like a man without hope.

Now he hadn't shown up to supervise his work crew. Had she acted too late, or was he already gone?

"He probably had to man the store," Amanda suggested as she ushered the children into the schoolhouse.

"I hope so, but I'll stop by after school to be sure."

Only after the school day ended and the last child set off for home—three of them with kittens—could Pearl consider the events of the morning. Though she'd glanced out the windows periodically, she didn't spot Roland's tall figure with the familiar rolled-up sleeves.

Amanda tidied up the room, arranging the slates in the cupboard since the children had tossed them in willy-nilly. "What made you change your mind about the rally?"

Pearl finished noting the last child's assignment grade. "Roland promised to stop the machinery after Saturday, at least until they finish sawing the incoming logs. He said all his men will be busy at the mill."

"Are you certain it didn't have something to do with who was doing the asking?"

Pearl felt the heat in her cheeks. "Certainly not." Though to be truthful, she might not have considered her actions in the same light if Garrett Decker had been the one building the glassworks. Perhaps that was the problem. She shouldn't have a different standard for Roland. "Well, it might have come into play."

"I'm sure it did. Fiona says—"

"Fiona? Why does she care about the school?" The moment she asked, she knew the answer. Fiona was trying to capture Garrett's attention, and the children were the quickest way to his heart.

Amanda huffed. "You know why."

"I'm sorry I asked." Yet Pearl watched her friend's reaction with interest. Could she be forming an interest in Garrett Decker? "You don't think she cares about Sadie and Isaac?"

"Only as much as they'll lead her to their father. Oh, dear!" Amanda pressed a hand to her mouth. "I shouldn't have said that, but she is so obvious. I don't know why

Garrett doesn't recognize it. He thinks she actually bakes the bread and sweet rolls that she brings over."

"She brings food to Garrett's house?"

"Oh, yes." Amanda rolled her eyes. "And spends far too long flirting with him. Honestly, I don't see what any man would see in her. She's so…so, oh, dear, I shouldn't say such things about anyone, but she practically throws herself at him."

Pearl smiled to herself. Amanda's indignation meant she was growing fond of Garrett, in some way. "Garrett must realize what she's doing."

"Hugh didn't realize Lena was trying to capture his attention."

"Maybe he did. Maybe he sought it."

Amanda sank onto a bench. "Then I truly am unlovable."

"Oh, dearest." Pearl rushed to her friend's side. "You are a beautiful daughter of God. Never forget that. The right man will see your true beauty and cherish it. You must believe that."

"But I don't want to go through this again." Amanda's lip quivered. "I'm going to be like you and stand on my own."

"On my own?" Though that's what she'd claimed to do, that ground had gotten murky since they'd arrived in Singapore. She could not have taught school without Mr. Holmes's generous donation of primers. The townspeople had repaired the roof and cleaned the interior. Roland had supplied the paint to freshen the walls. Everyone had a part in this school. "We are never on our own."

"But you're so confident and able to take care of things."

Pearl had never thought of herself quite that way. She did what was necessary, but that usually meant relying on the assistance of others. She hugged Amanda. "I couldn't run the classroom without your help. You take care of the laundry and our room. Everything would be a mess without you."

Amanda brightened somewhat. "But will a man ever notice that?"

"He will. You can be sure the right man will notice every little thing about you."

The way Roland had noticed her. The thought made her shiver. His sapphire-blue eyes and sheepish smile melted her heart. If he left Singapore, he would take part of her with him.

Pearl rose. "Let's finish up here. I want to look over the coats in the store. It's getting too cold for just a shawl."

"Could you make certain there's no problem with Sadie bringing Cocoa home?"

"Of course." But most of all she wanted to make sure Roland was still there.

Business had been brisk enough at the store to keep Roland busy all day. He could almost shake off that horrible memory that had taunted him at the river yesterday. From that exact spot he'd seen Eva's boat capsize into the icy waters. Worse, he'd precipitated her flight into the river. They'd argued. He'd wanted to tell his brother the truth about their relationship before she'd met Garrett. She vehemently opposed it. When he refused to bend, she'd stormed off. Not long after, for a reason no one understood, she'd taken the boat across the river and got caught between the rushing logs and chunks of ice.

If he hadn't pressed the point…

He shook his head. Nothing could change the past. No one could forgive his role in the tragedy, either. Garrett said he had, but only in words. The anger and hurt resurfaced over and over, sometimes in barbs, other times in withdrawal. Thus far Isaac and Sadie didn't know, but eventually they would. Then he would lose them all.

The figures in the ledger blurred. He blinked his eyes repeatedly, but they wouldn't clear. He rubbed his eyes.

The doorbell tinkled. Not another customer.

"I'm closing for the day," he called out.

"So early?"

Pearl's strong voice made him look up. Her chestnut-brown hair glowed in the last rays of the late-afternoon sun streaming through the windows. Her independent streak made her more beautiful than Eva had ever been. Given a choice between the two, he would choose Pearl every time.

The thought shocked him.

Pearl stepped to the counter with a smile. "I came to look at the coats."

Roland pulled his thoughts back to business. "The coats."

"Winter coats. We spoke of them yesterday."

"Of course." Roland shook his head. "The cloak I mentioned is in the stockroom. I'll be back in a moment."

He whisked through the store, glad for a moment to recover his wits. Pearl was nothing like Eva. Yes, they each made demands, but Pearl's weren't for her own comfort. She fought for the children and wanted the church so they could reach the unbelievers. For others.

He leaned against the stockroom worktable and drew a deep breath. The cloak. He suspected she didn't have the money to buy a winter coat. If she had, she wouldn't have toughed out the cold in that moth-eaten shawl of hers. Now where had he put that cloak that he'd ordered for a customer who left town before it arrived?

Roland took so long that Pearl feared he'd forgotten about the coat and disappeared into the kitchen to cook supper. The last rays of a brilliant autumn sun had settled into the soft glow of twilight before he returned. In his arms was the most exquisite dark green woolen fabric.

He shook it out before her. "Will this do?"

She hesitated to touch the cloak's elegant fasteners and braided trim. It flowed with a quality she could never hope to afford, even at cost. "It would be too dear."

"Try it on," he urged, that twinkle back in his eyes. "It won't hurt to see if it fits."

"This is made for a lady in hoop skirts rather than this common dress."

"That's why I thought it might be long enough for you. Every other lady who has passed through town swam in it." He held out the cloak to fasten it around her shoulders.

Though she could never hope to afford such a garment, it couldn't hurt to try it on. For just one tiny moment she could stand in front of the glass and pretend she was a grand lady.

"All right. But just to try it on. That's all."

She turned, and he draped the cloak on her shoulders. Its luxurious, soft wool enveloped her at once in warmth. But it was the brief touch of his hands that made her skin tingle and her cheeks heat. How could one man have such an effect on her?

"This way." Roland extended his arm. "Have a look in the mirror."

She slipped her hands through the openings and set a hand on his arm. Once again, his presence made her stomach flutter and her head spin. She moved across the store one careful step at a time, aware of everything about him. The smell of soap, the crisp collar, the shadow of late-day whiskers, the deep blue of his eyes. He stopped before the large glass.

She gasped and her hand went to her mouth.

"Is something wrong?" he asked.

She shook her head, overcome by the image before her. On a New York street, they would be considered a lady and gentleman of means, not an orphan and a storekeeper. Tears rose to her eyes.

"Something is wrong," he said.

She shook her head again. "I—I look…" She couldn't say it.

"You look beautiful." He drew her hand to his lips and kissed it lightly. "You are a lovely woman, Pearl."

A tear slipped down her cheek.

He swiped it away with his thumb. "Why the tears?"

"I've never worn anything this lovely."

His brow furrowed. "Why not?"

"Orphans don't receive fine clothes." That came out more bitter than she'd intended.

He drew in his breath, not sharply but enough to know he was surprised. "I'm sorry. I had no idea."

She shook her head again, unable to speak. What had provoked her to tell him she was an orphan? Now he would know she had nothing and no one in this world. Moreover, he would rightly suspect Amanda came from the same situation. That could destroy her chances with Garrett.

"Please don't tell anyone," she begged.

He hesitated, looking her over. "I'll honor your wishes, of course, but it's not shameful to lose your parents at a young age. It's tragic. I was fortunate that mine passed on after Garrett and I were adults, though they never saw their grandchildren."

Pearl was relieved that he'd shifted the focus. "I'm sure they would be pleased by what you've both done with your lives."

His smile was taut. "And your parents would be proud of you."

She had to look away lest he see the truth. Her parents wouldn't be proud. Her parents hadn't wanted her.

She undid the clasps on the cloak. "This belongs to you."

He stopped her from removing it by placing his hands on her shoulders. Again that entirely too pleasurable sensation rippled through her.

"Consider it yours." It came out ragged, and he cleared his voice. "Please."

"I cannot. It's too costly."

"It's out of style and will never fit another woman."

She couldn't accept his reasoning. He must be offering this because he pitied her, the poor little orphan and all. She squeezed her eyes shut. "It's so beautiful that someone will want it."

A finger lightly touched her lips and she shuddered under the memory of his kiss, brief as it had been. "No one will want it. I planned to send it to the poor when I returned to Chicago."

The poor. Her.

She set her jaw. "At least let me repay your cost."

He hesitated, and she could feel the air vibrate from his presence. "All right."

She dared open her eyes and saw him grinning at her. "What is it?"

He shook his head, but the grin never left. "You drive a hard bargain." The smile faded. "Sometime consider accepting a gift."

She felt her face flame and began to yank off the cloak.

Again he stopped her. "It will cost you one dollar."

"One dollar?" This fine cloak must cost far more than a dollar. Then she remembered his admonition to receive with gratitude. She wasn't a grateful receiver. Never had been. She bowed her head and then summoned the courage to look him in the eye. "Thank you."

He smiled.

Chapter Eighteen

As promised, the steam tractor left the construction site, which sat largely idle except for the driving of dock pilings into the river bottom. That work took place far enough from the school that the noise wasn't any louder than the whine of the sawmills. Pearl didn't see Roland unless she went to the store, and then more often than not Charlie waited on her. Roland was always busy with one or more of the lumberjacks and sawyers that arrived by boat and on the rafts of logs.

Each day Amanda wandered the docks asking if anyone named Jake or Jacob had arrived. Thus far two had, but both were older than her brother. One was missing two front teeth and the other was bald. Both apparently thought Amanda wanted more than information, and Mr. Calloway had rescued her from their attentions each time.

"I'll ask Roland or Garrett to tell us when he arrives," Pearl suggested. "One of them is bound to know. Then they can make proper introductions, and this sort of misunderstanding won't happen again."

Amanda picked at the lace on her skirt. "What if they forget?"

"They won't. I'll check every day."

"Then I suppose it's all right."

Pearl ended up speaking with Garrett Decker, since she couldn't get Roland alone. Garrett was the better choice anyway. If he gave Amanda the news, her excitement might bring the two of them together. Yet days and weeks passed without the mysterious third Jacob appearing in town.

Amanda's disappointment grew, and Pearl tried to focus her attention on the schoolchildren. She did especially well with the younger children, but Sadie was clearly her favorite, and the seven-year-old clung to Amanda's side whenever they went out of doors.

With the weather growing cooler, the children spent less time outside. Soon their restlessness turned to the usual classroom shenanigans, like the boys picking on the girls by yanking on their hair. Primers got misplaced, and a huge toad ended up in the cupboard. Angela Wardman shrieked when she pulled out a stack of slates and found the toad staring at her. Since no one would confess, Pearl made the entire class scrub the slates and cupboard. She then sent them outside to play and release the pent-up energy.

"I don't know what's gotten into them." She sighed to Amanda as they tidied up the mess left from the cleaning efforts. "Could it be all the noise from the mills or the extra men in town?"

"I don't think so. Most of the children don't live in Singapore." Amanda pondered a moment. "Maybe they miss the kittens."

With the advent of cold weather, all the cats had been sent to winter homes.

"We can't keep them here overnight," Pearl said.

"Perhaps they could visit during the day, one at a time, and the children can take them home at night."

Pearl was skeptical, but something needed to be done. Even Isaac had begun to misbehave. "It's worth a try, but I'll be glad when these lumberjacks leave and things get back to normal." Amanda blanched, and Pearl realized the callousness of her words. "I'm sorry. Jake is sure to appear soon."

He did not. The warehouse filled with lumber, and Fiona's concerts had to be shifted to late afternoon at the boardinghouse, where dozens jammed into the parlor. Pearl and Amanda stayed away during those times, uncomfortable with the crush of men in such close quarters. Generally they walked around town or visited the store, but the first Saturday of November, Amanda suggested they visit Louise, who was doing famously at Mrs. Elder's house.

"For the most part I'm simply a companion," Louise said as she served tea. "I read to her and we play the occasional duet on the piano. I'm dreadful, but she doesn't seem to mind. Her hand has grown so shaky that I write her correspondence for her, but she still signs everything. She does retire early, which leaves me a great deal of time to read and study on my own."

"You study?" Amanda said with much surprise. "Of your own volition?" Pearl's friend had always found learning onerous.

Louise babbled on blissfully. "The Elders have a large library, with many volumes on shipping. Mr. Elder was a sea captain, you see, and has collected numerous books on the subject. I find it fascinating. Many ships are lost this time of year. Apparently the winds and the storms are savage here."

"Interesting," Pearl said, though she didn't find either shipping or the weather all that fascinating. "How is Mr. Elder?"

"Very well. He dotes on his wife. They are absolute dears, and I have grown to love them like my own parents." At that a wistful look crossed her face.

"You must miss your mother and father. Do you plan to return home?" Amanda asked.

Louise shook her head. "My father passed on some years ago, and my mother lives with my sister." She shuddered.

Pearl sensed a family disagreement and tried to turn the conversation. "Did your husband leave you enough to care for her?"

Louise paled. "Only debt."

"I'm so sorry." Amanda squeezed Louise's hand in sympathy.

Pearl admired her friend's ability to console and form attachments. Amanda gathered people to her with warmth while Pearl managed to drive them away with ill-timed comments.

By the time they left, Pearl wondered why they'd waited so long to visit. Louise was delightful, well-educated and gracious.

Amanda agreed. "We should have come sooner, but I was afraid she would be like Fiona."

"I don't think anyone could match Fiona's temperament."

"Fiery."

"Unlike the weather." The breeze was cold, and Pearl hugged the cloak tightly around her shoulders. "November has come in with the smell of winter."

"Just like Louise said it would. You must be glad for your new cloak."

Pearl had written a note of thanks to Roland the evening he gave it to her and left that note with Charlie weeks ago. She'd expected Roland to at least mention that he'd received it. He could step away from customers that long.

Instead, any passing comment had to do with how well Cocoa had fit into the family. Even his brother had grudgingly accepted the little ball of fur, and Cocoa had taken to sleeping on Garrett's lap. The image of the burly man with a tiny kitten had made Pearl laugh. It was the last joyous moment they'd shared.

Pearl and Amanda had apparently timed their return perfectly, for the concertgoers were just then drifting out of the boardinghouse.

"Can't wait to head back to the city," one of the men said to another. "Won't be long now."

"Can't come soon enough. Been working steady since last November," another replied.

"Hear tell a steam tug's coming in to haul out the barges. Then we'll head out."

Amanda gasped and then raced ahead of Pearl to catch up to the men. "Aren't any more lumberjacks coming to town?"

The men paused long enough to notice how pretty Amanda was. Pearl caught up and stood by her friend's side.

"Miss Porter is looking for a man named Jake who is two years older than her. Do you know him?"

One of the men peered at her. "I seen him upriver, but he didn't come down on the log drive."

Amanda clutched Pearl's arm until it ached. "Where did he go?"

"Up Allegan way." The man shrugged. "Don't know where he went from there. Might've taken a train to the camps up north."

Pearl could feel her friend's strength crumble. "Thank you, sir, and good night."

The men resumed their conversation and drifted away. The conclusion was clear. The torrid pace at the mill would soon draw to a close. Young Jake would never arrive. Men would leave, and construction on the site of the glassworks would resume.

"I'm so sorry." Pearl wrapped an arm around her friend and searched for something to cheer her. "Tonight at the prayer meeting could you ask Sadie to bring her kitten to school on Monday?"

Maybe seeing the little girl's joy would bring back the light in Amanda's eyes.

Roland eyed Garrett's determined stride toward him along the river's edge. No doubt his brother was upset about something. For some reason, he wore his best suit and an ill-fitting black hat. He looked like a preacher about to give his first sermon.

"Aren't you going to the prayer meeting?" Garrett huffed when he arrived. "It's already past supper time."

Roland turned his attention back to the four men laying planks on his new dock. "This has to be done tonight. Go on without me."

Garrett didn't budge. "What's more important to you? This project or God?"

He said it as if some great calamity would befall Roland.

"I'm sure God understands. I will be at services tomorrow morning." Roland lifted a sledgehammer. "I have some spikes to drive."

"Pearl's been asking about you."

That drove a jolt of curiosity up his spine. "What does she want to know?"

"First off, she probably wants to know when you're going to call on her again."

"I'm busy," Roland growled. It still stung that she hadn't said another word about the cloak. In spite of his protests otherwise, giving it to her had cost plenty. One little word of gratitude would go a long way, but she seemed to avoid him whenever she entered the store.

"Too busy to answer her note?" Garrett said, needling him.

"What note?"

"Amanda says that Pearl left a note for you at the store."

Roland shook his head. "She must be mistaken. I never received a note."

"Humph. Seems to be a discrepancy somewhere."

Roland eyed his brother. "Trust me, I wouldn't have forgotten any note that Pearl sent my way." The ringing of a handbell meant that the prayer meeting was about to get underway. "Shouldn't you be getting Isaac and Sadie up to the school?"

"Miss Amanda took them."

Interesting. That was the second time he'd mentioned Amanda Porter. Moreover he'd used her given name, and he'd entrusted his children to her care. Maybe his brother was finally developing an interest in her.

Garrett nodded at Roland's work crew. "Maybe they'd like to attend the meeting."

"I don't think they'd be accepted in work clothes."

"The Lord accepts all of us as we are."

"The good congregation is a bit less tolerant."

Garrett grunted his displeasure yet again, but this time he gave up the cause and trudged up the hill to the school. Roland watched his brother, feeling more than a little guilty. He should attend this special gathering, but the dock would be needed soon to store the loaded barges until they were ready to be towed out onto the lake.

Pearl walked past, alone, and her gaze naturally drifted toward him. When she saw that he'd spotted her, her gaze snapped back to the path in front of her. What was that about? The easy banter between them had suffered over the past month, but his gift of the cloak had seemed to smooth things over.

Judging from her reaction, it no longer did, even though she had no problem wearing the cloak.

"You can go on up to the meeting, Mr. Roland," Evans said.

Roland hadn't realized his foreman had joined him. "There's work to be done."

"The men could stand ta rest a spell."

Roland surveyed the men, who were indeed looking tired. He'd pushed them since before sunup. With darkness closing in, he might as well put a halt to the workday. Maybe he could get them here early Monday morning.

"All right," he said, relenting. "Ask the men to be here at dawn on Monday."

Evans touched a finger to his cap. "Thank you kindly."

"I'll expect extra effort."

"Yes, sir. If you hurry up, you might catch her."

"I'm not trying to catch up to anyone."

Evans grinned. "Yes, sir. Whatever you say."

Apparently no one believed him. Roland would set Evans and everyone else straight.

"I am not courting Pearl Lawson," he yelled.

Pearl froze at Roland's bellowed statement. If she'd needed confirmation of his recent coldness toward her, she'd just received it. She straightened her back and marched on.

Inside the schoolhouse, the benches were already filled. Amanda had joined Sadie and Isaac and Garrett. Pearl found a spot standing beside the cupboard. The door opened again, ushering in the roughly clad construction workers and Roland, looking just as sweat-stained as his men.

He glanced in her direction, and she quickly looked

away. She could hear the men moving and silently pleaded Roland wouldn't stand near her.

Meanwhile, an unfamiliar and rather scruffy man walked to the front with Mr. Calloway. The congregation murmured, some not so quietly. Pearl hazarded a glance to see where Roland stood. He was opposite her. Their gazes met, and something tangible stretched between them. Though his gaze did not waver, she looked away.

Mr. Calloway hushed everyone with a shrill whistle. Once they'd quieted, he said, "We got ourselves a real treat this evening. Brother John's come down the river on circuit and before we settle down into prayer, he's going to give us a message."

Pearl stared. Mr. Calloway couldn't mean that the wild-haired man dressed in a ragged coat and patched trousers was a preacher. Yet, the wiry stranger nodded vigorously with every word.

"If Miss O'Keefe would lead us in 'My Faith Looks Up to Thee,' we'll get started," Mr. Calloway said.

He joined Mrs. Calloway as the congregation stood. Fiona stepped to the front opposite Brother John and waited for Mr. Calloway to give her a note on his harmonica. She then launched into the song. The congregation joined in, and Brother John sang with utter abandon. The words flowed off Pearl's lips, requiring no thought. She'd sung this hymn so many times that each word was stuck in her memory.

"Take all my guilt away," she sang, and her conscience pricked.

Was she guilty of causing the rift with Roland? Had she spurred that declaration of disinterest in her? The coolness of his gaze sent shivers up her spine. She turned back to the hymn but heard none of the remainder.

Lord, show me where I have failed.

The prayer did not take away the churning in her stomach.

When the last word had been sung, the congregation sat, and Brother John stepped to the pulpit.

"Brothers and sisters in Christ." His voice boomed through the room, sufficient to overwhelm any growling machinery. "What did you think when you first saw me? A ne'er-do-well? A pauper?"

Pearl shrank against the cupboard.

"You all know the story of the Good Samaritan, but let's turn to that story again in Luke, chapter ten, beginning with the thirtieth verse and look at it with fresh eyes. What did the priest and Levite see that made them walk past? What assumptions did they make?"

Pearl opened her Bible and tried to hide behind its pages. Every word of Brother John's message seemed written specifically for her. Had she not judged Roland without listening to his side of the story when he had to turn the church back into a bunkhouse? This very evening she'd judged him irreverent for working instead of coming to this meeting. His lack of a response to her note might have been due to being busy at work. He might have declared he wasn't courting her to protect her position at the school. He knew that marriage would cost her. Why shouldn't he allay gossip with the truth? He wasn't courting her. He had shared nothing more than kindness.

By the end of the message, she had to fight back tears of shame. During the prayers that followed, she poured out her heart to God. As the congregation sang the closing hymn, she came to a decision. She must take the first step.

Roland had slipped to the back of the classroom, doubtless so he could leave the moment the benediction was given. She tucked her Bible under her arm and edged toward him. In spite of her efforts, the hymn ended before she could reach him.

Roland and his crew ducked out of the church.

Pearl slipped around those standing between her and

the door. She bounded outside. The wind had picked up and now sent the fallen leaves dancing across the ground in the light of the nearly full moon. Pearl hurried down the steps. Roland was already headed down the hill.

She ran after him. "Roland!"

The wind carried her cry back up the hill. She cupped her hands around her mouth and tried again.

This time he stopped and turned around. For a second something like delight crossed his face. Then one of his men said something, and his expression turned to stone.

What was going on? She pulled the cloak tight, lest the wind wrest it from her shoulders and closed the gap between them. Each step brought more uncertainty. What should she say? Every practiced phrase evaporated under his scrutiny.

Lord, give me the words.

She drew a breath.

"Is there something wrong, Miss Lawson?"

Not Pearl. No smile. No hint of camaraderie. All traces of friendship had left their relationship.

She battled panic and fear. "No." Nothing else came to mind.

"Then why did you stop me?"

She glanced at the men trailing back toward town. Roland clearly wanted to join them.

Please, Lord.

Then she recalled that the Good Samaritan had extended grace when not expected. That's what she needed to do.

"I just wanted to thank you. Again." She looked into his eyes and her resolve wavered. "This cloak, your kindness, it all means so much to me."

Could a man tremble? If so, Roland had for a brief moment.

Then he composed himself and his mouth twisted into

a wry smile. "I'm sorry, but the construction will begin again Monday. We'll have to burn the debris and then begin digging the foundation."

What had she expected? For him to rush into her arms? Of course he wouldn't, not in view of every man, woman and child who'd attended the meeting. What a fool she'd been to think otherwise. He'd meant every shouted word. He was not courting her now, nor would he do so. He couldn't. Neither could she.

She swallowed the bitter disappointment. "We will manage."

He nodded curtly and hurried after his men. She watched him go and tried to salvage what was left of her pride.

Chapter Nineteen

The winds increased all day Sunday and through that night so that by Monday morning several ships had taken refuge in the river. From her perch on the boardinghouse porch, Pearl counted three sailing ships moored to the docks lining the waterfront and two steamboats at the wharves heading upriver. The barges, loaded with lumber, had been tied to the outside of the schooners. None would sail in this howling gale.

Even inside the boardinghouse they had heard the pounding roar of the waves.

"We should pray for the sailors," Amanda had whispered when Pearl finished her devotions early this morning.

They'd kneeled on the hard wooden planks and laid out their petitions. Amanda prayed for the children, as always. Pearl prayed for God's protection, but her mind kept straying to the encounter with Roland on Saturday and his avoidance of her after Sunday services.

Even now, her gaze drifted to the mercantile, where oil lamps blazed. He would be up and about, ready to begin the day. She gripped the railing, hoping for a glimpse of him.

Too soon, Amanda bustled out of the boardinghouse.

"I'm ready. Gracious!" She grabbed her hat, which nearly blew off her head. "What wind!"

Pearl surveyed the leaden clouds. "I fear a storm is brewing." She shivered beneath the cloak, which whipped about her limbs. "We should hurry to the school before the rain falls."

"Or snow." Amanda followed her off the porch. "It's certainly cold enough."

"Either way, we'll need to get a good fire going in the stove to keep the children warm."

"And dry their coats and hats and mittens."

"That, too." Pearl pulled the cloak tight, but the wind tore it from her grasp. After the second time that happened, she gave up and let it flap like an angry green bird.

"There are Sadie and Isaac," Amanda exclaimed.

Pearl had noticed that lately, Garrett brought out the children at exactly the time Amanda passed the store. They would exchange the barest of greetings before he left the children in their care.

"Need to get to the mill," he said this morning, holding onto his hat, but not hurrying away.

"I brung Cocoa," Sadie said, holding out the bundle she'd been clasping to her chest.

"Brought," Pearl said, correcting the little girl. "You brought Cocoa."

Amanda bent over Sadie. "Let's hold tightly to her. We don't want her to get away."

The girl shook her head solemnly. "I won't let go. Promise."

Pearl sensed that Garrett wanted to talk to Amanda, so she made an excuse about needing some paper from the store. "Go on ahead. I'll catch up."

Garrett frowned. "A woman shouldn't make that walk alone."

"Come with us, Papa," Sadie pleaded.

As Pearl expected, that was all the encouragement he needed. She watched them walk away together, and her heart ached. They looked so much like a family. She swallowed and turned away. No matter how much she tried to tell herself otherwise, she did want this. An independent life might sound adventurous, but it would also be terribly lonely. She shut her eyes against a gust of wind that blasted the sand against her face and imagined Roland by her side, escorting her along the boardwalk to church or to their very own house.

How that hurt, for it would never happen. He had made that perfectly clear Saturday.

She drew a breath to gather her composure and stepped out of the wind on the store's porch. The building was angled in such a way that it blocked the worst of the wind. She shook the sand from her cloak and skirts. Why, she had no idea. The moment she stepped back on the road, she'd be coated with it again.

The door pushed open, and Charlie peered at her. "Can I get you anything, Miss Lawson?"

She swallowed the disappointment that it wasn't Roland. Naturally he'd be at the glassworks site, resuming construction as he'd promised. She glanced up the road. Amanda, Garrett and the children had gone sufficiently far that she wouldn't catch up to them, but she did need to buy that paper that she'd used as an excuse.

"A few sheets of paper, please." She followed Charlie into the store and was surprised by the cleanliness and the smell of soap. "It looks nice in here."

"Mr. Roland said he couldn't sleep and so he came down and spruced things up a bit."

"Indeed he did."

Charlie stopped at the counter. "What kind of paper do you want? For writing letters?"

That hadn't occurred to her. "Stationery. Yes, of course.

I used my last sheet writing that thank-you note to Roland, er, Mr. Decker."

Charlie blanched and patted his coat pockets.

"Are you out of stationery?"

"No, miss." His shoulders drooped. "I forgot to give yer note to Mr. Roland."

"You did?" No wonder Roland had reacted the way he had. He must think her ungrateful. But then she had thanked him Saturday evening. Though it hadn't broken the impasse at the time, he hadn't been able to sleep last night. Maybe their friendship wasn't over after all. "Thank you, thank you." She impulsively hugged Charlie. "You dear boy."

He shook himself free from her embrace. "You're glad I didn't give it to him?"

"No. Please do give him the note. I'm just...oh, it's impossible to put in words. Just know that I'm relieved." She danced toward the door, her spirits buoyed.

"Don't you want the stationery?"

"Set aside a whole box. I'll pick it up after school."

She practically skipped through the door. The clouds parted just enough to allow a ray of sunshine, but she didn't need the visual confirmation. Today would turn out gloriously.

"We're gonna hafta burn all this." Evans pointed to the huge pile of branches and limbs.

Roland shook his head. "Not today. Not with this wind and the woods tinder dry. We'll do it after the storm, if it rains and the winds calm down."

"Then what do we do the rest of today? We can't dig the foundation with this in the way."

Roland had already considered that. "We'll check with the tug captain to make sure he's secure at the dock and see if he needs any fuel. We've got plenty of cordwood if they need it." Roland motioned to the pile of limbs.

Evans grinned. "Good thinkin'."

"We can check with the other steamboats, too. We might as well make something off this pile of debris."

Roland set the rest of the men to chopping the limbs into fuel for a boiler furnace. If the steamers in port didn't need any, a future boat might. Then he and Evans headed for the tug moored at his new dock.

They found the captain in the engine room with grease up to his elbows.

"Trouble?" Roland asked.

"Jus' a little adjustment to the engine." The man stood and stretched his back. "Happens all the time. What can I do ye for?"

"I wanted to make sure the mooring is holding. Do you need more lines?"

"Nope. She's holdin' fine."

Evans gave Roland a pointed look. Since boarding they'd noted the sideways tug on the mooring lines. Some of those looked a bit weathered. With the back and forth rubbing against the pilings, one or more might snap, setting the tug adrift.

"Need cordwood?" Roland asked. "I can give you a good price."

"How good?"

Once Roland named the price, the man was eager to buy.

"It's not seasoned," Roland pointed out. He didn't want any debate after delivery.

"Seldom is," the master joked. "Ol' Bessie'll take anythin' I give her."

Roland figured Bessie must be the boiler. Some engineers and captains liked to name more than the ship.

Once they'd settled on a price and quantity, Roland and Evans stepped off the tug.

"Don't like the look of them lines," Evans murmured when they got out of hearing range.

"Me, either. Tell the men how much wood to bring down and double-check with the captain at that time. If one of those lines parts, he'll be ready to deal. I'll stop back after checking with the other steamers."

He looked down the dock in time to see Pearl leave the store—his store—with a flush to her cheeks. Why had she been there? Pearl never stopped in the store before school. She and Amanda walked together to the schoolhouse. Seeing Pearl alone meant something had happened. The flush in her cheeks sent his mind racing. Had someone propositioned her? He clenched his fists.

What if it was Garrett? He often met Amanda and Pearl with the children. What if they'd sent Amanda and the children ahead? Roland deserved that after shouting to the world that he wasn't courting Pearl. He couldn't let people like Evans go around spreading rumors that might get her in trouble.

"Fine-looking woman," Evans commented.

The twinge of jealously escalated into a full-blown firestorm. "She's off-limits, understand?"

Evans drew back. "Didn't say I was interested."

"Good. Make sure none of the men approach her."

Evans hesitated.

"You have your instructions," Roland barked.

Evans gave him a questioning look but held his tongue. The shake of the head was Roland's only clue that he'd crossed an imaginary line.

He scrubbed his jaw and tugged his coat a bit tighter against the wind. Pearl had disappeared behind a stand of low cedar and fir. He waited until she emerged, now with her back to him. Every instinct told him to go to her, but that would only inflame the rumors that he was trying to squelch. For her sake, he had to keep his distance.

He watched her pass the construction site, climb the slope and disappear into the school. Only then could he recall what he'd planned to do next. On the way to the steamships, he'd stop by the store and see what had happened to put a flush in Pearl's cheeks.

Perhaps it was the wind or the impending storm, but whatever the reason, the children were restless. Even Cocoa wouldn't settle down. She prowled from table to table, hopping on top to look out first one window and then the next. Amanda would shoo her down, but a few seconds later she'd be right back atop another table.

Instead of settling the children, as Pearl had intended, the kitten was riling them up.

The wind blew ferociously. Though the bits of leaf and tree seed flung against the building sounded like rain, no drops fell.

"Who can tell me what two plus four is?" she asked.

The older children's hands jumped into the air, but she waited for one of the young ones to answer. They looked back at her with wide eyes but said nothing. At last she called on Isaac.

"Six. And two times four is eight."

"Very good, Isaac."

"I'm going to work in the mercantile like my Uncle Roland."

Interesting. Usually a boy wanted to follow in the footsteps of his father. "I'm sure your father uses a lot of arithmetic in his work."

Isaac shrugged. "The store has lots of things."

"Pretty things," Sadie announced.

The children laughed.

"Not nearly as many nice things as the store in Saugatuck," Angela informed them. "We have ribbons and dolls."

Sadie clammed up, her gaze cast down.

Pearl's heart went out to the little girl. She seemed to take the slightest comment as criticism. If someone didn't set her mind in another direction soon, she would suffer through school. Angela hadn't meant anything by her comment beyond the usual childhood pride in their hometown. Sadie didn't understand.

Amanda moved forward to comfort Sadie, but Pearl shook her head. Sadie needed to stand up for herself. "Now we're going to work on our own. I will write a problem for each grade level on the blackboard. Copy it onto your slates and work out the solution. When I call you, come to the blackboard to show your solution to the problem."

While the students worked, Amanda approached Pearl's desk, kneeled beside it and whispered, "Why did you stop me? Sadie needed to be comforted."

"She needs to stand on her own."

"Look at her."

Pearl could see the tears in Amanda's eyes. She loved that little girl too much, like a daughter. If only Garrett Decker could see that. She glanced at Sadie, who stared at her slate with her right thumb in her mouth and no chalk in her other hand.

Pearl sighed. "Perhaps later."

Clem Bailey's hand shot in the air. "May I use the privy, Miss Lawson?"

"The necessary," Pearl amended, hoping to instill a bit of delicacy in the students. Thus far her efforts had no effect, and she sent the boy off with a wave of her hand.

She'd learned early on the hazards of not allowing the children to avail themselves of the privy. The first week she'd made Evelyn wait until playtime, but the little girl couldn't hold it. Pearl ended up mopping the floor while Amanda consoled the poor girl who'd suffered jeers from the older children.

The next hour passed with relative calm. The children settled down to complete their problems and then display the answers on the blackboard. Sadie came up with the right answer in front of the room even though she'd written nothing on her slate. Last week she'd done just the opposite, writing only on her slate and refusing to write on the blackboard in front of the class.

That girl stymied Pearl. There was a bright, intelligent girl inside that protective shell if only Pearl could break through. Amanda made more progress, though Sadie had not communicated any reasoning for her peculiar behavior. Amanda gravitated to Sadie, and the little girl clung to her with a fierce attachment that would only cause problems if Garrett continued his refusal to consider remarriage. Amanda would not wait forever. Already her gaze drifted about the church. Pearl's friend was only happy in the company of a gentleman.

Pearl inwardly sighed. She'd hoped the morning meeting with Garrett would lead to an attachment, but he remained emotionally aloof except for his children.

"I smell smoke," Angela Wardman announced, drawing Pearl from her thoughts.

The children murmured.

Pearl instantly looked to the woodstove, which they'd stoked all day against the chilly winds. "I'm sure it's just the stove. I'll check it while everyone continues their reading assignment."

The children at least pretended to read, but their eyes followed her to the stove. There was a faint smell of smoke around it, but nothing different from usual. Then she looked to the rear of the classroom, where smoke curled under the door. A glance to the windows revealed the telltale flickering orange. Pearl's heart stopped.

The woods were on fire.

Chapter Twenty

"Get the fire pump from town," Roland ordered Evans.

The man took off at a run. It would take time to bring the steam pump up to pressure, but it was their best hope for getting a solid stream of water on the growing blaze.

"I want every bucket and shovel put to use." Roland assigned each man, but the winds were whipping the small flames into a blaze.

One spark. That's all it had taken. Roland had looked up from the sawing operation at the exact moment the tug's stack spewed soot into the air. Amid the dirt had been a few sparks, embers likely. One touched the dried leaves, and a flame soon licked upward. He'd raced down the slope to beat it out, but the flame had taken off through the dried leaves and twigs. Though he'd yelled to his men to drop their saws and help out, the wind-fed fire soon gained the upper hand.

"Four buckets, Mr. Roland," one man reported.

That wouldn't be much help against this growing blaze.

"Dig," he barked. "Throw dirt on the blaze."

Maybe they could smother it before it got to the huge pile of debris. If they could turn it back on itself and force it to the river, they might extinguish the growing monster. He positioned his men with the shovels and wished he had brought the steam tractor back to the work site today, but he hadn't wanted to upset Pearl the very first day, not after reading her gracious note that Charlie had finally given him this morning. He'd misjudged her badly and treated her worse.

He glanced to the top of the hill. The school stood in the potential path of the fire.

He grabbed Tuggman, one of the crew chiefs. "Tell Miss Lawson to take the children away from here." He pointed to the school, and the man took off.

The fire streaked up the slope, following the piles of leaves that had been created by dragging the felled trees. Though his sweat-stained men flung shovelfuls of sand and dirt on the flames, the fire was winning. Only twenty feet of open ground stood between it and the debris pile. If that caught fire, nothing could stop the blaze from consuming the timbers and beams piled high for the construction of his glassworks.

He had to stop that blaze. It took but a moment to assess the situation. If they could clear every bit of tinder from the expanse between the fire and the debris pile, they might stand a chance of stopping the blaze's progress. Unfortunately, his decision to keep the steam tractor off-site today left him without the one piece of equipment that he could have used to stop the fire. It could drag the entire debris pile to the river. Likewise the wooden beams. Without it, they must rely on their hands.

Roland ran toward his men, barking out orders even while he raked away debris with the only tool available to him, a crosscut saw. When one of his crew grabbed the other end, they were able to drag it along the ground and rake aside leaves and twigs. Men with shovels followed behind, scooping up what he'd missed.

The men worked as a solid unit, focused on the task

at hand. Good men. Most were bachelors, but some had wives and children elsewhere. Wives. Children. Roland looked up the slope toward the school. Surely Pearl had been warned by now. Surely they were all safe. Then where was Tuggman?

"Boss?" the man on the other end of the saw called out to him.

Roland had let his attention wander at the worst possible time. The blaze was gaining on them. He grabbed his end of the saw and dragged. They scooped up another swath of debris, but the wind tugged the dry leaves from the pile and sent them swirling back onto the ground they'd just cleared.

He looked back to direct the men with the shovels when the fire found a scrub pine at the edge of the clearing. With a great sizzle and roar, the tree ignited like a torch. Now the fire moved from treetop to treetop, carried by the wind. The entire hillside to the east of the clearing was ablaze.

Seconds later, the debris pile lit.

Roland grabbed a shovel and flung dirt at it with all his strength.

"Boss." Evans appeared at his elbow.

Roland couldn't give up. If he could stop the fire here, they might save the schoolhouse. "Where's that fire pump?"

"Stuck."

Roland stopped shoveling long enough to look back toward Singapore. Sure enough the heavy pump had bogged down on the sandy road too far from the river and too far from the fire. Old Tom, the only horse in town, neighed and fought the twisted harness. Two of the men worked to get him free. Once loosed, he bolted back to the stable. Even if the men did catch him, in such an agitated state he wouldn't be much use pulling the pump from the loose sand.

"Get the men to help you move it."

"Tuggman said we can't budge it with his men alone. Can we take some of Raiford's crew?"

"Tuggman?" Roland heard nothing past that. Tuggman was supposed to tell Pearl to move the children to safety. Roland whipped his head back toward the school, his heart in this throat. "Did he warn Miss Lawson?"

"I don't know."

"When did he join you?" Roland grabbed Evans by the shirt collar. "This is important. Lives are at stake."

"He came down the hill not long ago."

Then he must have warned them. Roland looked back up the hill. Fire and smoke shrouded the scene and blocked the path. He hoped Evans was right and Tuggman had gotten everyone in the schoolhouse to safety.

The children started sobbing while Pearl and Amanda hurried to bundle each in his or her coat.

"Take your primer and slate," Pearl instructed, mostly to take their attention off what was happening, but most of the children were too upset to obey.

The fire appeared to be down the hill. They would be able to escape toward the northwest in the direction of Goshorn Lake.

"Amanda, lead the children up the hill away from the flames."

Her friend opened the door, and a terrifying quantity of smoke rolled into the classroom. The children began coughing, and Amanda shut the door.

"What now?" Amanda asked, her eyes wide with fear.

The youngest students clung to her. Any moment now, they'd succumb to panic if Pearl didn't take charge. She glanced out the window. The flames had raced near, but she couldn't give in to fear. These precious children needed Amanda and her.

Help us bring the children to safety, Lord.

The prayer calmed her enough to focus.

"Soak your handkerchiefs in the water bucket and put that to your face," Pearl instructed.

Naturally the older boys postured that they could handle a little smoke.

"Do it," Pearl demanded. "Use your handkerchief to help the younger students."

This time they responded to her no-nonsense tone.

She next paired up an older child with a younger one. "Miss Porter will lead, and I will follow. Hold onto each other's hand and stay close together. We will get through this."

She reached the end of the pairing. Twelve students should come up even, but Isaac stood alone without a partner. Who was missing? Clem Bailey had come back from the privy long ago, and no one else had asked to leave. Pearl began to count again, but Amanda had already taken off with the first students, and the remaining pairs were hurrying out behind her. Had three students gone together or had one of the little ones stuck to Amanda's side? Like Sadie.

"Where's your sister?" she asked Isaac.

"She went to get Cocoa."

Pearl drew in her breath. The kitten! She'd completely forgotten about it.

"Sadie!" Pearl looked beneath the tables.

"She's not in here." Isaac pointed at the windows. "Clem took Cocoa with him when he went to the privy."

Pearl reeled. That meant Sadie was outdoors in this. Most likely she'd gone to the privy to look for Cocoa. Knowing Clem, he might have closed the kitten into the structure. Fury gave way to terror.

"Follow Miss Porter." She pushed Isaac out the door after the last pair.

"I have to get Sadie." His thin shoulders squared and his little jaw set. For that instant he looked so much like his father and uncle that Pearl's heart nearly broke. That poor child had taken on the responsibility for his family at too young an age. When this was over, she'd give the Decker brothers a piece of her mind, but now all that mattered was getting every last child to safety.

"I need you to take my place at the end of the line and keep the children together."

"But Sadie," he protested.

"I will find her and bring her to you."

He wavered, not sure he could trust her.

"I'm counting on you," Pearl added. "I need you to keep the other students safe and to tell Miss Amanda to go away from the fire and toward Goshorn Lake. She doesn't know the woods around here. You have to be her guide."

His lip trembled. "You promise to get Sadie?"

"I promise."

He nodded solemnly and hurried after Amanda.

Pearl closed the door to the school, coughing in the heavy smoke, and then raced to the east around the building. Flames swept through the treetops and licked at the trunks, swept along by the wind. She pressed her sleeve to her face, for she'd neglected to dampen her own handkerchief, and edged along the building just out of the reach of the flames. On this side of the school stood the water pump and the privy in the far back, at the edge of the woods.

"Sadie!" she cried out.

The smoke was too thick to see, but she heard a small sob.

"Where are you?" Pearl plowed forward.

More sobs.

Panic threatened to cripple Pearl. She had to find Sadie. Why wouldn't the little girl tell her where she was? Because she was terrified. She'd gone back into the protective shell of silence.

Lord, help us. Help me find Sadie. Save her, Lord. Take my life, if You will it, but save that precious little girl.

A gust of wind cleared the smoke, and Pearl saw Sadie. She stood in front of the privy, the kitten hugged to her chest, surrounded by flames that tore through the dry grass and leaves. Soon the fire would reach her.

Pearl looked left and right. To get to Sadie, she must cross the flames. Pearl drew in a deep breath and plunged through the fire.

Roland heard the first of the bricks crack from the heat. More followed. The wooden beams he'd stacked for the roof of his glassworks created a bank of heat so fierce that no man could get near. Flames shot thirty feet into the air. All his work, all the investor's money, was vanishing in this fire and there was nothing he could do to stop it.

"We've got the fire pump loose." Garrett appeared at his side.

Roland looked back to see they had indeed moved the pump into position. Lines were being laid to the river, and the steam engine boiled. "It's too late. The bricks are cracking. There won't be anything left."

"Don't give up." Garrett glanced up the slope. "You got the children out of the school?"

"I sent Tuggman to warn them."

Garrett growled, "I'm going up to make sure."

The similarities to two springs ago did not escape Roland. In a flash he saw that day again, Garrett asking about his wife while Roland raced for a boat to rescue her. They'd argued, and she'd stormed off after calling Roland selfish and inconsiderate. She'd taken the skiff they kept tied to the shore upriver. The rushing water and chunks of ice had proven too much for her. The skiff capsized and sank. He'd run back to town for another dinghy, the *New Dawn*, the very one that the kittens had been found underneath. Though he'd rowed with all his might, by the time he got there, she was gone. Dead. It was all his fault.

Now, Garrett's children were on the other side of that fire.

"Wait." Roland grabbed Tuggman while holding Garrett at bay. "Did you warn the students at the schoolhouse?"

The man went ashen, and Roland had his answer. He didn't wait for another word but sprinted up the hill, dodging the flames. Garrett was on his heels and soon reached his side. Together they raced through the burning woods until they reached the clearing where the schoolhouse stood. Flames lapped its southern wall, but to the north the woods were as yet untouched.

"There!" Garrett pointed high on the hill, where the children huddled around the dark-haired Miss Porter.

Garrett sprinted toward them. This time Roland trailed behind.

"Papa!" Isaac separated from the huddled group.

Garrett aimed for his son, falling to his knees to envelop the boy in a bear hug.

Roland caught Amanda's frantic gaze.

"Pearl?" he said.

She pointed toward the rear of the schoolhouse, already enveloped in flames.

This couldn't happen again. His family would not lose someone they loved to tragedy. His niece and nephew would not sob through the nights. He could not fail them this time.

He could not lose Pearl. Not now. She didn't even know that he loved her.

Chapter Twenty-One

Sadie shrieked over and over, one little finger pointed at Pearl as if she was a monster.

"It's me, Pearl, Miss Lawson. I'll save you." Her face felt singed, like when she'd opened the oven door and the flame leaped at the sudden influx of air.

Still Sadie shrieked.

Pearl looked down. Her skirts were on fire. She dropped to the ground and pounded her bunched skirts against the ground until she'd extinguished the flame.

Sadie sobbed, still clutching Cocoa, who clawed at her with desperation.

Pearl looked back. The flames had drawn closer. There was no way out except through the blaze. A flash of memory from long ago scorched through her mind. The heat, the smoke, the bright orange flames. She'd been in a fire before, when she was very little, almost too young to remember, younger than Sadie.

She clutched the girl close. Sadie was a tiny thing. She couldn't weigh more than half a sack of flour. The little girl was too scared to run. Pearl must carry her—and the kitten. Sadie would never let go of the yowling, terrified Cocoa. She loved that kitten. Cocoa's life mattered so much that she would not abandon it to save her own.

Unlike Pearl's father and mother.

She brushed aside the bitter memory of looking out the orphanage window week after week for her parents' return. Now was no time to dwell in the past. This girl needed her.

The flames rose in a wall between them and the schoolhouse. Perhaps they could escape through the woods. Pearl glanced back. The woods were ablaze. A burning limb dropped onto the privy. Soon it would catch on fire, too.

She must act now. She must run through the flames holding the little girl and pray that somehow she'd make it without catching fire.

Lord, cover us with Your protection.

Pearl lifted Sadie. "Hold tight to Cocoa and press your face into my shoulder."

Sadie obeyed, and the squished kitten planted its claws into Pearl's chest. Pearl drew a sharp breath and prepared to run.

Then she saw a man racing toward them waving his arms.

Roland! Relief coursed through her veins.

He ran to her right, where the flames were lower, and held out his arms. "Hand Sadie to me first, and then I'll get you out of there."

A mere three feet of burning ground separated his outstretched hands from the edge of the flames near her.

Pearl trembled as another fragment of memory returned. The flames surrounded her, and her papa took her away from her mama. Then she hadn't seen her mama for a long time.

"Pearl!" Roland shouted. "Hand Sadie to me."

Could she trust him to return for her? Her father and mother never came back. She shook off doubt. Sadie mattered most. She began to hand over Sadie, but girl and kitten clung to her, the latter with its claws dug into Pearl's dress.

"Let go of Cocoa," Pearl begged.

The little girl dug deeper into her shoulder.

Pearl could not do as Roland suggested. She must risk all to save Sadie. Lowering her head, she ran through the flames, eyes shut and covering as much of Sadie as she could. Her foot struck a root, and she stumbled, falling to her knees. The heat sizzled around her. Her lungs begged for air, and she breathed. The air scorched. The smoke choked.

Spare Sadie, Lord. Save this little girl.

Summoning her last ounce of strength, she crawled forward. Strong hands pulled her from the heat. Roland. His deep voice rumbled like thunder but she could not make out what he said. Something, a heavy cloth, smothered her, and she felt blows to her back and legs. She couldn't stop coughing. He lifted Sadie and the kitten from her grasp.

Roland. She tried to speak his name, but nothing would come out. She tried to look, but her eyelids would not open. Each breath hurt. She struggled to her feet.

"Follow me," he said.

She reached for him and got only air. The effort cost the last of her strength. She collapsed to the ground, unable to breathe, unable to speak. One hand reached for him.

Above the crackle of flames she felt the thud of his footsteps running away.

"Uncle, uncle," little Sadie sobbed as Roland ran to safety.

The kitten bounced in her arms, but he would not let Sadie or her beloved Cocoa go, not until he reached Garrett. His lungs burned from the smoky air and his face felt singed. His muscles protested with every step, but he would not quit.

This time he would get everyone to safety. This time he would not fail.

The fire raced through the treetops, nearing the group huddled in wait for him. They must leave.

"Go!" he tried to shout, but the noises of wind and fire and men desperately attempting to stop the blaze prevented anyone from hearing him.

Though his legs threatened to falter, he pressed on. Only a hundred feet farther. Only fifty. Almost there.

Garrett met him and took Sadie from his arms. Roland bent over, winded, hands on his knees until he could catch his breath.

"Papa," she sobbed, "help Teacher."

Pearl! Roland whipped around. She wasn't there.

"She was right behind me," he said, but sinking dread clenched his stomach. "I'm going back."

Garrett grabbed his arm. "It's too late. You'll never get through. The schoolhouse is already on fire."

Though his brother was right, Roland couldn't leave Pearl. "I have to go. I have to."

He tried to shake free, but Garrett had a viselike grip on his arm.

"Let go." Roland pounded on his brother, but Garrett would not release him. "I can't let her die, too."

"You didn't let Eva die. She chose to cross the river. She knew how dangerous it was."

Roland stared at his brother. After all the fights these past two years, he'd never expected to hear those words from his lips. But now was no time to make amends.

"Pearl," he choked out. "I love her."

Garrett nodded solemnly. "I know. But these children need you. Miss Amanda can't do this on her own. She needs our help to bring everyone to safety."

"You can do it."

"The little ones are too scared to move. They need to be carried."

"But I can't leave Pearl." Roland started for her again.

Garrett tightened his grip. "Would she want you to help the children or go after her? You can't do both."

Roland knew the answer, but he couldn't accept it. "I can't let her die."

"It's too late. We only have the chance to save the children if we act now."

Deep down Roland knew his brother was right, but he could not accept it. "Pearl."

"We must trust God to protect her."

"God watch over Teacher," Sadie repeated.

From the mouth of babes?

Roland looked up at the blazing treetops and down at the men who worked to stop the fire from heading toward town. "We'll take them west toward Goshorn and then over the dune."

"Once we get to the dune, we'll be safe. Go find Pearl then."

By then Roland knew what he'd find. His heart shattered.

The fire's heat singed, but the ground felt unnaturally cool. Pearl pressed her face against it, first one side and then the other, while she tried to summon enough strength to rise. She could not feel her legs, could barely sense her arms.

She dug her fingers into the ground and pushed up.

The effort spent the last of her strength, and she collapsed to the ground.

Around her, the fire roared. The popping of cedar trees mingled with the sizzle of pine needles. The schoolhouse must be ablaze by now. Nothing could slow this wind-driven fire. Nothing could spare her.

All those years ago she had called out for her mama when her papa carried her from the fiery room. He had given her to someone. She couldn't recall who. Then he went away. She remembered another house, a strange place filled with people she didn't know. A gray-haired woman would pat her head and say "poor child" over and over, but all Pearl wanted was her mother.

"Mama," she whispered into the cool ground.

Her mama had returned with Papa one day, but she wouldn't hold Pearl or even look at her. Pearl had hugged her, but Papa had pulled her away and said her mama was too sick. The next day, they left the strange house full of people and brought Pearl to the orphanage.

A sob escaped Pearl now, both for the hurts she hadn't understood back then and for the pain of these memories. Why had they sent her away? Because she was bad? Had she caused that fire?

Perhaps Miss Hornswoggle was right, and her parents had died. Or at least her mama. Whatever happened, Pearl never saw them again. And never would until she crossed into the next life.

That step could happen now unless she fought. Images of Amanda and the schoolchildren and Roland drifted through her mind. So many people here cared about her. So many depended on her. She must try.

Once more she summoned all her strength and rose to her elbows and knees. She squinted into the smoke and crawled a couple of steps until the pain became too much. Again she collapsed.

Ever since giving up hope that her parents would return for her, Pearl had taken charge of her life. She had worked hard at the orphanage and studied harder. Every waking moment was pointed toward this end—to help children succeed by giving them the gift of an education. Was that all to be snatched away before she'd even begun?

"Why, Lord?" she sobbed, her lips forming the words though nothing would come out.

Why now when she was doing the one thing she thought He'd destined her to do?

The Lord is my strength and my shield; my heart trusted in Him, and I am helped: therefore my heart greatly rejoiceth; and with my song will I praise Him.

Was that familiar verse from Psalms telling her something? Had she overstepped her bounds?

"Help me!" This time something came out of her throat, but the gentle croak vanished beneath the howl of wind and fire.

No one would ever hear her. She could not walk, could not even crawl. Without help, she would die. Pearl no longer had any control over anything. Her life hinged not on what she could do for herself but in what God would do for her. All she could do was submit her life to His care.

Utterly depleted, she laid her face against the cool ground and surrendered control to her Lord and Savior.

The fire still raged. The wind still howled. Pain numbed her mind, and each breath still hurt. Yet everything had changed. Peace settled over her. Whatever happened, He was with her.

A single cool drop splashed on her cheek. Then another and another. Rain.

Tears bunched in her eyes and slipped over the bridge of her nose before falling to the cool earth. God was with her.

Chapter Twenty-Two

Roland carried two little girls to the top of the dune. From there they could see the homes and businesses in Singapore. To the southeast, the fire still raged, but the driving winds would keep it away from town. Soon it would run into cleared land and lose its fuel. The fire would die. Had Pearl?

He set down the now-squirming girls as his brother joined him.

"Go," Garrett said. "Miss Porter and I can take the children home from here."

Roland didn't need more encouragement, but Garrett gave it anyway.

"You did the right thing. She would be proud of you."

Roland wasn't. The entire terrible trek west had reinforced his guilt. Yes, the fire had begun from the tugboat, but that tug would never have been there if he hadn't built a dock for the glassworks factory that now would never happen. As he ran toward the blaze he realized that the project that had once possessed his every waking moment no longer meant a thing.

All that mattered was Pearl.

If he found her charred remains, he would never forgive himself. He should have made sure she followed. He should have looked back. He should have listened to her concerns about the construction site. He should have found another place for the school. The list of charges against him was long. No judge would acquit him, certainly not God.

At the top of the wooded slope, the carnage became evident. His building timbers had burned away. The bricks were cracked rubble. The woods had largely burnt and the schoolhouse was a smoking hulk of charred wood.

He stumbled forward. Pearl couldn't possibly have survived. Yet he could not abide anyone else finding her. He could not bear to think of another soul touching her.

"What a fool I am," he cried to the God he had set aside in the name of progress. Selfish dreaming might be a better name for it. Yes, it would have helped the town, but at what cost? Had he taken the time to bring everyone together? Had he ensured others shared that dream? No, he'd plowed ahead, dreaming of riches, not the benefit to others. His name would go on the glassworks. His bank account would grow. How worthless and conceited.

He had thrown away the things that mattered most—his family and the woman who made him reconsider every decision he'd ever made. She'd brought him back to church. Now he knew that wasn't enough. If he'd given her a chance, she would have led him straight to the Lord. Instead, he'd let her down. He'd let everyone down.

"I was wrong," he called out to God. Like the penitent of old, he struck his chest with his fists. If anything would bring Pearl back, he would do it, but even the most righteous human did not bribe God.

He dropped to his knees. "Your will, not mine."

The words should have sapped his strength, but a drop of rain splattered against his uplifted face. Then another and another. Each one poured hope into him as if from a bucket. He clambered to his feet and ran.

Whatever he found, whether Pearl lived or died, the Lord would be with him. Somehow, deep down, he knew that would be enough. Yet hope built with each step. The remnants of the fire had moved south. The area around the school smoldered. He pressed his shirtsleeve to his nose to filter out the choking smoke. He'd left his coat with Pearl after dousing the flames on her skirt.

Pearl, oh, Pearl. What would he find?

He slid down the slope and hurried around the smoking remains of the schoolhouse. Then he halted, shocked.

The hand pump, inexplicably dribbling water, stood in the center of the open backyard. Beneath it, in the trail of the streaming water, lay Pearl, her clothing no more burned than when he'd left her. His coat lay behind her, where she'd once lain and from where she must have crawled.

He stumbled toward her and dropped to his knees. "Pearl?"

He touched her shoulder.

She did not respond.

He cupped her soot-covered cheek, which was streaked with perspiration…or tears. It felt slightly warm. Was she alive?

He placed an ear on her back and heard the most wonderful sound on earth, the beating of her heart.

"Pearl," he choked out through the tears. "Oh, Pearl."

He pressed his lips to her cheek.

She stirred, ever so little, but it was enough to send hope surging through his veins.

"Thank You, God." The whispered words filled with emotion.

Then he gathered her in his arms.

* * *

Waiting had never been easy for Roland. After carrying Pearl to the boardinghouse and placing her on the bed in her room, Mrs. Calloway shooed him downstairs to the parlor, where Amanda and Fiona turned eager eyes in his direction.

"How is she?"

He shook his head. "Not awake. We need to send for a doctor."

"Mr. Calloway already left for Holland," Amanda said.

"Holland," Roland repeated dully. Why didn't Singapore have its own physician?

"Mr. Calloway said that was the closest doctor."

Roland scrubbed his jaw. "That's probably true. The doc in Saugatuck heads upriver this time of year." But that meant a long wait. "It'll take hours."

"He took Old Tom," Amanda said hopefully.

Roland breathed a sigh of relief. Old Tom might balk at pulling the heavy fire pump, but he could bring Ernie Calloway to Holland faster than a man could walk. "Good. It won't be long, then. How are the children?"

Amanda brightened. "All safely home. Once we were within sight of the village, their spirits lifted, though they're worried about Pearl."

Roland couldn't blame them. "Me, too." He wondered for a moment how Sadie was doing. She'd been through too much for her tender years.

"I'm sure all will turn out well." Amanda rose. "I'll go look in on her."

"Mrs. Calloway said everyone had to leave the room," he said.

She gave him a pitying look, one that women used to indicate he simply didn't understand. "I'm Pearl's dearest friend. Mrs. Calloway will welcome my help."

Everyone apparently only included him.

"Moreover, it's my room, too." Amanda tucked her embroidery into a basket before leaving the parlor.

They shared a room? That shouldn't have surprised Roland if he'd been observant. It fit with Pearl's inability to purchase primers, a new dress or a winter coat. Though Amanda's gowns were finer, she, too, wore only a couple different ones. Pearl had carried only a carpetbag when she landed in Singapore. He'd assumed she had sent her trunks to the boardinghouse, but what if all she owned was in that single bag? She had let slip that she was an orphan. He'd assumed she'd been raised by relatives, but what if she hadn't?

He hurried after Amanda and caught her on the first step of the stairway.

"Miss Porter. Amanda."

She turned, her violet eyes more somber than usual. "Is something wrong?"

He shook his head. "I wondered if you could answer something for me. It's about Pearl. She mentioned she is an orphan."

Amanda turned her face from him. He couldn't help but notice how tightly she gripped the railing.

Something about that statement bothered her, but he could not stop now. "Did she live with your family?"

Amanda's shoulders drooped. She shook her head.

"But you said you are close friends, and Pearl said you grew up together. She must have lived near, perhaps with a relation?"

She turned troubled eyes toward him. "Please don't ask me these questions. Pearl needs to give you the answers."

What was she hiding and why? "I mean no harm."

"I know that, Mr. Decker, but Pearl is the one who should give you the answers you seek."

That sounded ominous, as if Pearl had something to hide. Impossible. She was the most open person he'd ever met. She spoke her mind, sometimes without thinking first, but openly nonetheless. He could not believe her capable of deceit. And now she lay in grave danger, if her unresponsiveness and Mrs. Calloway's concern were any indication.

"Shouldn't we contact a family member?" he persisted. "Send a letter or telegram?"

She shook her head ever so slightly. "That won't be necessary." Then she practically sprinted up the staircase.

Odd. Very odd. Either Amanda had complete faith in Pearl's recovery or Pearl was estranged from what family she had. Unless she had none. Roland drew in his breath. After losing his parents, Garrett had become his only family. Roland had nearly wrecked that with his foolish longing for Eva. Lust. Best call it what it was. Roland hated to lose to anyone, and Eva had been a pawn in the terrible struggle between Roland and his brother. Though Roland had never touched her after she abandoned him for Garrett, he still wanted her. No wonder she'd run from him.

Roland felt ill. No wonder Christ had condemned not only the coveting, but also the covetous thought. He needed a heap of forgiveness, but before he could plead before God, he must humble himself before his brother.

As if on cue, the front door opened, ushering in Garrett and the children, all dripping wet.

"Uncle, uncle," Sadie cried, throwing her arms around his legs.

"Let's get those coats off," Garrett said.

Once the children's slickers had been removed, Roland picked up Sadie and gave her a bear hug, overwhelmed by gratitude that this little one had survived. Thanks to Pearl, who'd risked her life for Sadie.

He set her down. "Any bumps or bruises?"

"Cocoa scratched me." She held up a wrist with a red welt where the frightened kitten had gouged her.

Roland kissed the spot. "There. All better. How is Cocoa?"

"She's hiding behind the bed."

"Not surprising. You were very brave to rescue her."

The little girl's eyes filled with tears. "Miss Lawson saved me."

"Yes, she did." Roland looked up at his brother, who shot him a questioning look in return. Roland shook his head. "But now she needs to rest and get better."

"Like Cocoa?"

"A little like Cocoa."

Fiona appeared in the parlor doorway. "I thought I heard you two darling children. I happen to have a game of jacks all set to play. Would you like to join me?"

The two children squealed their agreement, and Garrett shot Fiona a look of gratitude. She smiled back, and Roland wondered if he'd guessed wrong about Amanda and his brother. If Garrett could communicate with Fiona simply with a look, then they'd spent more time together than he'd realized. Roland was beginning to see just how little he knew about his brother.

Once the children had left with Fiona, Garrett grew solemn. "Any word?"

"Ernie took Old Tom to fetch a doctor from Holland, but you probably already knew that."

Garrett nodded. "It'll be a couple more hours before we can expect them, then."

Roland knew this, but hearing it confirmed dampened his already turbulent feelings.

Garrett must have seen his pained expression, for he leaned close to whisper. "Did she wake?"

"Once. Well, not completely. She stirred and murmured something when I first found her."

Garrett nodded gravely. "We must take that as a good sign."

Then why did he look like a man waiting for a funeral? Roland attempted to swallow the sawdust in his throat and failed. "She's a strong woman."

"That she is." Garrett looked down at his scuffed and worn boots.

Though Roland's brother could afford new footwear, he would not buy anything that wasn't practical. Unlike Eva. She adored the frivolous and beautiful. Like Amanda, she glowed when dressed in a pretty gown with her locks curled. Roland sighed. Maybe Garrett and Amanda weren't such a good match. She could be too similar to Eva. Speaking of which, Roland had unfinished business that he could not put off any longer.

He cleared his throat. "May I have a word with you?"

Garrett looked up, curious. "If you need money to cover your losses on the factory, I'll do my best to help out."

"No. That's not it. Not even close." Roland drew a deep breath. Garrett had been exceptionally kind today, but their relationship would never strengthen until he cleared the air. "I need to confess something." He swallowed. "This might hurt. Do you want to step out onto the porch for some privacy?"

No one sat on the porch in this weather. In fact, Ernie Calloway had put the chairs into the barn for the winter.

Garrett eyed him suspiciously. "What is it?"

Roland stepped outside, and his brother followed. Only after he closed the door and they moved to the far end of the porch would he speak. The rain still fell in sheets, and the spray off the railings misted their clothes.

"What happened?" Garrett prompted, his arms crossed in front of his chest.

Roland's heart thumped against his rib cage like an angry bear in a cage. There was no getting out of this now. "I wronged you."

Garrett's brow rose but he said nothing.

Roland continued, "Eva and I were more than friends before she went to you." He drew in another breath and hesitated a moment in case Garrett's anger exploded. It didn't. "I know now that I drove her away. She wanted love and encouragement and devotion. I could only think about my plans and my future. I thought she fit into it. I was wrong."

Garrett nodded curtly.

Roland knew that was his signal to proceed, but it got more difficult from that point forward. "I tried to make her into what I needed. When she left, I was furious, even envious. I couldn't understand what you had that I didn't."

"What did you do to her?" Garrett growled.

Roland held up his hands. "At least let me finish before you pound me senseless. That's why I couldn't attend your wedding and why I accepted the store manager position here in Singapore. Then you followed me here. I couldn't stand to see Eva every day. In my mind it rubbed salt in the wound. Then..." He hesitated before this difficult part.

"Then what?"

"I'm ashamed of what I did." Roland swiped his brow, which in spite of the cool temperatures was sweating profusely. "I talked to Eva."

"Talked to her."

"Asked her why she preferred you, suggested she would have done better with me. That's why she left in the skiff that day. If I hadn't pressed her, she would never have died."

The blow came without warning, but not a fist to the jaw, which would have knocked Roland senseless. Instead, Garrett clapped him on the shoulder and gave him a solid shake.

He looked Roland in the eyes. "You must forgive yourself. God has." His grip relaxed. "And I have. Long ago. I knew about your relationship with Eva."

"How?"

"It was obvious by the way you two acted around each other and the way she begged to leave, as if her life depended on it."

"It did," Roland said bitterly.

"That was her choice. I spent a lot of time these past two years trying to figure out what I could have done to change that day."

"You couldn't have done a thing."

"I could have listened to her, really listened instead of dismissing everything she wanted as frivolous foolishness. You see, you're not the only Decker who thought he knew what was best for everyone around him. It took a lot of reading God's Word and really paying attention to what it said to see what a fool I'd been."

"I was the fool."

"We're all fools until we put our lives in the Lord's hands. Now let's go inside out of this rain and see if Mrs. Calloway has any news on your Pearl."

"My Pearl?" Roland didn't miss the wording.

"Yep. Yours." Garrett grinned. "If you stop acting like a fool."

Pearl awoke with a start, and the blissful dreams of Roland kissing her cheek vanished under a blanket of pain. Each breath made her cough. The tiniest movement of air against her legs hurt.

She coughed again, and the memories flooded back. The fire. Roland must have begun burning the debris piles, and the fire got out of hand. He should have known better with all that wind.

By the time Angela Wardman spotted the smoke, the blaze raced toward the schoolhouse. She'd sent the children out of the building with Amanda, but Sadie was missing. She'd found the little girl surrounded by fire and had walked through the scorched ground to get to her. A second later, the fire had grown. Roland wanted her to hand over Sadie, but she couldn't extricate the girl and kitten from her arms. So she'd run through the fire. After that, the memories faded except for the feeling of being left behind. Alone. Abandoned.

Then where did that dream of the kiss come from? She tried to lift a hand to her cheek but her arm felt incredibly heavy.

"That cough is going to last a while," an unfamiliar man said over her head.

She squinted to make out a silver-haired, bespectacled man in a black suit.

"I've dressed the burns on her legs with carron oil and covered with cotton wool. Check the dressings twice a day and reapply oil and cotton wool as needed. The patient should be kept in bed for two weeks and only moved when necessary. You may give her a spoonful of laudanum if the pain becomes too much."

So, the man was a doctor. That must mean she was the patient.

"I'm fine," she rasped, barely audible. The effort hurt, but she must know. "The children—"

"Don't speak," Mrs. Calloway ordered in her most authoritative boardinghouse tone. She thrust a slate and piece of chalk at her. "Write."

Pearl flexed her fingers. They worked, but she could not lift her arm to take the slate, least of all to write. The very thought exhausted her. Still, she had to know if Sadie had survived.

"Perhaps later," the doctor said, removing the slate from Mrs. Calloway's hands. "If you have a spare room, I will stay the night and check on the patient in the morning."

"Of course. We can put you in the green room just

down the hall. Let me show you there." Mrs. Calloway's voice drifted away along with the patter of footsteps.

Pearl let her eyes slip shut.

"Dearest." Amanda's familiar voice danced into Pearl's consciousness. She clasped Pearl's hand. "You must listen to all the doctor tells you. You must get well."

Pearl opened her gritty eyelids to see tears in Amanda's eyes. Was her condition so serious that Amanda feared for her well-being? Pearl tried to tell her that she was all right, but her voice failed. Her friend could tell her about the children if only Pearl could ask, but without the use of voice or hands, how could she?

Sadie? she mouthed.

Amanda's eyes widened and then she squeezed Pearl's hand. "Perfectly fine. All the children are unharmed."

Pearl let out a breath of relief, but that was soon followed by irritation. None of them would have been in danger if Roland hadn't decided to burn on such a windy day. How could he?

Amanda bubbled on, oblivious to Pearl's thoughts. "Roland carried Sadie to safety. She's completely untouched except for a few nicks where Cocoa grabbed hold. Oh, and the kitten is fine, too. It's amazing how they escaped the blaze. The whole schoolhouse and yard was on fire. We gave up hope, but somehow you all survived. No one can believe it."

Pearl let her eyelids slip shut again. Not somehow. God had protected that little girl, just as He had protected her all those years ago. Maybe her papa had prayed the same words she'd prayed years later, to spare the child if not the adult. Or maybe God had heard her own cries for help.

Her head hurt. She must rest. Two weeks at least, the doctor had said. Two weeks! How would the children continue their schooling without a teacher or a schoolhouse? She tried to ask Amanda, but nothing would come out of her mouth. She couldn't even lift her arms to write. She lay helpless in a bed, utterly dependent.

And it was all Roland's fault.

Chapter Twenty-Three

Pearl wandered in and out of slumber for days. November's bleak light faded to darkness and returned again with barely a notice.

"You must eat something," Amanda urged, soup bowl in hand. "A little broth will do wonders."

Pearl pulled herself up on the pillows and winced. Her arms worked like normal and the coughing had stopped, but the tiniest movement of her legs brought tears to her eyes.

"Oh!" Amanda set down the soup. "I should have put another pillow behind your back."

Pearl rubbed her eyes, which still felt gritty. "I need to get back to the classroom." Though still hoarse, at least she could speak.

"First you must eat." Amanda held out a spoonful of the liquid.

"I'm not a baby. I can feed myself."

Amanda, always patient and understanding, beamed. "You're feeling better."

"I can't seem to shake the cobwebs from my mind."

"Perhaps a little broth will help."

Pearl sniffed the offering. Chicken. Her stomach rumbled. It would do. She took the spoon and managed to get most of the spoonful into her mouth before falling back against the pillows, exhausted. "What is wrong with me? It's only been a day or two."

"Four, actually."

"Four?" Pearl couldn't comprehend how that much time had passed without her knowledge. Then she spotted the bottle of laudanum. "No more medicine. I need my wits about me so I can teach school."

Amanda bit her lip and lowered her gaze.

"What is it?" Pearl asked. "What happened?"

Her friend pasted on an artificial smile. "Have more broth. You need to get stronger first."

"Before what?"

"Before returning to teaching." Amanda held out the bowl. "Have some more."

Pearl swallowed another spoonful. "Now tell me what happened."

Amanda held up the bowl. "Not until it's all gone."

"That's blackmail."

Amanda nodded cheerfully.

Though the effort taxed her strength, Pearl's stomach appreciated the offering. When she finished, she handed back the spoon and dropped against the pillows. "Now tell me what's going on."

Amanda set the bowl and spoon on the little bedside table that had appeared from somewhere in the boardinghouse, likely a more costly room. "Dr. Van Neef said it'll take a bit for your throat and eyes to fully recover, but they should improve each day. Roland brought some horehound drops that'll soothe your throat."

Pearl bristled at Roland's name. Though some of the memories were murky, one was not. Roland had set fire to that burn pile on a windy day. He had caused everything. "I don't want anything from him."

"But those flowers brighten the room."

Only then did Pearl notice the vase of chrysanthemums on the bureau. How he had found them this late in the year was a wonder. Naturally Amanda loved them, for she was drawn to every beautiful thing.

"Take them away."

Amanda frowned. "Don't be such a grouch. They belong right there."

Pearl could see she would get nowhere with Amanda, whose eyes sparkled with the prospect of matching her to Roland. Time to put an end to that. "Forget it."

"Forget what?"

"You know what. Your matchmaking."

"Me?" Amanda's mock surprise was proof enough.

Pearl motioned to her throat. "I need to rest."

Amanda took the hint. "I'll take the soup bowl downstairs." She pulled open the bureau drawer and removed a stack of letters. "Perhaps you would like to read a little."

No one wrote to Pearl. Ever. How could she have a stack of mail?

"The children sent notes." Amanda teared up again. "They love you."

Pearl's heart filled to overflowing. Sure enough, the top letter was from little Sadie. Dear, precious Sadie. As Amanda slipped out of the room, Pearl held the note to her face and drew a breath of the fresh paper. Sadie couldn't write much more than her name, but she'd sent Pearl a note.

Thank You, Lord, for saving her. And me.

A little pain was a small price to pay.

An adult, probably Sadie's father, had written "Miss Lawson" on the outside. Pearl unfolded the piece of paper. As she'd suspected, the "note" contained no writing other than Sadie's name in block capital letters with the *D* backward and the *E* splayed out like fingers reaching to play a full octave on the piano. The rest was a drawing. The schoolhouse was on fire, and flames surrounded it, a little girl and a grown woman. A kitten clung to the girl.

Pearl choked back a tear. The poor girl. Drawing what had happened must be a way to make sense of it. She looked back at the sketch. Away from the school stood a man. Her father? Farther away was a boy. Isaac, no doubt. In the other direction, where there should be trees, Sadie had drawn a steamboat with its smokestack belching soot. Peculiar. Did it represent her wish to get away from the fire?

Pearl's hand dropped, and the other notes scattered across her lap. All were addressed to her. Many bore the telltale writing of her students. By now, she could differentiate Angela's hand from George's. Each child's writing was distinct. Each note she would treasure.

Then she came upon four notes, all written in the same adult hand. No family sent four wee ones to her school. It could not be from a parent. She unfolded the first to find a finely written letter, each line perfectly straight. Her gaze drifted to the signature.

Roland.

Her jaw clenched.

He could not buy her forgiveness with a simple letter, not when his actions had nearly cost the children their lives.

Saturday while manning the store, Roland whistled as he put the finishing touches on his package by tying the ribbon into a big bow. He held up the finished product. "What do you think?"

Sadie surveyed his effort, first by tilting her head one way and then the other. "It's all right."

He would have to consider that good enough.

"But you should draw a picture on the paper," Sadie

added. "Teacher likes pictures. Miss Amanda said she really liked the picture I made for her."

"I'm sure she did." Roland touched a finger to her nose, making her giggle. "Especially since it came from you, but I'm not much of an artist. She'll be much happier with your new drawing that we put inside." He patted the brown paper wrapped package.

Sadie thoughtfully considered what he'd said. "Was my mama an artist?"

Roland knew the questions would eventually start to come, but Eva's memory still brought a twinge of guilt in spite of Garrett's forgiveness. He concentrated on Sadie, whose dark hair reminded him of her mother. "Your mother loved everything beautiful. When she lived in Chicago, she liked to visit the art exhibitions. I think she would have been an artist if she'd had the opportunity." He smiled. "Maybe you'll be the artist in the family."

She giggled at that and ran off to play with Beth Wardman, who arrived with her mother.

"Any news on the school?" Debra Wardman asked.

"We're going to use our church cabin on Pine Street. It'll be ready next week."

"But who will teach?"

"Miss Porter, Miss O'Keefe and Miss Smythe have agreed to lead the children in their lessons until Miss Lawson returns to the classroom."

Mrs. Wardman looked skeptical. "What will they use? Most of the primers and slates were lost in the fire."

"New ones are on order and should arrive within the week."

"At what cost?"

"None, Mrs. Wardman. An anonymous donor has paid for them." Him. He'd placed the order the very next day.

"Praise God!" Her concern melted into a smile. "That's the best news I've heard all day."

"Is there anything I can get for you today?" Roland was eager to deliver his gift, and with Charlie off on deliveries, he had to wait on the customers until the boy's return.

By the time he'd filled Mrs. Wardman's order and had her sign for the purchases, Charlie returned. Though Roland had intended to leave Sadie at the store, he decided Pearl might want to see the little girl. It wouldn't hurt his chances, either.

He helped fasten the buttons on Sadie's coat before donning his own. Then he hefted the bulky package and they made their way into the blustery November afternoon. Though heavy clouds scudded across the sky, it had yet to rain or snow. Fortunate, since he didn't want this gift to get wet.

After considering all possible ways to thank Pearl for her heroic sacrifice to save his niece, Roland and Garrett had settled on this. She needed it and deserved every penny that it cost.

"Why are you giving Teacher a present?" Sadie asked for the umpteenth time.

"It's from all of us to thank her for saving you and Isaac."

Sadie tilted her head to look up at him, the old repaired rag doll tucked in the crook of her arm. "Are you going to give Miss Amanda a present, too?"

That was a fair question, but one he had no answer to. When Roland had mentioned adding something for Amanda, Garrett had stiffened and reiterated his intent not to marry. Though Roland had tried to convince his brother that this had nothing to do with matchmaking, Garrett would not relent.

"We gave her the flowers, remember?"

Sadie nodded vigorously. "But she said they should be for Teacher. We need to give Miss Amanda something just for her."

"I'll tell you what we'll do. When we get there, you give Miss Amanda a big hug and a kiss. I think she would consider that the best gift of all."

Sadie scrunched up her nose, apparently unconvinced. "That's not a present."

"To grown-ups, that's the best present they can get."

"Are you going to hug Teacher?"

Roland coughed and extended the coughing spell until he could think of a good response. "It's different between adults."

"Why?"

Why indeed. Sometimes Roland wished his niece was still the quiet little girl she'd been before Pearl and Amanda arrived. No, that wasn't quite true. This little girl skipping along the boardwalk was more precious than the biggest factory. Maybe it had taken disaster to wake him up to the bounty right in front of him. Since Pearl had arrived, life had taken on a new shine. Thanks to her, he and Garrett had reconciled. Family and faith now took the top spots in life. He actually looked forward to church services tomorrow.

"We're here," he announced, glad he wouldn't have to answer Sadie's probing questions.

Mrs. Calloway answered the door. "Mr. Roland, Miss Sadie, come on in. I just took some gingerbread out of the oven. Would you like some?" She bent to help Sadie out of her coat. "Miss Amanda is already there."

Sadie rushed back to the kitchen. After spending so much time here, she knew the boardinghouse as well as her own home.

Mrs. Calloway straightened. "Well now. May I take your coat?" She eyed the gift. "Someone's about to have a fine day." She chuckled. "But I expect it's not me. She's upstairs. I'll go on ahead and make sure she's ready for visitors."

She headed toward the staircase.

He waited.

She turned around and beckoned him to follow. "She'll be right pleased to see you."

He followed but hung back. When he first arrived in Singapore, he'd stayed at the boardinghouse, second room on the left. The same room, he now realized, that he'd carried Pearl into the day of the fire. Mrs. Calloway stopped before that door again. After rapping lightly, she cracked the door.

"You have a visitor," she said.

Roland couldn't hear Pearl's response, but Mrs. Calloway beckoned him near. She then flung open the door, revealing Pearl seated in bed, the threadbare shawl draped around her shoulders.

The moment she spotted him, her eager smile faded.

Pearl struggled to calm her emotions. Mrs. Calloway had given her no warning and no chance to chase Roland away. In fact, the moment the door opened wide, Mrs. Calloway vanished, leaving Roland alone, tall and stunningly handsome with his dark hair and cheeks flushed from the cold. His black wool coat was of the finest cut and quality, and he held in his arms a large, paper-wrapped package tied with red ribbon.

If she hadn't been so angry with him, she would have braved the pain to run to him. Every fiber of her fickle body cried out to go to him, but her mind struggled to make sense of the man who stood before her. Charming one moment and unthinking the next. He had risked children's lives to burn debris on a windy day. On the other hand, he had returned for her. He had cradled her in his arms and carried her to safety. During each one of the long days confined to the bedroom, she had relived that gentle kiss to her cheek. Even now the very spot hummed from the memory of his lips.

"I'm glad to hear you're recovering." He stepped in the room.

Too close. She put up a hand to stop him. "I'm sorry, but without a chaperone…"

"Of course." He backed away. "I will call for Mrs. Calloway or Amanda."

"Don't bother them." Though her voice came out petulant, she couldn't regret it. After all, he had caused this.

An awkward silence followed. She pulled the quilt higher though she wasn't cold. He shifted his weight from foot to foot.

Finally, he cleared his throat. "I'm glad the cough has left. Is the pain better?"

She hated to admit that it was. "Somewhat, but Dr. Van Neef said it will take some time before I'm back to normal."

"Naturally." He looked around the room. "You must find such a small space confining."

"You can't imagine." She pressed a hand to her mouth. The last thing she needed was to agree with anything he said.

His lips curved slightly. "Might I at least give you this gift?"

"Why would you think it necessary to give me anything?"

He set down the package on the bureau and retreated. "It's from all of us, but especially Sadie."

"Oh." Now she felt terrible.

"The red ribbon was her idea. She said you look pretty in red." He grinned, and that irresistible sparkle returned to his eyes. "I happen to agree."

Pearl had to duck her head to hide the heat rising in her cheeks. How was she supposed to stay angry with him when he said things like that? "She is well, then? And Cocoa?"

"Both in excellent health. Sadie is showing no ill effects from the incident other than asking a great many questions."

"Questions about what?" Pearl picked at the sad fringe on her shawl.

"Ah, that is for her uncle to know."

"And me to find out?" Pearl challenged. Something about the man brought out the fighting spirit in her.

He laughed. "That's the Pearl I love."

Love? That word made her stiffen. Could those feelings she had for him truly be love? Could the fact that he displaced everything else in her mind indicate the sort of affection that would last a lifetime? Or was this one of those passing fancies that led to heartbreak? After all, he could not be trusted to take care of the innocent and vulnerable. Why should she trust him with her heart?

She turned her face away from the door. "I'm tired. Please let me rest."

He hesitated, probably waiting for her to relent. She could not. To give in would be to accept and condone such carelessness. No, she'd made up her mind. Her life would be dedicated to her students. There was no room in it for a man who'd proven faithless.

Even though he had come back for her.

Chapter Twenty-Four

Pearl greeted the news that the church had reopened with some satisfaction. Amanda reported the building full for the first service.

"You should have heard Roland sing." She sighed. "Such a beautiful tenor."

Pearl didn't want to hear one word about Roland, but Amanda peppered her with references from sunup to sundown and then some. Even her report that the school would reopen included Roland.

"He arranged for us to use the church. Isn't that perfect?"

"It's the only logical choice." Pearl shifted in the rocking chair Mr. Calloway had dragged upstairs two days ago.

Though the former cabin was the perfect place for a school, she could not see what part Roland needed to play in this. It wasn't as if he owned the building. The still-absent Mr. Stockton did. With a lull in sawmill operations he had no need of the extra space. Only one question remained. Had she been fired?

"Who will teach the classes?" Pearl held her breath.

Amanda beamed. "Louise and Fiona and I are taking turns. Roland ordered brand-new primers and slates."

"He did? How could he afford that?"

Considering how much of a fuss he put up when she first arrived, this turnaround made no sense. The materials for his glassworks must have burned up. He should have less spending money, not more.

Amanda shrugged. "I wouldn't know."

Naturally. Amanda had never needed to understand the cost of daily living. The Chatsworths had paid for the necessities. Amanda would only know the sting of not having luxuries. Pearl swallowed the bitter realization that want would follow her all her days.

"Aren't you going to open the present?" Amanda repeated the question every day.

Pearl gave the same response. "I can't."

Amanda, ever the romantic, clucked her tongue as she riffled through the stack of letters beside the package. "You didn't even read his notes."

Pearl had read Roland's notes, but she would not tell her friend that, even to stop the questioning. His fine script had drawn her. Few men wrote so meticulously, and she'd expected the content to match. Surely he would apologize or at least explain why he'd pushed forward with setting the burn pile ablaze on such a day. None of the notes even mentioned what had happened. They brimmed with family details, like Sadie's ability to care for Cocoa or how Isaac was helping out at the store.

Not one word of apology. Not one word about how he felt.

The letters might have been written to a mother or a sister or even a friend. That's what annoyed her more than anything. Had the kiss been a dream?

Amanda ran her hand over the package. The paper

crackled. "Sadie asks every day if you like it. I tell her you haven't felt well enough, but that's no longer true, is it?"

Amanda had a way of pricking Pearl's conscience. How could she explain? "Whatever it is, it will be too dear."

Naturally that explanation did nothing to stifle Amanda's curiosity. "It feels like cloth. Maybe it's a blanket."

"A blanket? Why would they give me a blanket?"

Amanda shrugged. "Sadie might think you need one."

"It's not from Sadie, even if it does say that on the outside."

"You did look!" Amanda ventured.

"Only at the outside. My point is that no matter what's written on the gift, it's really from Roland."

"Now you're being ridiculous," Amanda said. "You refuse to open it just because you think Roland bought it?"

That did sound childish, but Pearl couldn't give in. "Sadie could not possibly afford to buy me anything."

"Who said anything about buying? Perhaps Sadie is giving you something of hers."

Pearl's breath caught in her throat. What if Amanda was right? What if Sadie was giving her a prized quilt or blanket?

"She wants you to get well," Amanda added.

Pearl relented. "All right." She pushed to her feet, and the shawl dropped from her shoulders. Pearl shivered as the cool draft from the window hit her. "A blanket might be welcome."

"Sit. Sit." Amanda leaped to her feet. "You're only to move when necessary."

"I will go mad if I can't do something."

"You can open this." Amanda lifted the bulky package from the bureau and laid it on Pearl's lap. "It's the right weight for a blanket."

"I suppose you're right." Pearl fingered the ribbon. Red.

Chosen by Sadie because she thought red looked good on her. Her throat constricted.

Amanda perched on the edge of the bed, hands clasped with excitement. "Don't keep me waiting."

Pearl untied the ribbon and ran her hand over the names written on the paper with a thick pencil. *To Teacher from Sadie.* She'd seen enough of Roland's writing to recognize his precise script.

"Hurry," Amanda urged.

Pearl folded back the paper to reveal stunning green silk cloth. This was definitely not a blanket. The scoop of a neckline and dainty buttons covered in the same green fabric left no doubt. "It's a dress."

"Oh, how beautiful." Amanda ran a hand over the silk. "It will look so pretty on you, and you need a new dress after your everyday gown was ruined."

"I can't accept it. Just as I suspected, it's much too dear."

"Only because you think Roland bought it."

"That's not true."

"Isn't it? If you learned Garrett purchased it would you feel the same?" Amanda didn't wait long for Pearl to respond. "Just what I thought. Why should it matter? Why have you put up such a wall against Roland when he's the one who rescued you from the fire?"

"Because he's the one who started that fire."

Amanda gasped. "You can't mean that."

"He told me he was going to burn the branches that Monday. He should have known better."

Amanda's eyes filled with tears. "So you're going to hold it against him? For how long?"

Pearl couldn't answer. She didn't know.

"You told me to forgive Hugh. You told me the only way I could move on was to forgive him."

"This isn't the same," Pearl muttered, though deep down she knew that it was.

Amanda stood, her color high. "Yes, it is. It's exactly the same. You said that holding a grudge allows the other person to have control of you. I believed you. I trusted your judgment. Now you won't even follow your own advice?"

The truth behind the words drove them deep. They stung. They hurt. They convicted. Yet she could not take the step that Amanda demanded. She tossed the dress onto the bed, and a slip of paper floated out.

Amanda picked it up, and her eyes filled with tears again. She pressed a hand to her mouth and held out the paper.

Pearl trembled at what might be written on it, but when she took the paper, she saw only Sadie's name, spelled perfectly with the *D* facing the correct direction, and another drawing. This one was similar to the other one except that flames spewed out of the tugboat's smokestack and rained down on a woman and a little girl.

Her heart stopped. The last picture had shown soot coming from the tug's stack. This one showed flames. Was Sadie trying to tell her something? Sadie did sit near the window that faced the river. Cocoa had gone missing by then. What if she was looking outside to see if Clem had taken Cocoa with him? What if she had seen what happened?

Pearl gasped, her hand to her mouth. She had leaped to the wrong conclusion. She had misjudged Roland, had blamed him when he was blameless, had thrown away his demonstrations of affection. He had reached out to her at the very time his dream burned to the ground, and she'd turned him away.

What a cruel and selfish woman. While claiming defense of the children, she'd really been building a wall around her heart. A wall of prideful self-reliance.

O Lord, what have I done?

The sobs wrung out of her with the same fierceness as the day her parents abandoned her.

Roland tried to drown out the sting of Pearl's rejection by singing the hymns with all his strength. Eight days had passed since he left the gift in her room. He'd heard nothing and received no word. Little Sadie had grown quieter each day. That hurt most. If Pearl needed to shun him, he could accept it, but not that precious little girl. Sadie had been through so much, and Pearl knew it. Why punish an innocent child? This silence of Pearl's made no sense.

Lord, give me patience. I know I'm supposed to forgive and wait, but can't You send someone for Sadie? She needs a mother's love.

That was the problem. Pearl wasn't Sadie's mother. No one would be, if Garrett meant what he said. Last Sunday, Roland's brother had greeted Amanda cordially but didn't invite her to sit with them in church. This Sunday she didn't arrive at all.

The hymn ended, and he glanced out the window. Snow raced along the surface of the dunes like windblown sand. It wasn't snowing hard enough to accumulate, but it was cold. Maybe Amanda didn't feel well enough to go out of doors. Though he hoped to see Pearl, she wouldn't be ready to leave the boardinghouse yet. She certainly wouldn't go outside.

He turned his attention back to the visiting pastor.

"Be quick to listen, slow to speak and slow to anger," the man said. "Sound advice but difficult to follow."

That was true. Roland had spent his life speaking first and thinking later. Listening? He'd fallen far short of that ideal. Could that be what had upset Pearl? He'd never truly listened to her, even when she gave up a priceless nugget of information. An interested man would have leaped on her revelation of losing her parents to comfort her and ask where she had lived next. He'd related his own losses, which was neither helpful nor compassionate.

How he'd failed.

No wonder she'd turned from him.

If only he could have another chance. The apostle Peter got a second chance. The criminal crucified at Christ's side got a chance at paradise. Could he?

The door opened with a rush of cold air.

The pastor looked to the back of the room and smiled. Like everyone else, Roland turned. There stood Amanda. And Pearl, wrapped from head to toe in the green cloak and leaning on her friend's arm.

He'd gotten his second chance, and he wasn't going to ruin it. He rose, but Amanda shook her head. He sat back down, disappointed, but then he saw the one thing that could make his heart soar.

Pearl smiled.

Pearl had not expected such a wave of emotion at the sight of Roland. It nearly sent her knees out from under her.

"Let's sit here," Amanda whispered.

Fiona moved over and Pearl gratefully sank to the bench. The walk to church had been exhausting. She needed to rest before the return. Still, her eyes could not help wandering to Roland. The men sat at each end of the bench with the children protectively between them. Like sentinels. The way it ought to be.

Pearl's throat tightened. Roland had always put his niece and nephew first. If she'd listened, truly listened, as the pastor was even now explaining in his sermon, she would have seen his love for them in every word and action. She would never have doubted him.

Today's conversation would be difficult, but it must be done. In spite of her lowly beginnings, Pearl had always held her head high, shielding her heart with a wall of pride. She did not outright lie about her past; she hid it. That, too, was deception. Roland deserved to know the truth. All of it. Only then could the air be cleared between them.

Still, when the closing hymn ended and the congregation began to filter outside, she could not will herself to move.

"Do you need help?" Amanda whispered in her ear.

Pearl looked, truly looked, at her friend, and for the first time heard the unspoken hope in her words. She clasped Amanda's hand. "Go to them."

Amanda's reply shone in her eyes and reflected in her beaming smile. "I'll be back."

"That's quite all right," boomed the very voice that sent a shiver through Pearl's spine. Roland winked at Amanda. "I can escort Miss Pearl back to the boardinghouse."

That was all the permission Amanda needed to hurry forward to greet Sadie and Isaac. Their father, on the other hand, had to face Fiona.

"He has his hands full," Roland chuckled.

"I'm afraid so."

He rounded the bench to sit beside her, but this was not a conversation she wanted to have in public. "Would you walk with me toward the dune?"

He glanced down at her legs. "Are you able?"

"With assistance." She managed a wry smile. "That's something God is teaching me, reliance on others. It seems I wasn't as strong and independent as I thought."

He helped her to her feet. "You're the strongest woman I've ever known."

She shook her head. "The most foolish and stubborn perhaps."

"You'll have some stiff competition in that category, I'm afraid."

They walked from the church and exited into the wind. It blew her cloak open, revealing the lovely silk gown.

"It fits!" His blue eyes darkened. "Sadie will be pleased."

"Miss Sadie must have a substantial allowance."

His laughter rolled out again and she'd forgotten how much she loved the sound of it. "Now that's the Pearl I love."

This time those words struck a harmonious chord inside her. If only…but once he learned the truth about her, once he heard her confession, that melody would fall into discord.

"I must speak with you. There is so much to confess."

He took her hand and led her away from the church, taking care to match his normally long strides to her painfully halting steps. "The confession is all mine. I was so selfish."

"No. Never. I was the selfish one."

"Listen, Pearl. I thought you ungrateful when your note was merely mislaid."

"But I was ungrateful. You sent this fine gown when you could not afford it, and I pushed you away. The least I could have done…oh, I'm so ashamed of how I behaved."

He stopped her and tilted up her chin. "Look at me, Pearl."

She did.

"You were hurt, wounded. You needed to protect yourself."

She shook her head. "The only thing I was trying to protect was my heart."

"As was I." His voice deepened. "You see, I once loved

Eva. Sadie and Isaac's mother. I was angry that she married Garrett instead of me. I threatened to tell Garrett everything about our time together before she left me to marry him. She begged me not to. I didn't listen, just like I didn't listen to your concerns about the schoolchildren."

"Please, don't—"

He didn't stop. "I wouldn't let you close, because I didn't want you to end up the way Eva did." He squeezed his eyes shut. "Dead. After our fight, she took the skiff and rowed across the river, but the ice and the strong flow tipped over the boat. She drowned and I couldn't get to her in time."

"You don't need to tell me this."

"Don't you understand, Pearl? I almost lost you the same way. I didn't make sure you were following me."

"You couldn't have done anything. You needed to get Sadie to safety." She had to make him understand. "That's what I prayed for, that Sadie would live even if I had to die."

His chin shook before he looked away. After a moment, he composed himself. "And you call yourself selfish? That's the most unselfish act I've ever seen."

"No more than you running through the fire to find me. I blamed you for starting the fire, but now I know that I was wrong. It was an accident, a terrible accident. I leaped to conclusions and didn't even try to learn the truth. I'm so sorry."

He held onto her hands as if to a lifeline. "There is no reason to be sorry, Pearl. I love you. Love forgives."

Oh, such words! But love could not be founded on anything but truth. "You need to know that I'm not exactly an orphan. That is, I may be, probably am now, but I don't truly know. You see, my parents abandoned me at the orphanage. I wasn't good enough."

He pulled her close and hugged her so tight that she

could barely breathe, but she didn't care. No one had held her like that since her papa sobbed before leaving her.

She gasped.

He held her at arm's length. "What's wrong?"

"It's vague, the smallest memory, but I think my papa wept when he left me at the orphanage. I remember him crying." Tears sprang to her eyes. "He didn't want to let me go, but he had no choice." She squeezed her eyes shut. "He said that he would be back as soon as he could." She drew in a shaky breath. "He must never have had the chance."

He drew her close again, this time cradling her in his arms and whispering the verses of "Amazing Grace" into her ear.

She was lost. But now she was found.

"I won't ever let you go, Pearl, if you will let me."

The words flowed down her spine, driving away every tear and every ache.

She drew in her breath. Was he saying what she thought he was? "Do you mean?"

"It means I would love you and cherish you in sickness and health as long as we both shall live. Yes, Pearl, it means that and so much more." He cradled her head in his hands. "You are my everything, my spitfire, my joy and my laughter. I can't imagine a day without you."

"Nor I you," she began before he touched a finger to her lips.

"I haven't much to offer you." His brief laugh turned to the desperate hope of a boy asking for his heart's desire. "But I will work hard to give you the kind of life you deserve."

"No."

The hope left his eyes. "No?"

"Not that! I meant that I don't want you to work hard

to give me anything. I want to work together with you to build a life."

"Together?" He shook his head. "Pearl Lawson, you are an unusual woman."

"Too unusual?"

"Never." That hopeful smile returned. "Are you saying what I think you are?"

She nodded and threw her arms around his shoulders. "Yes, oh, yes."

His lips met hers in an explosion of feeling that melted away the icy day. Gone were the harsh wind and pelting sleet. Pearl didn't care if the entire town witnessed it. Roland Decker loved her, truly loved her for who she was, not what she claimed to be.

"Oh!" She broke the kiss as a sudden realization shot an arrow through their plans. "I can't get married until my contract ends." She frowned. "And I still intend to teach school as long as I can."

To her surprise, he was chuckling.

"What's so funny?" she demanded.

He shook his head. "Just you, darling. From the first moment I adored your practicality. As for your contract, I can wait if you wish. A long courtship would give me time to consider our future."

"Don't you mean that it would give *us* time to consider our future?"

He laughed. "Precisely." He reached into his inner coat pocket and extracted a piece of paper. "However, if you are in a rush to marry, you could exercise this little addendum to your contract."

"What addendum?"

"One I worked out with Mr. Farmingham and the school board that releases you from the marriage clause if you promise to complete the term of your contract." He handed her the piece of paper.

Pearl read the brief paragraph and noted the date. "You did that *before* we reconciled?"

"I figured you'd come around."

She swatted him with the paper. "A bit presumptuous, don't you think?"

He laughed and gathered her close again. "Hopeful, Miss Pearl." His eye twinkled. "Knowing one's partner is the basis of a successful proposition."

"And a successful union."

His lips touched hers again. This time she let his embrace carry her away to that place where wrongs got righted, orphans found families and dreams came true.

* * * * *

Dear Reader,

When I first married, my new husband and I lived near the former site of Singapore, Michigan, and I was fascinated by its story. Like many lumbering towns, it sprang up on the shores of a river that offered a protected Great Lakes harbor for shipping. The history of many Michigan coastal towns leads back to lumbering. Some towns thrived, and some died when the timber was gone. Those that survived found another industry to push the town forward.

Though the characters and situations in this story are purely fictional, I wanted Roland to be that kind of visionary. He wants to put down roots and turn Singapore into a thriving community. For Pearl, who has no roots, this sense of place and an unbounded future holds a strong appeal. I can't wait to see how their plans turn out!

I love to read mail-order-bride stories. Those women had incredible courage and faith! They also must have been spurred to this drastic solution by devastating circumstances. Imagining each woman's story has been and will be a great adventure throughout this four-book series. I hope you will join me for Amanda, Fiona and Louise's stories.

Please visit me at christineelizabethjohnson.com and send me a note. I'd love to hear from you!

Blessings,
Christine

REQUEST YOUR FREE BOOKS!

2 FREE INSPIRATIONAL NOVELS
PLUS 2 *FREE* MYSTERY GIFTS

Love Inspired® **HISTORICAL**

Town founder Will Canfield has big dreams for Cowboy Creek—but his plans are thrown for a loop when a tiny bundle is left on his doorstep. With a baby to care for, the last thing he needs is another complication. But that's just what he gets, in the form of a redheaded, trouble-making cowgirl who throws his world upside down.

Read on for a sneak preview of
Sherri Shackelford's
SPECIAL DELIVERY BABY,
the exciting continuation of the miniseries
COWBOY CREEK,
available May 2016 from Love Inspired Historical.

"The name is Will Canfield," he said. "Thank you for your assistance, Miss Stone."

"You sure picked a dangerous place to take your baby for a walk, Daddy Canfield. Might want to reconsider your route next time."

The measured expression on his face faltered a notch. "Oh, this isn't my baby."

She hoisted an eyebrow. "Reckon who that baby belongs to is none of my business one way or the other." She gestured toward the child. "I think your girl is getting hungry. Better get mama."

"That's the whole problem." The man spoke more to the infant in his arms than to her. "Someone abandoned her. I found her on my doorstep just now." He glanced over his shoulder and then back at her. "The woman— the one who spooked the cattle. Did you see which way she ran? I think this child belongs to her. If not, then she might have seen something. She was hiding in the shadows when I discovered this little bundle."

"Sorry. I was focused on the cattle."

Clearly frustrated by her answers, Daddy Canfield muttered something unintelligible.

He grimaced and held the bundle away from him, revealing a dark, wet patch on his expensive suit coat.

Tomasina chuckled. The boys were going to love hearing about this one. They'd never believe her but they'd love the telling. Her pa always liked a good yarn, as well. At the thought of her pa, her smile faded. He'd died on the trail a few weeks back and they'd buried him in Oklahoma Territory. The wound of his loss was still raw and she shied away from her memories of him.

"Fellow…" Tomasina said. "As much fun as this has been, I'd best be getting on."

"Thanks for your help back there," Will replied, his tone grudging. "Your quick action averted a disaster."

The admission had obviously cost him. He struck her as a prideful man, and prideful men sometimes needed a reminder of their place in the grand scheme of things.

"Daddy Canfield," she declared. "Since you don't like guns, how do you feel about rodeo shows? You know, trick riding and fancy target shooting?"

"Not in my town. Too dangerous."

"Excellent," Tomasina replied with a hearty grin.

Yep. She felt better already.

Don't miss SPECIAL DELIVERY BABY
by Sherri Shackelford,
available May 2016 wherever
Love Inspired® Historical books and ebooks are sold.
www.LoveInspired.com

SPECIAL EXCERPT FROM

Love Inspired

*A marriage of convenience for widowed single
parents Joshua Stoltzfus and Rebekah Burkholder
will mean a stable home for their children.
Becoming a family could also lead to healing their
past hurts—and a second chance at love.*

*Read on for a sneak preview of
AN AMISH MATCH by* **Jo Ann Brown**,
available May 2016 from Love Inspired!

"Will you give me an answer, Rebekah? Will you marry me?"

"But why? I don't love you." Her cheeks turned to fire as she hurried to add, "That sounded awful. I'm sorry. The truth is you've always been a *gut* friend, Joshua, which is why I feel I can be blunt."

"If we can't speak honestly now, I can't imagine when we could."

"Then I will honestly say I don't understand why you'd ask me to m-m-marry you." She hated how she stumbled over the simple word.

No, it wasn't simple. There was nothing simple about Joshua Stoltzfus appearing at her door to ask her to become his wife.

"Because we could help each other. Isn't that what a husband and wife are? Helpmeets?" He cleared his throat. "I would rather marry a woman I know and respect as a friend. We've both married once for love, and we've both ost the ones we love. Is it wrong to be more practical this time?"

Every inch of her wanted to shout, *"Ja!"* But his words made sense.

She had married Lloyd because she'd been infatuated with him and the idea of being his wife, so much so that she had convinced herself while they were courting to ignore how rough and demanding he had been with her when she'd caught the odor of beer on his breath. She'd accepted his excuses and his reassurances it wouldn't happen again...even when it had. She'd been blinded by love. How much better would it be to marry with her eyes wide-open? No surprises, and a husband whom she counted among her friends.

She'd be a fool not to agree immediately. "All right," she said. "I will marry you."

"Really?" He appeared shocked, as if he hadn't thought she'd agree quickly.

"Ja." She didn't add anything more, because there wasn't anything more to say. They would be wed, for better or for worse. And she was sure the worse couldn't be as bad as her marriage to Lloyd.

Don't miss
AN AMISH MATCH
by Jo Ann Brown,
available May 2016 wherever
Love Inspired® books and ebooks are sold.

www.LoveInspired.com